# Genevieve Knows Too Much

Printed in Australia

Cover and internal design by Shawline Publishing Group Pty Ltd

First printing: August 2024

Shawline Publishing Group Pty Ltd

www.shawlinepublishing.com.au

Paperback ISBN 978-1-9231-7187-9

eBook ISBN 978-1-9231-7210-4

Hardback ISBN 978-1-9231-7221-0

Distributed by Shawline Distribution and Lightning Source Global

*Shawline Publishing Group acknowledges the traditional owners of the land and pays respects to the Elders, past, present and future.*

A catalogue record for this work is available from the National Library of Australia

# Genevieve Knows Too Much

## SUSIE ALLANSON

# Also by Susie Allanson

*Murder on his Mind: The Untold Story of Australia's Abortion Clinic Murder*

*Empowering Women: From Murder and Misogyny to High Court Victory*

For Benjamin, Georgia and Jules.

A black streak screeches, jolts over the gutter onto the footpath. A door flings open and a bundle rolls out, dumped by disembodied hands. The door slams shut and the vehicle reverses onto the road. Growl of the engine as it accelerates away.

Earthiness hangs in the air and ketones hover. Blood stains on fabric. A white face moans.

# I

# FANTASY

What a wonderful world.

Blue ocean waves roll onto sun-soaked beaches. A patchwork of cliffs angle upwards towards a cloudless sky. Children gambol at the water's edge, splashing and building sandcastles. Adults laze and swim.

'The Church Justice & Healing Mission moved into palatial new premises today,' says a voice with exquisite diction.

An aerial camera drone sweeps slowly across the beach and transmits a 360-degree panoramic paradise. Zooms in on the top balcony of a glitzy 15-storey building.

'The High Court ruled that for the purposes of being sued by victims of clergy abuse, the church is *not* a legal entity,' the voice-over explains kindly. 'However, the church *is* a legal entity when it comes to an array of tax exemptions and deductions and,' the voice pauses for added emphasis, 'when purchasing the luxurious Widgie Conference Complex.'

The bird's eye view of the balcony reveals a man reclining on an ornate lounge and sipping from a crystal glass refracting the sunshine in a rainbow. He is sunbaking nude. A small area of not-at-this-hour TV vision is smudged to a grey fuzz. The man jumps up in his birthday-suited glory, gestures dramatically with one hand while the other hand joins the blur of his genitals. He swats and mutely rants at the drone spying on his private Eden and his ugly indulgence. Swat. Slap. Swish. The man's face fills the screen, his profanities easily lip-read.

The narration continues, unhurried and calm, 'Sources suggest that a sum of $95 million was the asking price for the luxurious Widgie Complex. The Church will neither confirm nor deny the price paid.'

Footage shows the naked man, now fully clothed and smiling, his maxi frock unsuccessfully vying for attention with a blackhead stigmata on his nose. Archbishop John Bell's bejewelled hands flit about to emphasise his most sacred words.

'We don't have to tell you that. *Secreta Continere*! This is God's work. God is answerable to no man. But I can say, the church really got a good bang for its buck with this one. Of course, the place did need a significant reno to bring it up to scratch. How much was the renovation? I'm not telling you that! This is God's work. God is answerable to no man. My new premises, er, God's new premises, include offices, restaurants, wine cellar, casino, go-karts, gaming arcade, pool tables, bowling alley, roof top tennis courts, a pool and golf course. All the things the beautiful boys like, to attract the next generation of God's servants. And my own top floor 220-square penthouse with four carat, gold-plated glass windows for my stunning gold carat views.'

The drooling man of God report ends and the soothing tones of the voice-over are revealed to belong to *The LoDown* news anchor, Genevieve Parker, sitting elegantly at her *LoDown* news anchor desk. With a hint of mischief in her violet eyes, Genevieve observes, 'Archbishop Bell seems to have forgotten a chapel, hmm.

'And in related news, earlier today, the advocacy group for victims of clergy abuse, *Shame on Church Abusers & Racketeers*, widely known as *SCAR*, was evicted from its western suburbs premises and is currently homeless. Ms Jessica Beauvoir, *SCAR* CEO.'

With a graceful head tilt, Genevieve Parker cedes the limelight to a woman with frazzled ginger hair and wearing a *SCAR*-emblazoned t-shirt and the letters S, C, A, R dangling from each ear lobe. The woman's accessories perfectly match her agitated demeanour.

'Yeah-nah, most of our volunteers are victims of clergy abuse themselves, so they already know what it's like being homeless. We'll get through it like we always do.' Ms Beauvoir pulls her shoulders back with pride before they collapse under the strain of a simple honesty. 'Yeah-nah, not always. Lots of victims aren't with us anymore. Not all victims can be survivors – suicide, drugs, sh-*bleep*-t like that. The church – f-*bleep*-ing f-*bleep*-ers – are f-*bleep*-ing criminals and murderers. We just hope our homelessness doesn't stop us fighting for those victims being sued by the church for court costs. The church and them expensive silks against our one legal aid lawyer.' Ms Beauvoir looks about to cry, before she throws her fist in the air and yells, 'Shame on Church Abusers & Racketeers!'

Genevieve Parker resumes centre screen.

'Ms Beauvoir is asking for assistance to find *SCAR* another rundown house urgently,' Genevieve says so kindly that those viewers without a house to spare are already googling details about how to make a donation. 'You can contact *SCAR* with assistance, or *for* assistance,' Genevieve says as if she is delivering a kiss to her viewers' foreheads. Within the hour SCAR will be re-housed in bigger and better digs.

Gen's years in the hot seat as *The LoDown* news anchor, Genevieve Parker, is where she keeps her cool. No matter the pressures of being in the limelight, Gen is unflappable. She reports current affairs as if she has all the time in the world, the way a brilliant athlete slows down time to carry out feats, hypnotising to mere mortals.

Surrounded by the organised chaos of studio gadgetry and crew invisible to her audience, Gen is defined by a screen frame that is an intimate micro-world of soft polish and perfection. Genevieve Parker tops TV ratings and defies the wide world web's death knell for TV viewing. *The LoDown*'s audience is happy. The shareholders and network bosses are happy. Everyone can trust Genevieve Parker to deliver. Genevieve is drop dead gorgeous.

*Drop dead gorgeous*, Gen rues, as an ad break races along like a game of tag. Maz taps on her desk with last minute copy edits and line-up changes. The work placement student tops up her water. Colwyn flutters a makeup brush across her forehead and upper lip. Gen is drop dead gorgeous thanks to makeup and camera angles and a challenging regimen with beauty and fitness experts. And where would she be without eye drops?

Gen's eyes blink rapidly. Is the lighting unusually bright tonight? An impertinent irritability needles and pricks a hole in the skin of her news anchor alter ego. Gen sighs through the hole, deflated. She is centre stage with the ugliest stories of the world, painting eyesore masterpieces of humanity. Does humanity exist? Gen tries to find it in herself and reveal it in the stories by radiating professional composure and warmth, and offering a smattering of carefully prepared, off-the-cuff comments. She hangs out for the one or two feel-good stories tacked on the end of the broadcast, if there is time: like a baby landing happily in its mother's arms while the rest of the world slides into the rising sea of melting ice caps.

The pinprick cracks and shivers along Gen's spine. Everything feels false and fucked up, she told Gael last night. But the curse was a disappointment to her. Gen said the F word so neatly that it lacked the casual harshness required to make the point. Gael wasn't listening anyway. He didn't notice. He has no interest in her career. What did he say the other night? She's nothing but a jumped-up show girl?

How insulting and cruel, Gen thinks now. But at the time? She apologised, of course, as if she had insulted and shamed him. As if she were a nuisance in his life and so desperately lucky to have found a man who would put up with her. No matter. Here she is centre stage as *The LoDown* anchor, adored and on top of her game. She is Genevieve Parker, in charge and at the controls.

'What the fuck am I doing?' Gen says aloud just as the vision cuts back to her. And she nails that ugly *fuck*.

The entire production team freezes. The control room director curses in her ear, then says, 'That just went to air, Gen. Get it together, whatever it is.' The floor manager contorts her face into a bright smile for Gen to copy.

For the first time in her career Gen watched, but failed to see, the floor manager's perfectly formed fingers complete their perfectly formed count-down count-in. *Unusual and disgraceful,* thinks Gen. She should be shocked and overcome with shame.

But, who the fuck cares? Gen does, does she? Fuck it.

*OutRageOnLine:*
*BOMBSHELL GENEVIEVE DROPS F-BOMB.*
*SEE News Anchor's disgrace.*
*Parents furious and frantic about effect on kiddies.*
*GET FREE $100 FOR FIRST THREE BETS ON BETCHA! WHEN YOU SIGN UP FOR PORN&POPCORN.*

In the split second between *fuck* and realisation, Gen has welcomed viewers back with her dazzling smile and violet eyes. Her voice conveys authority and sexy sincerity. Genevieve Parker delivers. Genevieve cares. On with the show.

'Ex-prime minister Julian Pope announced today that a Royal Commission into, quote, "the unconscionable practice of changing girls into boys and boys into girls" unquote, would commence next month. Country-wide protests, by those involved in gender-kindness health care, say the commission's focus on religious views, rather than medical facts, causes untold distress to some of the most vulnerable members of our community. They want the enquiry *off* the table.'

In the brilliant spotlight of the nation's gaze, Gen sweeps her arms in a breaststroke across the glass-topped desk. Two waves of papers fly and flutter and fall like starburst. A digital notebook, pen and glass of water spill, bounce, roll and shatter. Off, all of it, *off the table*. Her desk, host to political sophistry, not-news-news and all the nastiness of the world, is wiped clean.

Gen blinks as she recognises her sweeping away as a mere fancy; an impulse played out in her imagination. The world's evils are still writ large on the pristine papers in front of her. Her other news-reading accoutrements sit aligned just so. With a quiet horror, she scrawls across her brain: *Focus!*

After the half dozen quick news items that follow her fuck up and fantasy dummy spit, Genevieve sparkles a smile that curves sublimely. She teases her viewers.

'Sensational footage of Barb and Angelica's public stoush, and the latest in sport, when we come back.'

The director and the floor manager both express concern about Genevieve's earlier impropriety. Consciously deciding to ignore them both, Gen maintains a pleasant, attentive face and nods occasionally. She doesn't hear them at all. This is a skill and a necessity in this job where worlds and words collide. In the blink of an eye, Gen must select what she tunes in to and out of. Words in her ears from the director. Words written on the tele-prompter and screen beneath her glass-topped desk. Words mouthed silently by the floor manager. Words in Gen's own mind. Words, words, words. Seconds tick as she makes big and small decisions within an exquisitely paced performance. But Gen does it perfectly. She always does. She prepares meticulously and then flies by the seat of her pants. It all appears so effortless and understated. Naturally perfect.

Except that time. How did Gen miss the count in? How did she curse on air? She never swears at work and never, never swears on air. That footage will already be going pandemic online. *Fuck*, she thinks, before angrily reminding herself that *fuck* is what got her into this mess. *Take a breath and concentrate,* she tells herself.

Gen sits at her news desk concentrating and readying for the resumption of *The LoDown,* ignoring the fucked-up elephant in the room stampeding into the worldwide web. Make-up artist, Colwyn, is all silent attention as he dusts areas of shine on Gen's face and applies another layer of plumping gloss to her lips. An undisciplined eyebrow rises quizzically, but Colwyn reins it in with a frown and departs. With a blank expression, Maz places a rewrite and amended line-up on Gen's desktop with a cursory finger point.

'Is Toby's edit complete, Maz? The Facefreeze and Liquorice piece?' Gen asks.

The departing figure of Maz turns a thumb downwards. 'Bumped for a late footy scoop, Gen.'

Gen checks the changes, her mind meandering around the question of Facefreeze's toxicity. Approaching her 40th birthday, but not looking a day over 25, Facefreeze is an essential part of Gen's demanding beauty routine. It puts off the day she may need to take more extreme measures. Before that day, she'll probably be long gone. Her male on-air colleagues can amass grey hair, wrinkles and chub, but Gen and her female colleagues must be forever young and beautiful. Mother says so, too. On Gen's 30th birthday, two of the tiniest, teeniest lines appeared between her eyebrows. Her mother said so. How kind of Mother to give her a heads up, muses Gen as she scrawls across her brain a far too common reminder to herself: *Do not fall down the Mother rabbit hole.*

But what if Facefreeze is toxic? Gen wonders. What if that is the reason she is off her game? Maybe Facefreeze messes with your neural pathways. A brain orders a face to shape itself into whatever expression is meant to match an idea or emotion, and the Facefreeze-affected feedback signal responds. Negative. Lost connection. Over and out. Nerve endings may be dying. Pathways may be coalescing into the meaningless squiggles of dementia. In 20 years' time, when scientists finally recognise the damage, it will be called Facefreeze Fried Brain: a global female (with a smidge of men) epidemic. Gen will present an award-winning story about it, she decides optimistically. But if she is to last that long, Gen definitely needs to maintain her regular Facefreeze treatment. Ha.

Gen thinks of such absurdities as a distraction from her grinding reality. No one appreciates the pressures of being so exposed and so beautiful. The years of hard slog and constantly having to exceed expectations. The upkeep and self-conscious surveillance in the face of trolls and stalkers. Gen shivers as she experiences a flashback to a particularly ugly troll-turned-stalker saga. She snaps herself out of that ghastly freeze-frame and back to her musings about her own face freeze-frame.

Gen's routine is unrelenting but, she has to admit, once started, Facefreeze is very hard to stop, rather like an addiction? Self-sabotage? It killed off Genevieve Parker's signature frown: a frown so beautiful, so full of pathos and gravitas, and Gen traded it for a cosmetic façade of early twenties beauty. So, she contrived a Facefreeze-contaminated sequence of movements to substitute for her adorable frown and to signal the serious business of tragic and preposterous segments and Breaking News! stories. *What does that even mean?* Gen puzzles. *Breaking News? What, you have to smash it into smithereens over the audience's heads? Or is it news that breaks your heart?*

Gen feels her heart crack a tiny bit and wonders if she is literally cracking up. First the glare of the lights, the hole that cracked open and now her heart? But Gen knows she's got to hold it together. There's so much she must keep underground. This is not the time for holes or cracks. *Breathe and focus*, Gen orders herself, and Genevieve Parker is back.

'Excuse me,' she says, holding her hand to her ear and her alluring gaze on her audience. 'Breaking news just in, ex-prime minister Mr Julian Pope has become the nation's prime minister – again.'

In the kitchen of The Dodge, the official residence of the prime minister, *The LoDown* is a murmur in the background as an ignored television prattles on in the lounge room.

At the kitchen sink, Prime Minister Julian Pope moans, 'I'm just not feeling myself, Nance.' He clasps a sudsy dinner plate from his wife, who is washing the dishes, and wipes it with a golden-laced tea towel, presented to him by an oil-rich prince. Dried and gleaming, Jules carefully places the plate into a packing box, one of many scattered throughout The Dodge.

'Well, dear, it takes a bit to recover after a cholecystectomy. And you did have complications,' says his wife with a sigh as she passes him another dripping plate. 'It was recurrent gall stones or' – she exclaims like a cut-throat regent – 'out with your gall bladder! You know, dear, I've heard people say you have rocks in your head. Really, though, it was rocks in your gut. But they do say that our gut is another type of brain, and so...'

As Jules returns from depositing the dried plate in the box, he recognises that Nance's sentence has trailed off and she's gazing out the kitchen window in front of her. The swirl of the dish-washing mop has stopped still in her hand, its tendrils floating in the cloudy space of sink water as tiny soap bubbles pop out of existence, one by one. Jules leans in and peers out the window too at the magnificent gardens of The Dodge: manicured lawn, pruned sticks of the rose garden, abundant azaleas and towering magnolia, crepe myrtle and jacaranda. *Here she goes again*, Jules thinks as he resumes his dish-wiper stance. Nance is not actually looking at anything.

Whenever he can, PM Julian Pope indulges in this delightful post dinner ritual at The Dodge. It is a good old-fashioned husband and wife wash-up and natter. He owes her that much, he reckons. But the PM never likes these ponderous moments his wife is prone to. She does his head in sometimes. They remind Jules that she is in fact a brainiac and was a post-doc fellow in some bio-science or other. He swept her off her feet at an awards night, discovered she was the fuck of his life, and that was that.

Nance was head-strong and heading headlong and head-on to heady heights. But she fell head over heels for Jules and lost her head. She was headed for the head job and ended up with Jules and a different type of head job! Jules grins at his sophisticated wordplay on the word *head*, a little habit he developed when he first entered *parleyment* and sat on the back benches. A man with such a superior brain as himself needs a stimulating brain game when things become boring.

Jules waits out his wife's absence. Caused by girlie germs, Jules decided years ago. But he has to hand it to Nance, other stay-at-home mums have nothing on her. She produced precious child after precious child, although a boy never eventuated. Jules will probably never forgive her for that. Five girls. Girls, girls, girls. Surrounded by 'em all his life: girls, one sister, a mother, five daughters, a wife. Surrounded by all those girlie germs. Jules shudders all over, like he's being electrocuted.

*She is a faarking good little wifie though. Faarking! Get it?* Jules chuckles. Oh, he is in fine form today despite his health doldrums. But ingenious wit or no, Jules feels suddenly miffed, puffs his cheeks out, sighs long and loud and finishes with a lethargic lip-trumpeting raspberry. He really hates to see a woman with a cogitating mind. A woman's body is complex enough. But a woman's brain? Now that is faarking terrifying. God really shouldn't have bothered with brains for women.

He straightens the bib on his floral apron and realises with relief that the dish mop is again sloshing about the plates. His wife hands him a piece of wet crockery with a final regal judgment. 'The gall bladder is out and good riddance.'

As Jules dries and stores a bowl in a box, his annoyance builds. He returns to his dish-drying position beside his wife and whines, 'But it's been almost four months, Nance. I've been taking my meds and seeing the doc. I've been doing everything right, but this belly is so swollen. Hangs over the boxers when I powerwalk. Gets my spandex all out of shape when I cycle. I swear this gut is getting bigger, not smaller.'

'Impossible, Jules,' Nance harrumphs, scrubbing furiously. 'You men are hopeless patients. You have no idea what real pain and a real swelling stomach is. Your suffering is nothing compared with what we women go through. I'll give you swollen. Remember when I was pregnant with Chastity? I couldn't get up out of a chair and I had to wear your triple E runners and have someone else lace them up for me.'

'I guess my belly is quite small – in comparison,' Jules concedes. 'But I've still got nausea, Nance–'

'Nausea! I vomited every day I was pregnant with Virtue and I wasn't much better with Prudence, remember? You really need to get things in perspective, Jules, and stop moaning.'

Jules feels his wife's impatience like a sling shot striking him flush on his nose. He pointedly refuses to take the plate Nance is holding in his direction and she places it in the draining rack instead. He really expects a little more sympathy from his wife of 22 years. He must make her realise how serious it is.

Jules makes a concerted effort at control and consciously dons his deep and authoritative PM-in-the-House voice. 'Now, Nance, I really think you should take this more seriously. You know how I sometimes pretend to nod off in the House as a *faark you* when an opposition member has the floor? Well, the other day, I nodded off for real. I nodded off while a vote was taken on the new budget. No one even realised I'd slid off my seat and without my vote it didn't get over the line, Nance. The headlines were shockers, *You Snooze You Lose, Pope Dreams Dashed, Pope's Budget BluezzzZZZ.* They had such fun with it all, at my expense, Nance.'

'You have to admit, some of those journos and bloggers are very clever,' says Nance with a smile and far too much pleasure, as far as Jules is concerned. To add injury to insult, Nance then gleefully flicks the dish mop with extra exuberance and a spray of dirty water hits him full in the face. Then a high-pitched yelp almost blows his eardrums and gives him such a fright.

Good god, that girlie-girlie squawk was him, Jules realises. How humiliating. He mops his face with the damp tea towel and decides it has all become too much. That woman, his woman, has stepped over the line.

'It's not funny, woman. Whatever this lethargy is, it's not normal and it's not fair. It's killing me, Nance. You're killing me. And you're meant to be on my side, Nance. *My side.*'

Nance ignores the dishwashing, turns to Jules and says tenderly, 'Look, dear, my little schnookems sweetie pie. The specialist is very pleased with your progress, isn't she? It's probably just a bit of normal post-op inflammation, or gas, or a touch of male hysteria and neuroticism, dear. Apparently that's rampant these days.'

Choosing a doctor is always so fraught for Jules. Should he go for a man who obviously is an expert, worked hard for his position, got there on merit, and doesn't mince words or action? Bu-ut whose touchy-feely prods and pokes are a bit too, well, to be straight up about it, just a bit too homo-sex-su-al for Jules' liking.

Alternatively, does he go for a woman who has got there on the shirt-tails of a man, as part of some radical feminist affirmative action quota, blah, blah blah. Bu-ut whose touchy-feely prods and pokes are really quite delightful and always stoke the macho in him so that he feels so-o good. Hmm, such a dilemma.

This time, he let Nance make the decision.

'I know exactly who you're going to,' she announced. 'Dr Roberta Roberts is the best in her field.'

So that was that. Jules consulted the woman, was operated on by the woman, and continues to consult the woman. And now look where it's got him. Faarking hell, she removes his gall bladder and he ends up with a belly like an obese pig!

'You know how I like to look good, Nance. The People expect me to look good. I must be the fit, youthful PM with the strong, hunky bod. The marketing guys say my body and active lifestyle are pivotal, *pivotal*, Nance, in winning the men's and the women's vote. The men want to *be* me, and the women want to be *with* me,' Jules smirks. 'The men want to be in my *shoes* and the women want to be in my *pants*.'

'Julian!' rebukes Nance before laughing flirtatiously and returning her attention to the sink. 'You are shameless. But are you the PM at the moment? I thought you were the ex. I've rather lost track.'

Jules automatically takes a dripping saucepan from Nance, as his mind shifts momentarily to sex. For the first time in his life, Jules' libido fades in and out, rather than being his constant luscious companion.

'Yes, well, I'm back to my cycling and powerwalking, but this faarking post-op belly blubber is killing me in the polls. I'm the team captain, coach, and star player of the nation, Nance–'

'Jules, you've never played a team sport in your life.'

'Well, maybe not,' Jules concedes, his hands circling the tea towel about the saucepan. 'But I'm the quintessential sporting champion and hero to the whole faarking country, Nance. But what about now?' Jules' face crumples and he relinquishes the saucepan and tea towel to the kitchen bench. His hands hang loose and helpless. A child's stuffed clown. 'I don't feel like me, Nance. I feel like one of Them, not Me. A Loser, not a Winner.'

Nance runs her pink plastic gloves down the sides of her pinny to dry them and pats his shoulder gently.

'Oh, my little schnookems sweetie pie, it will all be all right. You just need a bit of time, dear, a bit of rest. It will all be okay.'

Her words touch him in a way that reminds him of the time he did the dirty deed with those centrefold twins and they rained down rose petals and kisses all over his naked body. Jules feels a slight stirring down below, nestles his head in his wife's arms and snuffles. Nance pats his back and rocks him back and forth.

Finally, Jules pulls away, cocks his head to one side and wonders, 'Do we have any of those ice-creams, Nance? You know the ones. Chocolate on the outside, orange on the inside?'

'Really, Jules?' Nance frowns and looks pointedly at Julian's belly, then attacks the dishwashing with an irritated vigour.

Julian matches his wife's irritation by picking up the tea towel and throwing it back down again before raising the ante with an explosive commentary. 'Faarking Christ, Nance. This faarking beer gut – when I haven't even had a beer for almost four months. This faarking beer gut will be the death of me *and* the country! The country's going to rack and ruin, Nance. I'm getting killed in the polls, and it's all because of this potbelly.'

'That's absolute nonsense, Jules,' states Nance matter-of-factly and looking sternly at Jules. 'You know you and the Bell went too far. When you and the Bell get together you just egg each other on too, *too* far, Jules.' Nance pulls the plug from the sink and the grey dross gurgles down the drain. She removes her apron, folds it and places it in a packing box with the words 'kitchen pinnies/royal presents' scrawled on it in black marker.

'You know, Jules,' Nance says, 'Because of you and the Bell, the women of the nation are planning a sex strike.'

Despite his current libido lull, a look of sheer horror erupts on Jules' face.

*Dear Rosie,*

*I'm not really sure where to begin. I think Today I Martha says I should it might be helpful if I write to you in long hand. That's going great isn't it? Apologies for the mess. But Martha says it's too easy to delete the important stuff when we use electronic writers, and that I've already deleted far too much of what is important to me. Martha says I ~~shouldn't~~ it's better if I don't edit or delete when I write to you, or when I'm in my session with her.*

*I'm unsure about all that. Editing is a forte of mine and requires sacrificing, that is, deleting, the less important to ensure a clear, uncomplicated story zeroing in on what is important. I'm hardly going to make the mistake of deleting from my life what's important, am I? If anything, I think my mind would benefit from a solid edit. It's always too full of too many thoughts. Well, almost always. Martha says you have to watch out for words like 'always vs never' and 'black vs white'. You're meant to look for the colours between the black and white. I'm not sure what that really means yet, but I always have loved rainbows. Rainbows always make me think of you, Rosie, always. Martha might not be right about everything, might she?*

*I will always love you, Rosie, always. Please forgive me.*

Gen's body fills and tightens with an agony threatening to burst. But all that breaks through is one teardrop. It rolls down her face and splashes onto the last word, *me*, so that it trails off into an ambiguous smudge. Gen trails off into the murky world beyond her penthouse window. She cradles her chin in her hand and gazes at the lights of the city against the indigo sky, the inky snake of the river shimmering in the headlights of traffic slithering in parallel along the boulevard. The night sky, woozy from the city lights, still yields up patches dark enough to backdrop the full moon and stars here and there.

'Here and there,' Gen whispers into the hum of silence around her and the void where her body should be. 'Are you out there, Rosie?' Time meanders on, while Gen slips through its scaffolding.

At some point in time and place and purpose, Gen's gaze returns to her handwritten task. She returns.

*Sorry, I lost myself there for a moment. Sometimes I just seem to disappear for a bit, can you believe it? I guess writing to you is much harder than I thought. My body aches with emotion and I lose my thoughts. Maybe I am going crazy.*

*Speaking of losing my mind, you'll love this: I literally fucked up on national TV. Everyone was shocked, including me. But a part of me was rather delighted too, proud of myself. I know, so wrong. The whole night I felt off kilter and was way off delivering my usual perfectly nuanced performance – remember Mrs Gibbons used to say that, 'another perfectly nuanced performance from Genevieve Parker!' But that was so long ago. It feels like another world. I guess it is.*

*But this is no time for me to be mucking up. So much hangs in the balance at the moment. I have to be beyond reproach and perfect. Well, Martha says I've expended far too much being 'beyond reproach and perfect', and I ~~should~~ embrace my imperfection. God, I've done it again. It's like learning how to talk again! Martha says ~~you shouldn't 'should' because~~ 'shoulds' are not helpful and not kind. They are demanding and judgmental. Apparently, I'm excellent at being judgmental – of me, but I don't have good judgment – of men. Where can I have learnt that?*

*All this is an experiment, I suppose, just writing whatever pops into ~~your~~ my head and crossing out mistakes as ~~you~~ I go. This has got to be the least planned and messiest writing in my whole life. Sorry.*

*Martha makes me stop and think about everything I try not to think about, and cannot think about, when I'm busy, busy, busy. Sometimes I don't want to go to my appointment. My stomach jumps about and I can hardly breathe. Me, Genevieve Parker, the cool, calm interviewer of power brokers and movie stars, is afraid of speaking with a lovely psychologist. Martha says all this is normal and that I'm not afraid of her, but I am afraid of what I'll find inside myself. That's why she's there with me and I'm safe. After the session, I usually feel lighter and freer as if I'm more the me I'm meant to be. As if, maybe, I can be me without you.*

> *Were we transplanted to a parallel universe of nightmares,*
> *you and I? If I could just wake myself up, could I find my way*
> *back to you and none of it would have happened?*
> *I miss you*
> *I love you*
> *Forgive me*
> *Love*
> *Gen*

Gen puts the pen down. Folds the letter. Places it in the envelope. Removes her dressing gown. Slips into her empty bed.

More than a week passes as Gen successfully wallpapers over cracks threatening to expose her imperfections to the world. She discovers that wallpapering is exhausting work and, to add to her woes, she's now awake when she should be asleep. Her phone display tells her the time is 3:11am and 35 seconds. When Gen checks again it is 3:13am and 17 seconds. *Who knew that one minute and 42 seconds could crawl by so slowly?* she thinks, before realising that if anyone knows that, she does. Gen's always been good with the maths of seconds and minutes. They matter in her job where she has to condense or elongate time. Gen bends time like light through a prism, she supposes. But it looks like time-bending is another of her talents confined to on-set reality only.

Gen lies on her back, wide-eyed and hostage to herself. The ceiling sucks up everything into a fuzzy static. She glances over at Gael, uncertain when he arrived in bed beside her. He looks blissful, while thoughts spin in Gen's head and pins and needles niggle her body. Her heart tick ticks, then stamps its foot, thump thump, and stomp stomps on the brink of tantrum, tightening its grip on her lungs. Thump-stomp-thump-stomp... Panic stations.

Focus on the breath, Gen hears Martha say. Gen pushes out the air from her lungs as best she can, inhales in a slow wave and exhales. She imagines a burbling brook tripping over pebbles and congratulates herself on conjuring such a soothing image. But even before she completes the thought, Gen's burbling brook ricochets off immovable rocks and becomes a rushing chaos.

*If still waters run deep, then busy waters run shallow?* Gen wonders. Is Gen shallow? Just an illusion of depth cast by slanted lighting and random rocks, while her heart is in too deep? Thump-stomp-thump-thump.

Gen lets that thought go with her breath. 'Pwhooo.'

*Notice, and let it go,* she tells herself, and immediately notices that her inside voice is the same as her outside voice. As a young adult, drama, debating and expensive elocution lessons polished and buffed Gen's voice until it gleamed flawlessly. Gen knows her voice is seductive, if not hypnotic. Her voice is perfect.

Perfectly irritating, she grumps now, it will not shut up so she can be mindful. All glitter and refracting light, with depths of… nothingness.

Gen resurfaces from nothingness, intent on mastering mindfulness. *Breathe iiiin and oooout,* she instructs herself as she experiences an exquisite sense of her chest rising and falling. So, Gael's sister had breast augmentation, Gen's mind ticks on. Her husband wanted the woman he loves to be mutilated and stuffed with a foreign object, just to please him. What sort of man does that? What sort of woman? Maddy has always been more boob than brain anyway, Gen thinks unkindly before, oh-oh, mindfulness, not mammary glands. Gen breathes and focuses on the soft weight of the doona, her head on the pillow, he-e-avy, si-inking, li-ight, flo-oating.

Gen can smell the scent of Gael and sex on her pillow. She used to love that smell, but she doesn't like it now and has an impulse to strip the bed and put on a load of washing there and then. That can't be right, can it? she wonders. She glances at Gael who's snoring softly, then whispers, 'Sorry,' to the mindfulness. *Mind fullness*, she realises, is exactly the problem. Her mind is too full. The washing drawer is full too, but unlike the fullness of her mind, all the dirty washing has been folded and neatly arranged. A place for everything and everything in its place. Some people understand the importance of a place for everything and everything in its place, Gen surmises with satisfaction. An orderly mind needing an orderly home–

'You're a control freak fucking bitch,' Gael interrupts. His words physically hurt. *Sorry, Gael, I'm sorry.*

Two hands around her neck. Two black thumb prints and eight purple fingerprints stamped on her arms and thighs.

Blank. Out of ideas. Out of her mind.

Into the vacancy spills every neatly folded piece of dirty laundry screaming and mocking, neat-freak bitch, fucking control-freak bitch, blah, blah.

'Sorry, I'm sorry,' she hears her voice say.

You're always sorry after everything, whore.

Blank. Nothingness.

*Now where was she? How can mindfulness be so hard?* Gen asks herself.

She focuses for a living. She is a master of concentration, or should that be a *mistress* of concentration? Typical, male terms elevate, and female terms demean. Gen contemplates the sleeping Gael curiously and feels inspired to just do what feels nice. Gen lifts her arms into the air and curls and swirls them like an exotic dancer. The motion softens her inner voice to a whisper. *So, when a woman sensually moves her arms at 3:31am in the morning either she is an exotic dancer or an insomniac?* And with that, Gen's voice finally departs. All she knows, and all she is, floats above her, weaving and undulating.

She reaches languidly for her ear buds on the bedside table. Music thrills through her and propels her onto her knees. She lip synchs into an invisible microphone like a rock star. Tumble-turns onto her tummy and completes ten push ups, her mouth silently screaming, lyrics whispering out of her. Then, who cares? She jumps to standing on the bed, swivels her hips and gyrates every part of her. She is nothing but the music.

She glances with smug glee at Gael. *Now who is blissful?* The bed bounces like a trampoline with Gael a lump flying up and down, up and down; an unseeing, deep breathing, bouncing blob. A nothing of a man.

'Don't,' the nothing of a man rolls over and sleep-whines. 'Don't rock the boat.'

Her heart misses a beat. Gen snatches the buds from her ears and dives to a lying position. The bed's boings lull to a full stop as she is still and panting, brushing tears from her cheeks, her heart swelling with yearning and grief. Gen's gut roils upward with fury and a murderous revenge takes form in her mind, then just as suddenly, her throat squeezes shut, her chest tightens, and her mind freefalls. Holes and gaping wounds. Smoke and mirrors. Black void.

Gen finally emerges to snuggle into Gael's sleeping body. Warmth emanates from his muscled shoulders, the soft curve of him and the fresh gardenia smell of his shampooed hair. Gen crosses into sleep.

As sunlight frills the border of the curtains, Gen wakes alone and haunted. So Gen does what she always does: she pulls herself together. She snips off the frayed edges of herself, patches over her raw emotions and draws herself up into Genevieve Parker. Work is her haven.

Gen walks to the studio, determined to revel in the familiar neighbourhood sights, the dance of sun and shade on her face, the reassuring busyness of traffic and people, and the small ritual of a long macchiato at her café. Normality.

Gen has Brian, her driver. She has her own racy two-door. But Gen often walks from her penthouse. The locals are blasé about seeing celebrities on their streets, unlike the mobs of starry-eyed fans elsewhere.

Gen arrives at the glassy and classless 12-storey building and takes the lift to the second top floor. Years ago, urgent cost-cutting made various staff redundant and evicted stunning leased art works, polished-wood furniture and potted palms whispering of exotic island adventures. A minimalistic shabby chic became the employee ambience by default. Except for those on the top floor whose jobs and big bonuses were saved, and whose executive offices are still stylish with expensive décor and glossy framed photos of studio stars, including Genevieve, lining the walls. Except also for the cheap fakery of studio sets sparkling with a fool's gold: glossy and decadent for glamour talk shows; loud, jarring colours and shapes for whizzbang game shows and sleek neutral tones and geometric lines for serious-minded news and current affairs like *The LoDown*.

In this workplace of illusion, organised chaos and true grit, Gen fits. With relief, she steps from the lift into the usual air-conditioning bubbles of chills and heat, the wafts of perfume, coffee and over-heating technology. After her early morning insomnia and haunting, she's made it. She's even remembered team member Maz's birthday.

They are already congregated in the staff room. Maz opens Gen's beautifully wrapped present, shocked and effusive about the scented candle leaning a little to one side.

'Not a Genevieve Parker original? Gasp! Thank you soo much, Gen.'

Gen knows her candle-making handiwork was worth it. Just like Toby appreciated the knitted beanie Gen made for his birthday last month, *That must have taken you a while, Gen. How lucky am I?* and Colwyn loved her home-brewed cider, *You've been taking online classes again, lovey? I love it! Oh, you!* Gen is a strong believer that the best messages of love are conveyed by a home-made gift.

Maz opens the card, examines the voucher enclosed, and is teary and speechless. Gen knows that the coastal weekend get-away for two is just what Maz and her girlfriend need. Just like Toby's skiing weekend went so well with Gen's hand knitted beanie, and Colwyn's country Beer & Cider tour was perfect with Gen's home brew. The very best gifts are both home-made *and* a little luxury that the person rarely would treat themselves. This is who Gen really is: someone who shares her generosity and sense of fun with those she loves. Gen feels warm and loved.

Today all goes surprisingly smoothly at work, Gen's haven. Now, during a break midway through *The LoDown* broadcast, Gen checks the running sheet, straightens her posture, neatens her papers, aligns her pen, checks the screens beneath her glass desktop, stretches her mouth in a practice smile, and twists the engagement ring on her finger so its brilliance is front and centre. *Where is Gael these days?*

The question comes unexpectedly like a hiccup in the infinity of her mind. He slips in and out of her bed, and in and out of her life. He's quite the slippery one these days. He's never there when she needs him. And even when he is there? Anxiety tingles unpleasantly in her jaw. Gen shivers and holds her breath. Shrugs her shoulders quite violently several times and breathes deeply. *Let it all go, aah.* Work is her haven.

But is it him or is it her? She nods imperceptibly to the floor manager as the last squawking finger is silenced with a strange thrusting hand movement denoting zero. Genevieve Parker is back live.

*Oh, what was that?* Gen hears air escape her lips in a blurting raspberry. *Really?* She runs a finger elegantly around her mouth to gather the spittle. *Was that an unvoiced linguolabial trill?* Gen wonders. How unusual. She didn't know she could do that. Gen doesn't know whether to be disgusted or delighted with herself. *Fuck,* she thinks.

*OutRageOnLine:*
*DROP DEAD GORGEOUS GENEVIEVE'S RAZZ SHAME*
*SEE News Anchor's disgrace.*

*Parents furious and frantic about effect on kiddies.*
*GET FREE $100 FOR FIRST THREE BETS ON BETCHA!*
*WHEN YOU SIGN UP FOR PORN&POPCORN.*

The director's voice swears in Gen's ear and the floor manager looks shocked.

For a split second, Gen stiffens her body against the shame. Steels herself against the resurgence of her early morning ghosts. Slams a lid down on the doubts dogging her romantic relationship and all that she cannot speak of.

'Welcome back,' says Genevieve Parker with a divine smile that segues smoothly into an adorably grave expression as she reports on the sorry state of the world. 'Climate change advocates warn that the Great Reef is completely bleached of colour. The nation's peak tourism body is in urgent talks with SAD: Scientists Against Disaster; MAD: Medicos Against Death: and BAD: Billionaires And Do-gooders. PM, er ex-PM, Julian Pope, says the nation is in the final stages of negotiations to sell the Great Reef.

'And in breaking news, we take you to our award-winning, roving crime reporter, Tim Merrin. Live at the scene of the latest violent crime in our beautiful city.' Gen signals the seriousness of this breaking news by tilting her chin gently downwards, blinking slowly once with her extension-enhanced lashes and holding herself and her audience just so for a dramatic second. This constellation of facial gestures is the post-Facefreeze version of Genevieve's signature frown that is adored by her viewers and bosses alike. Genevieve delivers. Genevieve makes everything all right. Genevieve is drop dead gorgeous.

'Drama today, Tim. What can you tell us, Tim?'

As the news coverage cuts to Tim Merrin, Genevieve rolls her shoulders rhythmically to loosen tightness.

'Well, Genny,' award-winning-roving-crime-reporter-and-live Tim Merrin replies, 'I am standing outside well-known Koroskova's

Jewellery Emporium where, as you can see' – Tim Merrin looks away from the camera momentarily towards neon police tape and a gentrified terrace, etched tastefully with the words, *Koroskova est 1927* – 'police tape remains around the area, Genny, as detectives continue to investigate how violent thugs smashed their way into the premises of this iconic jeweller in the early hours of this morning.'

As she listens to Tim's report, Gen resolves to speak with Tim about how a diminutive 'Genny' diminishes her authority. Tim has slipped up. Genevieve is her on-air name, and 'Genny' is neither her name on-air nor off. Gen hears a flicker of Martha at the edges of her awareness. *What do you make of that? That you accept others putting you down in your personal life, but in your professional role as Genevieve Parker? Never.*

Genevieve reappears on screen with a delicate downward tilt of her chin, a long blink and a serious, 'Hmmm. A worrying crime, Timmy Moron.' Wait. What did she just say? *Timmy Moron?*

The director's voice prompts, 'You right, Gen?'

She has skipped a beat in her heart and in the rhythm of the cross. She blinks once and recovers gracefully. 'What is the latest news in this shocking crime Tim, *Tim Merrin?*' she authoritatively beguiles.

For any other person, being authoritative and beguiling at the same time would be quite impossible, but Genevieve's beguiling authority has seduced many a new viewer and saved many difficult situations. The arrhythmia smooths into the gripping melody that is Genevieve Parker, as if the beat were never lost and *Timmy Moron* never happened.

'Oh, apologies, *LoDown* viewers,' says Gen with her hand suddenly at her ear. 'We seem to be having some technical difficulties. We shall return shortly to that story by *LoDown* raving crime reporter, Timmy Moron.'

Genevieve no-one-calls-me-Genny Parker looks down the camera and radiates glamorous competence to millions of screens. Mischievous surprise riffs through her.

One of the millions of TV screens tuned to top-rating show *The LoDown* belongs to middle-aged Aussie battlers, Carol and Reg. Their tele faces a modest, seen-better-days couch in a neat little lounge room. A soft rose fragrance rises from three classic blooms in a small vase on the mantelpiece. Poorly framed family portraits and holiday snaps hang from the picture rail circumnavigating the room.

Pride of place, over the mantelpiece, is hung a well-known bush scene painted by a renowned, and deceased, artist. Years ago, Carol cut the picture from a calendar and bought a frame she told Reg, 'suited it real well'. The small copy of an enlarged photo of a print of the famous original has always sung to Carol. It sings of the human condition, her own condition, and hums of solitariness and intimacy, vulnerability and courage. When she looks at that masterpiece she sees human beings lost and found, overwhelmed and embraced within the magical trees stretching to the Never Never. The blue dreaminess of the scene spills into the room and Carol's simple lounge décor is awash with its palette.

Carol is nestled deep in the threadbare couch that sits on the threadbare carpet and faces the famous painting. But it is what lies below the picture that now holds all Carol's attention. *The LoDown* is on the old TV that sits on a low cabinet set in front of the closed off fireplace and below the beloved picture.

Carol thinks she just saw Gen blow a raspberry and call Tim a ravin' moron, but then again, a week or so ago, she thought she heard the beautiful Genevieve say *fuck.* So, Carol knows she must be dreamin' because Gen would never do or say anything like any of those things. Carol decides it's just her own weariness and bleary eyes after working long days.

'I just need a nice little drink and put my feet up, is all,' Carol whispers to herself.

Carol's husband comes in with a hurrying little skip on his

58-year-old bare feet. Blue jeans button up under a small paunch and a greying singlet reveals weathered arms that are slightly flabby but muscular. A tattoo of a mermaid flows along his left upper arm so that whenever Reg flexes then relaxes his bicep, the nymph dances and Carol giggles.

In one hand, Reg carries a small bottle of beer. In the other, he juggles a half-filled wine glass as big as a coconut. With one well-practised motion, Reg sits down next to Carol, hands her the glass, 'Here you go, Cazza,' settles into the sofa, and swigs from his stubby. 'How's Gen doin' tonight, love?'

'She's gone darker still, Reg,' Carol replies soberly. 'Remember when her hair was as blonde as a surfie chick? Then she added those darker highlights. Now she's like a true brunette. Never seen such a thing before. They're all meant to be blonde, Reg. It's like a *presquement* for the TV girls. Pretty, nice boobs, long legs, blonde hair. You can't not be blonde.' Carol is genuinely perplexed by Genevieve Parker's hair make-over. 'But if anyone can carry it off, it's our Gen, Reg. Gen has what them beauty ads call *luminescent quality* and her voice just soothes your soul, don't you reckon, Reg?'

Carol imagines how the fashion bloggers would describe Gen tonight and says, 'Genevieve Parker wears a soft white blouse buttoned to a modest glimpse of cleavage. A solitaire pearl necklace nestles above, and she wears matching pearl earrings. A tailored peach jacket perfectly complements Genevieve's complexion and the surprise of her violet eyes.'

'Like poetry, love,' says Reg approvingly. 'Yeah, you could be one of them fashion floggers – ha.'

Genevieve Parker wanders into the intimacy of Carol's home like a glamorous friend popping in for a cuppa. Carol hangs on her every word and ingests the news as Gen tells it. Well, when she's not focussed on what Genevieve is wearing, or wondering about how Gen maintains her unblemished appearance. Carol can almost inhale Genevieve's perfume.

'She's such a lovely girl,' Carol says, and takes a sip of wine. 'Apart from her bad taste in men, and the occasional pair of fancy-pants knickers.' Carol and Reg huddle together and giggle like co-conspirators.

'Enough now, Cazza,' says Reg reining in his chuckles. 'Let's see what young Tim's got to tell us.'

They give their full attention to the box, where award-winning roving crime reporter, Tim Merrin, stands shivering in an overcoat against the evening chill. His hands clasp each other in heat-seeking co-dependence and prop safely at his waist. Occasionally they break free and flap like a seal's flippers. A subtitle running across the bottom of the screen says, BREAKING NEWS. TIM MERRIN. LIVE. Displayed in the bottom right-hand corner is the small *LoDown* logo, a pair of spectacles with the number 1 coming up from the centre. Like most viewers, Carol and Reg believe the logo is a bikini top.

Carol likes Tim. She likes Tim a lot. Such a clean-cut young man. So intelligent and handsome. His blue eyes whisper, *Run away with me, Cazza.*

'Ooh, he looks so cold, RidgyDidge,' pouts Carol using her lovey dovey nickname for her partner of 20 years. 'He'll need something hot and tasty to warm him up after this, poor love.'

'Shush, love,' says RidgyDidge.

'Koroskovas has been in the same family for *four* generations,' Tim tells Carol and Reg. 'Seventy-year-old Mrs Koroskova lives on the premises. She was *brutally* forced to open the safe, Genny. *The LoDown* understands that the thieves made off with jewellery that includes *priceless* heirlooms and ultra-modern nouveau pieces.'

'Ooh,' says Reg in a hoity toity accent, playfully nudging Carol with his elbow. 'Ultra-modern nouveau pieces, eh? Young Tim sure has tickets on himself.'

But Carol is transfixed by Tim's every word and every move.

'Detective Park,' Tim's saying as the screen obligingly expands its frame to include a young man in a suit and tie, hunched against the cold.

'Oh, he looks like he's umpiring a ping-pong match, Reg.' Carol watches the detective as he looks directly at Carol, then at Tim, back to Carol, back to Tim, pulling his shoulders back, smiling, frowning, then smiling again. 'Might be his first time on the box, Reg. Catching crooks probably doesn't leave much time for sprucing up your TV skills, poor love. Come on, mate, you can do it.'

With Carol's encouragement, Detective Park ignores Carol, looks steadily at Tim and tosses hackneyed police jargon around like Carol sorts the dirty laundry. 'Unknown perpetrators... unable to say at this time... canvassing the area... further enquiries... investigation ongoing.' Finally, the awkward, handsome detective looks directly at Carol and says, 'Anyone who may have information pertinent to the investigation please contact the Police Help hotline.'

'So, they got nothin', eh?' observes Reg.

'Viewers can rest easy knowing that our very best police minds are on the case,' Tim tells Carol, as in the background Detective Park is captured tangling with the police tape. '*The LoDown* will be first to bring you the latest on this shocking crime, Genny–'

There is an audible groan from the detective as he takes quite a spectacular tumble over the police tape. Tim Merrin turns towards the groan, utters, 'Oh, shit!' and runs to assist the detective.

'Aaw.' Carol smiles. 'Tim's rather heroic, isn't he, love? And don't you just love the way he calls Genevieve Parker *Genny*. Aaw. So cute. I wonder if they ever...'

Whatever Carol was wondering is left unspoken as she gulps from her wine glass, pulls her feet up under herself on the couch and snuggles into Reg. The Gen and Tim show is a fabulous aphrodisiac. An early night is in the offing.

Another couple decides on an early night, but for entirely different reasons to Carol and Reg. Jules and Nance are reading propped up on a wall of silk-covered pillows in their ornate hand-crafted mahogany king-size bed upholstered in distressed white, a gift from King Filipe XIII.

Sitting either side of the bed are ornate mahogany bedside tables, a gift from Wacko Jacko when young Immigration Minister Julian Pope helped expedite visas for Jacko and his chihuahuas. Jacko, a good friend of Archbishop Bell, knew a thing or two about bedrooms and distressed white, so the bedside tables were a perfect match to the bed. Nance's side table hosts a large vase sprouting long purple pencils of lavender exuding a quaint and calming veil of sleepy-time scent.

Jules and Nance make a studious couple in matching reading glasses and serious expressions: sharing the marital bed, but each in their own world. Nance's beauty mask crinkles with the occasional frown or smile as her story rattles around pleasantly in her head.

But Jules' literary world is being rudely intruded upon by restless, unsuccessful manoeuvres to get comfortable in his body. His heavy, uncooperative form aches and wriggles. To add to his misery, Jules' mind is rudely intruding too. Not just worries about the latest challenge to the leadership, the factional misfits or his fat post-op gut and uncooperative health, but mostly an unexpected, skin-crawling feeling of disloyalty, *disloyalty* to Nance.

How peculiar. Jules has never felt disloyal in his life. *What can it possibly mean?* he wonders. Forgetting Nance's birthday last week? No biggy. Missing Constance's ballet concert last month? Ha, men shouldn't have to attend such boring girlie girlie shows and, the sooner Constance learns that, the better. The little missy he fucked two months ago after the celebrity golf day? Jules doesn't feel a skerrick of guilt about that, but faark, is that how long since he's played hide the sausage? Two whole months. It's just plain faarking wrong. Thank God he made an appointment to see Ziggy. Only five more sleeps until he gets some faarking answers. Jules is certain that Ziggy will set him right.

Ooh, that's it. That's what's giving him this foreign, yucky feeling like he's some cheap bastard cheating on his wife, *cheating* on Nance. It's his appointment with Ziggy.

But why shouldn't Jules call his old mate, Ziggy? Nance has been so faarking unhelpful. She expects him to just keep on going back to that Dr Roberta Roberts. Well, Jules is a grown man, he can make his own medical decisions. And this decision is as clear as a no confidence vote in a rabid Greenie Leftie government. Doctor Bertie Zigwell and Jules go way back, to university in fact. Jules can't remember what the old boy ended up specialising in, but he's got to be better than Roberta Roberts. He's a man after all. Jules has every right to consult old Ziggy. Perfectly sensible course of action.

But no need to worry Nance about it, Jules reckons. He doesn't need to tell Nance about it at all. No need to bother the old ball and chain, the old commander in chief, the old unpaid maid. Not a word to Nance, or there'll be hell to pay.

So, too bad Nance, Jules decides as he punches the pillow and squirms into a new position, and falls into his word play. There comes a time when he just has to man up. Break free of the manacles. Forget the manners. Assume the mantle. Call on his mantic manhood to mandate *him*, Julian Pope, a man-boobs-free zone. Just be a man.

'Faark! It's impossible to get comfortable. Faarking impossible,' Jules yells throwing pillows at the wall, holding himself up with his two arms straightened behind him and looking like a whale lolling on the beach.

Nance ignores Jules, which makes him even more irate.

'Nance!' he booms

'Oh, what, dear? Sorry, dear. I just reached a particularly juicy part of the story where the young misfit Wallace comes face to face with the beautiful and evil–'

'Nance, can't you see that I'm dying here?!'

'Dying? Whatever are you talking about, dear? You're not having a heart attack, are you?'

At last Nance looks attentive and concerned and Jules feels vindicated in his victimhood.

'No, I'm not having a faarking heart attack. But at the rate I'm going I might end up with one. I can't get nice and comfy, Nance,' he whines. 'I feel chubby and befuddled and not comfy. The pillows and this bed don't fit me anymore. It's a faarking nightmare. Do something, Nance!'

'All right, dear,' says Nance with a begrudging tone that Jules does not care for at all.

He watches Nance bookmark the best seller and place it on the bedside table. She rounds the bed, picks up the ejected pillows and instructs Jules, 'This is a little trick I learned when I was pregnant with Patience and my tummy was getting in the way so much I couldn't get comfy in bed. And as I recall you were overseas and so no one was there to help me.'

'For faark's sake, woman, don't go doing the whole marital point-scoring thing. Just fix my problem, Nance.'

'Of course, dear, right then.' Nance is all business as she cleanly whips the doona off Jules like she's ripping off a band aid.

'Aaw,' he protests. 'It's a bit cold, Nance. You've sent a faarking chill right through me, woman.'

'Jules! Do you want to be comfy or not?'

Jules feels suitably chastened, remains silent and decides to follow his wife's instructions.

'Now,' Nance continues, her nightie flapping as she fluffs up the pillows, 'lie down on your side – any side, dear.'

'Well, that's easy for you to say, Nance. Should it be left or ri–'

'Lie on your right side, Jules,' Nance orders. 'The right is definitely your side. That's it. Now I'm going to pop one pillow under your head.'

Jules feels a pillow cradle his head cosily.

'And I'm just going to bend your top knee and prop it on this pillow. There, how's that?'

Jules has to admit this position does feel comfy.

'Right,' says Nance. 'I'll just put out the cat and–'

Jules doesn't hear what Nance says next. He is sound asleep.

Someone not in bed for an early night is Detective Senior Sergeant Jimmy Park. It's close to midnight when he walks in the door of his one-bedroom apartment. He's already frustrated with the Koroskova jewellery case and irritated that he was the idiot that had to face the cameras.

Jimmy's body slumps, his face sags and his cheeks puff misery out of his unhappy mouth in a sad sigh. He walks to the fridge and grabs a beer. Unscrews the lid and tilts the amber liquid down his throat in a thirsty scull. He burps. Heads for the bedroom. Strips off his clothes. Jumps in the shower.

As the water flows over him, Jimmy knows he needs a holiday. But when it comes down to it, he always thinks there's no one to share a holiday with, so why bother. Mates have girlfriends and wives, little kids and demanding jobs. He doesn't holiday with mates anymore. It's all he can do to see them for a round of golf or a beer. A shared holiday?

'Grow up,' Jimmy grumps out loud at himself and the world as he squirts shampoo on his hair and massages firmly.

But Jimmy's too young to be a grumpy old man. His financials are in good nick. He's got a good, if workaholic, job. And he's got his hair. It's all about the hair, he reckons as his fingers scrub his dark locks. Yeah, his hair's thick. And his face hasn't aged much. Just not the right face for some: not Caucasian.

Once upon a time, because of his face, Jung Min Park, aka Jimmy Park, was recruited and fast-tracked, mentored and promoted.

Top brass thought his was the right minority face for the force. Not enough faces like Jimmy's in the ranks of police officers and not enough bilingual officers like Jimmy. That's what his superiors and Jimmy thought, until someone dared to notice Jimmy's ethnic shortcomings, while failing to recognise their own racist ignorance.

'Oh, so you don't speak that language? But I thought you were one of the boat people?' Jimmy kept a straight face and replied, 'If only mate. The glamour of that experience, eh? No, mate. I'm from a completely different country. Came out on a jet plane when I was a little squirt.'

Now he reckons the boys in blue want more female faces and faces like moons peering out from the circle of a scarf or a turban. Jimmy is no longer in demand and his career progression has stalled.

Jimmy closes his eyes, and the shower spray flattens his hair as it rinses out the shampoo. He tilts his head back so the water smooths his hair off his face, one of life's little pleasures. Jimmy sets his head to normal and grabs the soap, slipping it under his armpits and over his body, sloughing the messy day off himself.

Once upon a time, football liked Jimmy's face too. Well, that, and he could play. Jimmy figured out early if he could play footy well, he could play life well. At school, he'd belong, be one of the boys and be embraced by the girls. And what's not to love about the game? His parents weren't natural embracers of the game, though. Footy wasn't studying, was it? You were meant to study night and day to become a doctor or a lawyer. They were never going to be the parents hanging over the fence barracking for Jimmy, making sure his gear was washed and ready, taking him shopping for footy boots and driving him to training and games. Jimmy rode his bike to training and matches. He cadged hand-me-down boots.

Turned out, Jimmy was not quite good enough to turn footy into a career. So Plan B it was. His ambition to join the police began when he was a little tacker. Something to do with Jimmy having had a stint of copping it from bullies before he learnt that quick legs and a quick wit could save him from bruises and humiliation. As a police officer, Jimmy would lock up the bad guys. There'd be no bruises and humiliation for Jimmy – well, only sometimes, Jimmy thinks as he rues falling over the police tape outside Koroskovas. But, hey, his parents might be a bit proud of Detective Senior Sergeant Jimmy Park.

Jimmy stands glum-faced under the warm water pondering how he doesn't quite fit. On the footy field he felt fluid, balanced. In life, he's a misfit, yeah, one foot in the world of his family and the other in the rest of his life. Not completely comfortable in one or the other alone. But needing the one to have any chance with the other. Hating and loving his difference. Disliking and relishing how he can stand out. *Everyone is balancing different worlds*, Jimmy reminds himself as he turns off the shower tap. Everyone is hiding something. Just some manage it better than others, *just manage it better*, mate.

Jimmy opens the shower recess door a crack and drags a bath towel into the shower recess where it's still warm. He dries himself vigorously as he chews over his pathetic situation. Maybe he needs to find his own better half, not the women he has sex with, but his soul mate.

'Yeah, and look how that worked out for you last time,' he says and sighs. His hand unconsciously stops over his chest where his broken heart is still mending. It's like he has stitches that refuse to dissolve, and instead they itch and stick out at weird angles and trip him up in matters of the heart. His heart is an aching, throbbing echo of what was, what might have been, and what will never be. His beating, bleeding heart.

As he steps from the shower, loneliness is all Jimmy feels. He smothers his wet eyes in the towel.

'Hmm,' says Genevieve Parker.

Three evenings after the late, lonely night for Jimmy, the early uncomfortable night for Jules and Nance, and the sexy night for Carol and Reg, Gen is back in her *LoDown* hot seat. Gen's fuckups are in the past, and tonight's *LoDown* has been going without a hitch – no visible ones anyway.

Gen has no real answer for her previous on-air gaffes, but she dealt swiftly with Tim who has just completed a live cross without one diminutive, patronising 'Genny'. Gen graciously decides to let bygones be bygones. Yesterdays and yesteryears are better off staying where they belong – in the past.

Unfortunately, her head is very much in the present. It is itching like crazy and she is desperate to scratch her scalp all over, with her beautifully manicured fingernails. Gen is used to resisting the smallest to the most irritating urge to touch her hair on air, or touch her face, or really touch anything other than the minor robotic movements with her pen or papers. Once she is dressed, she must not touch that clothing. Once her face is made up, she must not touch her face. And once Colwyn has her assembled – which seems a more apt descriptor than *styled*, given the amount of product used to keep her crowning glory frozen in glamorous time – she must never, ever let a fingertip stray towards her hair.

Gen digs deep, refusing to notice the accusing torment of her head itch. With a slightly clenched smile and a signature sparkle in her eyes, Gen signals a change of tone for the next story.

'Controversial sex therapist Dr Felisberta Freudenfrau has taken the country by storm. In an exclusive interview, *The LoDown*'s Toby Green finds out what all the fuss is about.'

'Ov course the male has the castration anxiety, but penis envy for the female? Ha, it is the male who have the vomb envy, no?' Dr Freudenfrau, a brooding old chook whose plump body nestles comfortably in her plump armchair, clucks indulgently as her opinions roll from her, like newly laid eggs, plop, plop. 'The man envies the voman's power to recreate life, you see?'

As Gen is freed from the camera's scrutiny, she dares a single finger scratch on the top of her head. She digs a little deeper into her scalp as she continues to watch the world renowned expert, Dr Freudenfrau, wax lyrical, pack her pipe bowl and strike a match. Flame to the bowl and pipe to the mouth, she sucks and riffs on her theme.

'But with such a pre-*ooph*–occu–*ooph*–pation, such an obse-*ooph*-ssion, the male's envy destroys what he cannot have. He murders the voman, you see?' Having sucked the pipe into action, the world-renowned therapist savours another blissful moment of silent and smoky contemplation before rousing herself and her audience with a demanding, 'You see?'

Toby coughs and enters the frame to pick up a glass of water, gulp, gulp, nod, nod.

As Gen watches young Toby's piece for the first time, her finger drops from her hair and she ignores staff flitting about her. He was all grin this afternoon, telling her it was a *feel good, sensational story, trust me*. Gen watches Dr Freudenfrau's 79-year-old grey eyes small and watery in her poultry face.

The doctor's hen head pecks up and down as she continues, 'The church and the Pope have severe vomb envy. He demands control over the voman's reproductive autonomy so that he can own the vulva, vagina and vomb. He murders the woman's self, her reality and her dream, no?'

The renowned psychoanalyst exhales another swirl of smoke, and Gen finds herself tracking its hypnotic path of ephemeral understanding upwards to– wait, what has the old chook just said? Gen's eyes widen as she realises: genitalia, sex, smoking, religion, prime time, children? Why has no one pulled the plug? Pull the plug!

But when Gen glances at the director and floor manager, they are both taking the opportunity a lengthier pre-taped segment offers, to focus on other matters. Toby's interview continues on.

'Dr Freudenfrau, how do you relate such insights to your work with troubled couples?' asks Toby sensibly.

Gen blinks and stiffens.

Dr Freudenfrau blinks and nods. Rocking back and forth like a hen working up another egg, the psychanalyst looks directly into the camera and advises solemnly, 'Have the sex. You are not the spring chickens you think you are. Have the baby. Live the dream in the child to remedy thee many, many, *many* vuck-ups of your own life. You must vuck and vuck, cluck cluck, vuck and vuck.'

'Vuck,' exhales Gen.

Dr Freudenfrau lifts herself from her roost to stand on skinny chicken legs. She sweeps her chicken wing arm towards the open door and squawks as she imparts her final egg of wisdom to Toby, 'Pay the $1500 to the Ruth on the way out. *Auf Wiedersehen.*'

'Vuck,' exhales Gen again. Two slender hands and ten polished fingernails attack her glorious crowning glory with a vengeance.

Following Toby's exclusive Freudenfrau interview, Carol and Reg check the TV guide to see what they'll watch next. 'Such a lovely girl, our Gen isn't she, Reg?'

'Yeah, but that last woman was a complete nut job, wasn't she, eh?' responds Reg.

'Well, I guess so, love. Bit hard to understand, wasn't she, with her big words? I really didn't have a clue what she was on about.'

'Me neither. I reckon she was smokin' somethin' a bit stronger than the usual, if you get my drift.' Reg winks and taps the side of his nose.

'Oh, Reg!' Carol says laughing, her fingers cascading down in a limp wrist slap on Reg's chest. 'It's amazing who is famous these days, isn't it though? I mean maybe we could even be famous, RidgyDidge. Maybe if I take up smoking a pipe and become a blogger influencer–'

'You'll do no such thing,' Reg says in mock outrage, grabbing Carol around the waist and giving her a good tickle.

Carol squeals and giggles.

'Shoosh now, Cazza,' says Reg pulling his arms from around Carol so he can prop them on his knees. He leans forward and concentrates intently on the box. 'The sports report's on. Some sports star's signed a contract for one billion dollars over five years. It's the largest contract in the history of the world, love.'

'It's obscene, that's what it is,' retorts Carol indignantly. She sits up straight on the couch, feeling a bit huffy that Reg has discarded her for some bloke who's got good ball skills. 'He's not saving the world, love. Harrumph.'

After the sports report, Carol says, 'Shoosh, Reg, Gen's back.'

'I don't like the Roosters' chances on the weekend, Terry,' laughs Genevieve. 'Fairley Fine, how is the weather looking over the next few days?'

'Oh, Fairley looks nice tonight, love, doesn't she?' says Carol.

'Guess so,' concedes Reg. 'But what she wears makes no difference to the weather, love.'

After the weather report, Genevieve Parker's beautiful smile lights up the screen radiating her serene reassurance to the world.

'I'm Genevieve Parker, and that's all from *The LoDown*. Good night.'

'Night, love,' Carol says to Genevieve Parker. 'Do you reckon she's got a new hairdresser, Reg? I mean her hair looked so *gorgeous Genevieve Parker* at the beginning, but it was all a-go-go afro just then. I mean she still looked lovely though, didn't she, our Gen? Ooh, shoosh, Reg, it's that Murder Mystery Cooking Show On Love Island.' And all is right with the world.

*The world is completely fucked up,* thinks Gen as she sedately shuffles her neatly aligned papers for the fade out. The charismatic and vuckingly ridiculous Dr Felisberta Freudenfrau was a nightmare.

Young Toby is Green in name and green in nature, Gen decides, and he requires closer supervision. Outraged viewers will be jamming cyberspace. After all her other stuff ups, Gen could be axed over this and that's the last thing she needs. So much depends on her continuing to be news anchor, Genevieve Parker.

Gen pushes her anxieties aside and resolves to stand her professional ground. She will be poised and reasonable. She'll convince the network big boys that a *LoDown* ratings bonanza awaits if the Freudenfrau disaster is handled the right way. Gen will save herself, young Toby and *The LoDown*. Genevieve Parker is smart and in control. For the next hour, Gen holes up in her office, scratching spasmodically at her hair as she develops a thorough game plan to address the complaints and threats from sponsors, viewers and regulators, as she waits for the esteemed Dr Felisberta Freudenfrau's poultry poop to hit the proverbial fan.

Nothing happens.

Gen has no idea that her loyal viewers did little more than wonder out loud about what substance the crazy, unintelligible old chook was smoking, before wandering off mid-interview for another snack or drink, taking a loo break, or arguing about whose turn it was to put out the garbage bins. Gen has no idea that Genevieve Parker's serene smile, like a fresh silky sheet, put to bed her audience's lingering irritations or doubts, and that all is right with the world.

Two hours after the Freudenfrau disaster that never eventuated, Gen arrives at a grand house in a beach-side suburb. A frisson of excitement thrills through her, and her hair, as she rings the doorbell and anticipates Gael opening the door: his smile and kiss, his arms wrapping around her. When they first met, Gael swept Gen off her feet. It was passionate and intense, and Gael moved in within a fortnight of their meeting. True love at first sight and forever.

Gael opens the door.

'Where the fuck have you been? You're late. And what the hell has happened to your hair?'

Gael spits his words out like a chilled wind flinging shards of ice in Gen's face and in her hair. She instinctively puts a hand to her hair but has no idea what can be wrong with her do. But then these days there always seems to be something about her that ticks him off. The cruel shock of him sets her heart thumping and her mind whirring. Yes, she is late. Yes, she's in the wrong. Definitely in the wrong. But, is this really how a fiancé greets the love of his life? For all her worldly sophistication and trappings, Gen has never known how a loving relationship is meant to be, but the more she speaks with Martha, the more this, Gael, doesn't seem right. It's *not* right, Gen decides determinedly. She and Gael are through. This relationship is over.

'I'm sorry, Gael,' she hears her small voice say. 'I am so sorry I'm late.'

He grabs her arm above the elbow. Moves her from the front door towards the family birthday gathering.

'I'm sorry, Gael,' Gen pleads quietly again, her eyes on his looming family all dolled up and drinking champagne in the luxurious home. She feels the pain of his pressure.

'You're hurting me, Gael.' Anticipates tomorrow's confusion and tenderness. The new tattoo on her upper arm: four blue fingerprints and one black thumb print.

'You know Papa expects punctuality, Gen. Way to sabotage him bankrolling my new business opportunity. You can be such a selfish bitch.'

What has she done to make it all go so wrong? She feels pathetic, but then all her other relationships eventually go wrong. She is the one constant, so, do the maths. *Try some new maths,* Martha's voice whispers in Gen's ear. New maths? Gen has no idea what this means. Instead, she just watches Gael. She sees his ugliness: a face all hard angles, eyes reduced to black slits, a powerful body crowding and hurting her.

'Smile, Gen,' he orders, an arm now wrapped tightly about her in a display of loving ownership.

And as he bustles her towards his family, Gen marvels as, in a heartbeat, Gael transforms from ogre to *Prince Charming*. His face softens and rearranges itself into ruggedly handsome. His mouth relaxes into a movie-star smile and his blue eyes sparkle. This well-built man emanates elegance and charming *bonhomie*, and suddenly, it's all so clear to Gen. None of this is for her. It's not about her at all. This isn't love. It's false. He's not her true love. He's a fake. Miniature Martha sits on Gen's shoulder smiling and nodding.

But the truthful, catastrophic insight, and the smiling elf, Martha, both slip like a birthday balloon from Gen's grasp and float away into the vast unknown, *gone*, never existed. While Gen transmogrifies into a stick figure with no substance at all.

'Look what the cat dragged in,' Prince Charming says. 'Here she is, my beautiful *LoDown* fiancée. My drop dead gorgeous Genevieve Parker.' He squeezes Gen to him so that she fears her body might snap. He looks at her threateningly. Adoringly. Everyone laughs.

'Oh you two... So in love, aren't you? Can't keep your hands off each other... Get a room, ha ha ha.'

Inside her body of twigs, something is pounding. Gen's heart throbs. Pathways of arteries and veins are a fault line surfacing in a sad fracture of her famous Genevieve Parker smile. She's cracking up. Can't breathe. Must escape.

'Hey, Gen!' squeals Gael's younger sister, Maddy. 'So much to tell you.'

Maddy's entrance is the signal for Gael to let go of Gen and move with the others to the lavish lounge. Gen's release from Gael frees her lungs and she inhales deeply and stifles a sob. It's just a normal family gathering in the twilight zone.

Maddy kisses the air about Gen's cheeks, hands Gen a glass of champagne.

'Our trip? Like, Oh. My. God. O. M. G. Gen! Like, A-maa-zing.

The coke was dirt cheap. Cocaine city. A-maa-zing. So of course we got into it. Sunbake, swim, then lunch and wine, then shots and cocktails and coke. Oh, my, God, Gen. The coke was a-maa-zing. Sleep in and do it all again. Total bliss. You don't know what you're missing. The stress, like, just melts away. You really should go Gen, it's amaazing. That big stick up your Genevieve Parker arse? It'd melt right away. You get maximum bliss for minimum dollar. Dirt cheap. Love your new hair BTW.'

Maddy's A-maa-zing, like, story and insults would be discombobulating, except that Gen is already discombobulated. Yet, she senses she is expected to say something in return.

'You're trying to get pregnant,' Gen states matter-of-factly, surprising herself that she came up with a solid fact when solid and grounded is the complete opposite of her current sense of reality.

'Oh, that,' Maddy replies dismissively and takes a slurp from her wine glass. 'Well that was, like, the stress I needed to get away from, wasn't it? One last hurrah and, of course, we've got back to the baby thing now. Wait 'til I tell you what I'm doing about that. But, Gen, like, the coke was soo cheap and soo good. It was a-maa-zing. Everybody was into it. Like Par-ty-ville. It was soo worth flying thousands of Ks. When we got home, the first thing we did was book cheap flights to holiday there again at the end of the year. Dirt cheap. We snuck some home in a bottle of talcum powder, like, ha-ha.'

'What?'

'You're such a worrier, Genevieve. Clearly we didn't get caught, did we? Lighten up, you're such a downer, Miss Prim and Proper. You only live once, you know.'

Gen recalls an underground room, a doctor relieving himself at a bucket, a rat scuttling across a bench and leaving a trail of faeces. The doctor had swept the tiny pellets into the white powder, and continued to cut the substance with a cheap additive that, he told Gen, had increased his profit ten-fold. The doctor's cocaine was snorted by sophisticated people partying in exotic locations, having sex in swanky offices, stumbling around nightclubs or filthy alleyways.

Gen steps out of her bizarre memory of one of her dangerous assignments years ago, to re-enter the bizarre world of Mad Maddy. Gen is out of her mind and into her body, feeling queasy and light-headed.

'Anyway, what do you think of my boobs? Like, amaazing, hey?' demands Maddy as she shimmies her boobs towards Gen's face.

Gen takes a small step back. Her mouth tastes bitter.

'Got a boob job while I was there, dirt cheap. Next time, I'm getting a pubesplant, you know, like, a pube transplant. Pubesplant get it? Ha ha. We all got lasered down there, didn't we? 'Cause that was the fashion. Got every last hair out of there so we had smooth, hairless dew flaps. But now, well, the Bermuda Triangle is back! And you can go any colour or shape you like, Gen, but, like, that's for next time. This time was all about the boobs. I went for a size triple D implant.'

'It's a little warm,' Gen says as the room becomes a sauna. Deafening surf rushes into her ears. An icy flame licks her body. Gen swoons. Nothingness.

Gen wakes to find herself lying on a couch. Prickling over her is a throw rug and a strange disjuncture of time, place and body wrought by unconsciousness. She has no idea how long she's been out. She hears people chatting, laughing and clinking cutlery as Papa's birthday dinner party continues in the background. The smell of barbecued steak is tantalising and Gen realises she's starving. Her head throbs, the lights are too bright, and she feels ridiculous. What is happening to her? As she wonders if she should see a doctor, flashes of her hellish evening return: vucking Felis Freudenfrau, cruel Gael and mad Maddy. All Gen wanted was a warm hug and a little sympathy. Is that really too much to ask?

'She's a-wa-ake,' Maddy sings. There is a lull in the distant conversation before the hubbub of chatting family voices resumes. The decision clearly has been made to ignore Gen's irruption into consciousness and focus on Papa's birthday celebrations.

'Oh, my, God, Gen. Like, really?' Maddy stands with one hand on her hip and the other hand cradling a large wine glass, as she stares down at Gen. 'You're pregnant, aren't you?' she stage-whispers dramatically, her head darting in paranoid glimpses over one shoulder and then the other. Maddy scoffs from her glass and sits down on the sofa.

Gen feels the pinching weight of her sister-in-law-to-be's bottom, yanks at the rug and sits up. Gen feels corralled anew, this time by Gael's more-boob-than-brain sister.

'I just knew you'd get pregnant before me. Like, boo hoo,' pouts Maddy.

Gen frowns and shakes her head.

'And here we are doing *everything* to get pregnant. Doing all the right things aren't we?'

Gen nods her head and grimaces.

'And, like, here you are just continuing on in your superwoman world and you just get pregnant without even trying. I mean, like, I've had three sessions with that famous sex psycho woman, Dr Feliss Froyf-f-f, Foyderfuck, er, F-f-f – you know the one who has the unpronounceable name and was, like, in all the mags?'

Gen looks blankly, while Dr Felisberta Freudenfrau's eggs roll into her mind threatening to scramble: *Remedy your many, many mistakes. Live the dream in the child. You are not the spring chickens. Cluck, cluck, vuck, vuck...*

'You don't know her? Oh, Genevieve, and, like, you're middle name is *LoDown*. Honestly, Genevieve *LoDown* Parker, you never have a clue do you? Always the last one to know aa-nything. Anyway, so, like, I've got Dr Frudierudie, I've got my reproductive massage, my Ovaries Visualisation, my Naturopath – and let me tell you some of those concoctions are hard to take – and of course, the Triple

F doctor. Oh, surely you know what FFF stands for Gen?' Maddy stands up to look down on the ignorant Genevieve Parker. 'Oh, my, God, Gen. I can't believe you got pregnant. The Triple F doc specialises in Feelgood Fucking and Fertility.'

'Sorry?' says Gen, raising a hand to wipe Maddy's spittle from her face, and a smile unconsciously playing on Gen's mouth. Her recognition of the absurd brings with it a surge of strength and clarity. Gael's sister is completely more boob than brain. That's not unkind, just a statement of fact. She's ridiculous, this is ridiculous, and Gen's whole evening has been ridiculous.

'And what is Paul doing to help with the triple F?' asks Gen, feeling mischievous if not vindictive.

'Paulie?' Maddy sounds surprised.

'Yes, Paulie, your husband. Has he been checked out, Maddy? His sperm count? Motility? Checked that his swimmers are doing free style not back stroke, swimming upstream not downstream–?'

'Oh Gen, like, you just don't get it at all, do you?' Maddy has righted herself from her momentary mental imbalance to climb back atop her completely mental view of the world. Wine sloshes from Maddy's glass onto Gen's forehead like a baptismal blessing. 'You sit up there on trillions of screens and, like, everybody thinks you know eev-erything, and really, like, you just don't know much at all, do you? You funny old thing.' Maddy laughs out loud at Gen, the funny old thing, and shakes her head as if Gen, in her old-age senility, has just asked the most inane question ev-er.

'You really don't get this at all, do you, Gen?' says Maddy, her eyebrows and tone rising and descending like a patronising school ma'am. 'Let me try to explain this to you so you'll understand, Genevieve *LoDown* Parker.' Maddy snorts with exasperation and sits back down beside Gen. 'So, well, it's really, like, a woman's issue, isn't it? And you know, you don't want to, like, undermine the man's confidence in his villyrility by suggesting there might be something wrong, when he's got to be jerking it where she's twerking it. You can't, like, undermine his ego when he's doing the pants-off dance-off. He has to be totally confident to get it up and hit a home run, Gen.'

Gen cannot stop laughing.

'For fuck's sake, Gen,' Maddy curses, standing up again to emphasise the seriousness of Gen's crime. 'How cruel of you to laugh when you're all nicely preggers and I'm not. Really! But' – Maddy flutters her eyelashes and composes herself – 'you *have* just fainted and you *are* pregnant and we *are* going to be sisters-in-law, so I forgive you,' Maddy says magnanimously, sitting down again and turning towards Gen. 'And so I'll explain it to you as clearly as I can.'

Gen would really rather Maddy did not. Gen sucks her laughter up into an unusual lip-puckering attempt at seriousness.

'Now, Gen, this is how it is. Men have to be sooo strong and sooo focused to press the baby button. You can't undermine him psycho-ogi – psycho-olg-illy by asking him to get checked out, like, O. M. G. Besides, it's always the woman's fault anyway, isn't it? I mean like all the treatments are for women, aren't they?'

Like a jack-in-the-box, Maddy stands, yet again, to look down on Gen imperiously.

'Gen, you really need to get a life. You just know nothing, *nothing*. Like, how the fuck are you going to have a baby when you don't know the first thing about any of this stuff? I really feel sorry for you, Gen, I do. I feel *really* sorry for you and your baby.'

'Sorry.' Gen hears herself say. *Sorry*. Gen's go to, automatic reflex around Gael. *Sorry*. Around his family. *Sorry*. Around Mother. *Sorry*. And now she thinks about it, around every man she has ever dated. *Sorry*. Why is Gen always the one who is sorry? Why does she have to be the understanding conciliator? The pathetic doormat one? *Sorry* is the sorriest, most overused word in Gen's vocabulary. She has nothing to do with Mad Maddy's, like, drug-addled pregnancy trials, like. Maddy and, like, poor little Paulie are in that on their own. Gen is not sorry and she is not sorry for not being sorry.

'I am unreservedly, remorsefully, sincerely, utterly, mortifyingly sorry, Maddy,' Gen says, but this time she is laughing as she says it. She can't stop. It's hilarious, hysterical. She is hysterical. Out of control and freefalling. Until Martha's voice catches her, holds her safe. *That's exactly right, it is ridiculous. You have done nothing to be sorry for, Gen. Would Genevieve Parker apologise in this situation? What would Genevieve Parker do?*

With a sharp intake of breath, Gen recognises a new truth. She stands up, neatly folds the rug, places it on the couch and leaves.

Somewhere between midnight and dawn, the full moon's luminescence beckons. Prime Minister Julian Pope peels off the doona and emerges from his king-sized hand-crafted bed wearing crisply ironed, striped pyjamas. He waddles to the floor-to-ceiling window draped on either side by conservative blue velvet curtains, and holds aside the sheer glass curtain.

The blue moon sits resplendent in the inky sky. Its mysterious magnificence is lost on Jules, but something about its round loneliness sets him pondering his own munificent universe. Yes, Jules is living the life he was destined to live, he thinks, aware that his body is standing taller with pride at that very thought. He is the leader of a great nation and has amassed untold wealth and power. He is adored by the people and looked to for wise counsel by others in high places around the world. Plus, he gets to live in The Dodge. The Dodge is surrounded by botanic gardens and is close to the beach boulevard. Both the gardens and the beach beautifully accommodate Jules' powerwalking and cycling. The Dodge is an easy commute to the nation's House of Parleyment and provides a showy setting for everything, from grand dinners with world leaders, to piddling doorstop interviews. The old world grandeur of The Dodge is perfect for a man of Jules' discerning tastes and traditional values.

'Tradition,' Jules says out loud with triumph. He could have lived happily in some earlier era, he thinks, *much earlier*. He quite likes *ye olde* unwinnable sink-or-swim test for identifying witches and the odd burning at the stake. What do those whingeing women call it now? That's right, the glass ceiling, chuckles Jules as he sees in his mind's eye, women hurling themselves at the ceiling and crashing to earth. Ha, maybe that's why so many of 'em suffer from migraine, ha!

Jules is forging ahead, along a new path for the nation, back to the good old days when men were men and women were women, just as God created them. In the pages of history, Jules thinks, his prime ministership will be unforgettable. He will leave an enduring legacy. Jules' vision for the future of the nation is clear, and he can see the path forward to a golden bygone era.

'Can't see a faarking thing now,' he tells the fat moon sitting in the dark.

Jules lets the sheer curtain fall back into place and heads to the *en suite* to pee. His ablutions flushed away, Jules pulls his torso tall, throws out his chest, sucks in his gut and examines his reflection in the bathroom mirror from both front and lateral angles.

'I am a handsome devil. Of course, I never want to be a lightweight, but strike a light, I haven't been exactly light on in the weight department lately. But after standing in the moonlight I look lighter and I feel light-hearted.'

Jules smiles and admires himself until he can no longer hold himself so erect. His body sags and his smile fades.

'Faarking hell.'

'Gen, wake up. Wake up, babe.'

She is a black smudge of a thought and a shape-resistant blob. Gen can't fit back into the world. She just wants to sleep. Sleep, aah, falling through clouds to soft eider.

But the doona is heavy with his hands. His words are breath on her face.

'Gen, wake up. Can you forgive me, babe? Wake up, babe, I need you.'

He sucks her out from the nebulous deep. She becomes contours and edges, substance and irritation.

'It is' – Gen squints at the alarm clock beside the bed – '4:02 am, Gael. I have to be up in one hour and 58 minutes.'

'Yeah, I know, but I just knew you needed me sweetheart. I had to do something to make up for last night. I was rude. I didn't look after you. I went out of my mind when I realised you'd left. You know it's just all Papa's shit and the business. I've got so much on my mind. I wasn't myself, babe. You know that's not me. I'm just under pressure–'

'Gael, go away. I need to sleep.'

'Fuck, Gen, if you're going to be like that. Here I am trying to make things right, but if you don't think our relationship is worth a bit of lost sleep well, yeah, I'll go right now. You're killing me, Gen. I love you. Surely there isn't a curfew on telling you I love you. I love you, Gen. I can't live without you.'

He loves her, truly, deeply. And she loves him. She is his, he is hers. Gen wraps her arms about him, pulls him down to her and kisses his lips. There is nothing else she wants to be doing at 4:03 am.

'Wait, wait,' he says. 'I got you something. I saw it and I just went, "that's Gen, she's gotta have it". Close your eyes, sweetheart.'

Gen obeys, her eyeballs hurting behind her eyelids as he flicks on the light. She hears paper rustle.

'Open, Gen.'

The light is a painful glare and she winces as she peers at a dazzling gem sitting in the palm of his hand.

'I love it!' she exclaims. Does she? It looks like something the Queen would wear.

'It's a symbol of our love, babe,' he says, looking from Gen to the gem and back again. He holds up the necklace, places it around her neck and seals the clasp. 'Our beating ruby hearts together and our forever in the circle of diamonds. It's yours and mine and ours. You and me, forever.'

'Forever,' Gen echoes. 'I will never take it off.' Will she?

For the next 22 minutes Gen and Gael are a tangled knot.

One minute after, Gen falls into a deep, satisfied sleep.

At 6 am when she wakes to a classical canon, Gen is alone in the bed.

*Dear Rosie,*

*There are things I haven't told you. Things I'm working on to try and put right what I can. This has been on my mind since the day I found your diary.*

*But we shouldn't get our hopes up. I know Hope is the essence of living. It energises and focuses. But you and I both know that unfulfilled hope can be lethal.*

*I miss you*

*I love you*

*Forgive me*

*Love*

*Gen*

# II

# POSSESSION

'I don't know why you want to have breakfast here, darling. It's all so, *so* grungy.'

The woman looks about the café with disdain, her red glossed lips curling to express her displeasure.

'Grunge is *so* last season. Who wants rough brick walls and mismatched tables and chairs? The germ-riddled cast-offs of people with appallingly bad taste who bought them for three dollars and sold them for two at some ghastly garage sale. You're always *so* behind the times, Genevieve. Really!'

This morning, Genevieve is almost inured to her sense that her life is playing out off-key. The weird feeling has been stalking her for more than two weeks now, while her perfect on-air persona has been riddled with blemishes: swear words and distracting fantasies, raspberries and raving morons, mis-timings and mad sex therapists, and crazy hair itching. Her love life is not faring much better. She was late for Gael's family dinner then fainted and she rudely left and almost ruined the best relationship she's ever had.

Gen stirs her hazelnut milk latte slowly and stares into its swirling cream as if she's reading tea leaves that haven't settled into her fortune yet: he loves her, he loves her not? Gael loves her, she thinks impatiently. He's so romantic – he must love her. Does he? And Gen loves him. She loves Gael with all her heart. Does she? How would she even know, she wonders miserably? She's never been any good at love and relationships, *no good at all.*

But this morning is not about Gen wallowing in romantic angst, she reminds herself severely. In fact, Gen should be feeling quite proud of herself because she's here, with washed, styled hair, and she didn't cancel or rebook. Gen showed up. Gen puts down the spoon and sips her coffee.

Gen's coffee companion has taut and oddly bloated skin. She tucks a blonde curl behind her ear, takes a sip from the white porcelain coffee cup and purses her lips before saying, 'But I must say my macchiato is quite delish. They may not know their décor, but they do know their coffee. So many barroosters just do not know how to do a good macchiato. The other day–'

A high-pitched beep does what Gen can never do: stops Mother during a rant. Mother glares at her phone.

'Oh, Genevieve, did you really have to blow a raspberry and drop the f-word on national television? Everyone I know is still having such fun at my expense, *still.* The whole world is laughing at me. *Me*!'

'I'm glad you're enjoying the coffee, Mother,' Genevieve gives a half-smile and places her cup in its saucer. She takes a breath and begins, 'Mother, I would like to know–'

Mother's phone interrupts again, this time with a soaring opera. She looks down imperiously at the gadget's rudeness, then brightens. Putting her hand up in a stop sign, Mother answers her phone. 'What's up, daarling?'

She mouths to Gen, 'Emergency, sorry,' then unmutes her voice, 'Oh, dear God, really? Your grandchildren? Look, darling, forget them. No, it's not about them, it's about you. Forget them. Shut the door, darling. *Now.*' The last word is a command. Mother rolls her eyes at Gen, twirls a finger in circles at the side of her head and mouths with a grimace, 'Going insane, darling.' Then Mother is back on task. 'Yes, darling, *now*. That's it. Take yourself to your happy place, yes, your happy place in your mind, darl–'

Gen reaches across, takes Mother's phone, snaps a small switch to red – off. Red – warning. Red – danger. Red – stop. But Gen doubles down and crosses against the flashing red stop hand. She's prepared to face the risk.

'Really?' protests Mother. 'You're disconnecting me? Really, Genevieve? You know Judith's four grandchildren slept over last night? Four! She's having a conniption. She turns to me for wise counsel, darling.' Mother flips her blonde hair with a frazzled, manicured hand. Her head tilts in a supercilious and irritated mood. 'Well, if she ends up jumping off the balcony or killing the children, it's on you Genevieve, *on you*!'

'I'm glad you're enjoying the coffee, Mother,' Genevieve says again, managing to ignore her mother's theatrics. *Well done*, smiles Martha sitting on Gen's shoulder. *Now breathe and re-lax*. Gen inhales smoothly, feels more assertive now that she has begun and is back at the beginning again. 'Mother, I would like to know my birth story. I don't think you've ever told me my story.'

'Whatever do you mean, Genevieve?' her mother replies, suddenly finding the cutlery enthralling, staring and fiddling at the metal contraptions as if she has never seen them before.

'I want to hear about the pregnancy and what happened on the day I was born. You've never told me my birth story.'

'Oh!' Gen's mother exclaims impatiently, throwing her red nail-polished fingers into the air as if she is sprinkling confetti. 'What is all this, Genevieve? Honestly you are *the* most self-centred person on the planet. Here we are having a lovely breakfast, mother and daughter, an opportunity to talk about my plans for my cruise, and you want to spoil it by asking *that*.' She begins to fold and unfold her serviette, brushing off the invisible confetti with her prancing fingers.

Gen is ready. She is patient and determined. She and Martha have workshopped this.

'Mother, it won't take much of your time, and we are mother and daughter after all. The story belongs as much to me as it does to you.'

Then Gen does something she has never done before, not once, in any of her most personally intimate and closest personal relationships, and especially not with Mother. Gen shifts into professional Genevieve Parker mode. She pitches her voice low and signals the seriousness of her request with a chin tilt downwards. A slow blink with her extension-enhanced lashes and eye contact hold with her audience – Mother – for a dramatic second. 'Mother', Gen says gently, 'I have told Paolo not to make you the smashed avocado with fuyu persimmon fruit, cardamom and rhubarb until I give him the nod.'

Red lips pout and Mother's countenance is quite put out. 'But, darling, that's the only reason I agreed to have breakfast here at this ungodly hour of 7 am. Yes, we mothers are meant to be self-sacrificing, but really, Genevieve, it's all about you, isn't it? Just so it fits in with your important routine, not mine, darling, *not mine.*' She shakes her head furiously so that her drop pearl earrings jingle furiously back and forth in *sympatico.* 'I really don't think you should hold my special persimmon dish hostage to some birth story, darling.' Mother's taut face aims for a frown and comes up lacking. 'I read about that persimmon cardamom number in Rogue mag. The reviews called it *orgasm on a plate,* which I could really do with while Jeremy is away–'

'Mother.' Genevieve News Anchor Parker's astute mind remains focused on her goal. Her hands stay firmly folded on her news desk – er, tabletop – as she cuts off Mother's expected digression with a kind, but determined, professional demeanour. 'I don't want to know about your sex life, but I do want to hear my birth story, just once, please, Mother.'

'Well, I'm not sure that discussing a birth story – anyone's birth story – can really skip the sex thing. And I'm not sure that you'll like the truth, darling. Do you really want to hear the truth?'

'Mother, the truth and nothing but the truth. Paolo is waiting for my instruction.'

'Oh, all right, but you won't like it.' Mother takes a sip from her long macchiato and begins, 'The troubles all began at the birth, you see. Well, of course, I missed almost the whole thing, didn't I? They accidentally-on-purpose spilt the ether all over me, or gave me too much of a dose of something in an injection. I really can't remember, can I? I mean, I was just the poor patient, wasn't I? It's all about the doctors, isn't it? Of course, today you'd sue the hospital for millions, but back then people didn't sue, darling. You would never sue a doctor, gods that they were. I mean the word *litigation* didn't even exist then, and if you did hear the word, you thought it was a new type of pasta, and to be frank, darling, I just really did not want to know.

'Knocking me out for so long turned out to be a blessed relief and a curse, for them and for me. It was a blessed relief from my wails and screams of agony, and a curse because, well, we'll get to that.' She sits up straighter, brushes the invisible confetti from the tabletop and draws breath.

'Mind you, it was over a day old before I got to see it – got to see you. They'd knocked me out cold for a whole day. When I finally came to, everyone had met the new baby, except me. I remember when the nurse brought in the little bundle for the first time she said, *Ten minutes either side, love,* and I didn't have a clue what she was talking about. I looked at that angelic face, your angelic face, and your big blue eyes with that touch of violet – even then there was that hint, you know, in your eyes.'

Genevieve senses her face softening and her chest loosening. Affection stirs towards Mother. Gen's violet eyes fill with the dreams of her mother's love. Here it is, Gen's very own beautiful birth story.

'I looked into your beautiful face, darling, into your violet-tinged blue eyes and I said, this is *not* my baby.

'And that was the curse, you see, because I knew that a mother was given a baby that was not hers. Some other mother was given my baby and I got hers. You weren't mine. That little bundle made my life hell from the moment I set eyes on it. They threatened to lock me up in the funny farm if I persisted with my' – Gen's mother pauses and waggles her red nails in the air around the next word – 'nonsense. So with my completely rational mind, I weighed up my options and I said, *Give me the baby*.

'I chewed on my anger and swallowed my disgust for every minute that ravenous piglet, you darling, sucked at my breast and guzzled the milk meant for my baby. And every day of that week I spent on the maternity ward, I politely fed that baby when they brought it. As soon as I got home, I used a bottle.

'Well, I guess it wasn't your fault you had ended up with the wrong mother. I started to feel a bit sorry for the little thing. But it was hard not to resent it. Fancy taking the place of my own flesh and blood.

'But you know, the worst thing, the most dreadful part of it all? I didn't know where my baby was. I'd carried her for nine months; I'd talked to her and patted her through my belly and imagined her whole life in my mind. I was excited and frightened and impatient for her to come out to meet me, and then I never even met her. I never knew where she was, where they had put her.'

Mother's eyes are haunted, animal.

'It was the most awful kind of emotional pain, darling. The most precious thing in my whole life ripped out of my body and out of my soul, darling, leaving a bloodied ache of emptiness. Worse than any torture you can imagine. And what made it unbearable was that I knew exactly what had been ripped out of me and what I needed back to feel whole again, to feel like me again. I needed *my* baby!'

Mother's face contorts in an ugly rage that is fleeting and forever. She smooths her face with a sweep of her hand over the serviette on the table. 'But I had no idea where my baby was. If my baby was sucking on some other woman's breast or sold into slavery. But I knew she wasn't dead. She could never be dead, darling. I know she isn't dead.

'So' – Mother tosses her head back into prim, upper class position – 'your father and I were a nice young couple, living in our nice new house, with our nice new baby. After I got home, I knew I could never tell my husband, your father, darling, the truth, not ever again. He'd been so shocked and heartbroken when I'd raised it all in hospital. I still remember the look in his eyes, staring at me like I was some lunatic he'd never seen before. I knew he wouldn't cope with the truth. So many people can't cope with the truth, can they, darling? So I shut up and got on with it. I got on with loving a baby that wasn't mine.'

Mother raises her macchiato to her lips, then stops. 'At least I didn't feel the same as other new mothers. I wasn't all anxious and jumpy at the baby's every cry, or worried if she was getting enough milk, or worried about the colour of her poop or – honestly, mothers worry so much about the littlest thing. I was calm and unrushed. You weren't really mine and so I just didn't feel your pain in the way natural mothers do.' Mother takes a sip. 'And it's certainly suited you, hasn't it? I mean look at you now: high-powered celebrity newsreader.'

Silence.

The silence of an emptied womb.

The object sitting across the café table from Gen takes out lipstick and compact. Looks at itself in the mirror. Draws the red crayon across two labia majora lips. Smacks them together. Pokes at the corner of its red-stained vagina with a bloodied talon. Clicks shut the compact. Pops it in its pouch.

The umbilical cord snaps. A wrenching, falling backwards through time. Set adrift from the mother ship and her beautiful, loving, funny birth story. Gasping, grasping. Untethered in the vast terror of infinite space and nothingness. Floating away, *away* until she is nothing but the dot of an eye. The dot of an I. The dot of a full stop.

Gen rises from the table. Stumbles to the door.

Mother's indignant voice echoes faintly, 'But what about my orgasm on a plate, darling?'

*OutRageOnLine:*
*INEBRIATED GENEVIEVE PARKER*
*took a tumble early this morning.*
*SEE News Anchor's disgrace.*
*Parents furious and frantic about effect on kiddies.*
*GET FREE $100 FOR FIRST THREE BETS ON BETCHA!*
*WHEN YOU SIGN UP FOR PORN&POPCORN.*

A couple of hours after Gen stumbles out of the grungy café, Julian Pope is in a doctor's consulting room. Behind a curtain, Jules takes off his shoes and peels off his clothes. He folds them into a neat pile, with the nappy pin, that holds up his trousers, on top, and sets the pile on the small foot stool – for those little, tiny people he assumes. He lies down on Professor Zigwell's patient bed and pulls the sheet over him.

'I'm ready, Ziggy,' he calls, feeling unusually vulnerable. What the faark is going on with him? The day started well enough with a bike ride along the beach boulevard. Faarking journos accosted him on his way back, but that's the jou–

Professor Zigwell pulls the curtain open with a dramatic swish and lowers the sheet so a platoon of Jules' pubic hairs stand straight up against the white fabric like bearskin helmeted guards ready to defend the crown jewels.

*Why the hell go through all this pretence of modesty when you just sweep it all away anyway,* grumbles Jules to himself.

'Here we are then.' Ziggy smiles broadly. 'Now, I do need some help with something that I think you'll quite like. Would you mind holding this special gizmo for me?' The doctor hands Jules a colourful, rattling object. 'Look, it rattles and rolls. I'm sure you'll figure it out. And now we'll just have a little feel here shall we?' Ziggy's hand palpates methodically over the round belly and down into Jules' groin. 'Hmm, mm, yes, quite. Now we're just going to have a sneaky peek inside with the ultrasound, okay? But first we need some magic tummy ice-cream.' Professor Zigwell squirts cold gel from a tube over the tummy. 'Might be a bit cold.'

Jules jumps as the icy sticky mess hits him. *Quite a nice little thrill,* he decides.

'Now, for our sneaky peek. Let's see, shall we?' Prof Zigwell moves the probe into the glug with an expert twirl, then twiddles it across Jules' stomach.

'Mm,' he says as he pushes the probe deeper. 'Mmm hmm. This might be a little uncomfortable, Julian, but just keep your eyes on the special gizmo and tell me how many colours you see.'

*Really?* Jules' eyebrows rise then frown and his mouth buckles with incredulity.

'Aha, hmm, yes, perhaps... I think I see what's going on.' Ziggy takes the gizmo from Jules' hands and pulls up the sheet to cover Jules up to his chin. 'I'll just step out for a moment, Julian. Yes, aah, yes, I think, um, one of my colleagues would be helpful. I'll be back shortly.' The door squeaks as it opens and closes behind Jules' old friend Ziggy.

Jules lies wrapped in the white sheet on the bed, his tummy looming above him. Left with his tummy and his own thoughts, Jules riffs on a morbid theme. This better not be a dead loss or a dead end. In the dead of night last night he was feeling like a dead duck, and Ziggy is so deadpan when what he needs is a dead cert. He has deadlines. He'll be as dead as a dodo if he doesn't break the parleymentary deadlock. This faarking gut will be the death of him.

With his brilliant, but morbid, word play, Jules feels more and more like a corpse. He wiggles his arms and legs – yes, he's alive – and looks around Ziggy's consulting room. There's a box of colourful children's toys and a doll's house with doll residents and furniture. A plump blue teddy and a soft cuddly duck sit on Ziggy's desk. On the wall is a poster with a measurement scale running up a giraffe's neck.

Jules examines the various certificates around the room. Bertram Rudolf Zigwell, eh? Jules never knew his middle name was Rudolf.

'Rudolf, the red nose reindeer,' Jules sings and hums. Yes, he'd keep that name quiet too. But there's no doubting the array of framed certificates is impressive, and Jules is reassured that Ziggy must know his stuff.

'Ooh, that's a very impressive one – "College of Paed-i-at-ric-Gas-tro-en-ter-ol-o-gists",' Jules says out loud to himself. 'Yes, Ziggy must know his stuff all right. He'll sort me out.'

Having canvassed the entire room, Jules becomes bored and a little impatient. He feels goose bumps on his arms.

'Where the faark is he? I'm the prime minister, for faark's sake. You don't keep the PM waiting like–'

The door opens and Professor Zigwell enters with a woman in a white coat with a stethoscope around her neck.

'Julian – Mr Pope, this is my learned colleague, Professor Zagid. She is renowned in her area of speciality.'

Jules glares. Not another bloody girl. Jules came to Ziggy to get away from the girls. He thought *colleague* was a male term. Women can't be colleagues, can they?

Jules jumps as Professor Zagid steps forward and places her stethoscope on his belly. He sees her furtive look to Ziggy and Ziggy's nod. Feels her warm fingers palpate his belly. Another exchange of looks between the two top notch specialists. She moves the ultrasound probe over Jules' belly. 'Ooh,' sends a shiver right through him so he knows that he is most definitely alive. Jules hates to admit it, but her twiddling performance is far more impressive than Ziggy's.

The two professors move away from the bed. Turn their backs to Jules. Jules hears a hissing of whispered doctor chat.

'Well, out with it,' Jules demands impatiently. Jules thinks he's been more than patient. 'I'm the prime minister, for faark's sake.'

Professors Zigwell and Zagid ignore Jules and continue their solemn whispered conferring.

To assert his prime ministerial authority, Jules stands and begins dressing himself. By the time the two esteemed doctors approach, Jules stands with dignity in his jocks, socks and shirt.

'We have confirmed the diagnosis, Julian,' says Ziggy soberly. 'I think you better lie down.'

'I've been lying down for the past hour. Just get on with it, Ziggy,' orders Jules despite his growing trepidation about what is wrong with him.

Ziggy says, 'It is confirmed.'

'What's faarking confirmed?'

'You are sixteen weeks and five days.'

'Sixteen weeks and five days what?'

'Pregnant. You are pregnant, Jules.'

'Pregnant? Sixteen weeks and five days? You mean' – Jules' lips move and an occasional finger count ensues as he makes a calculation – 'one hundred and seventeen days? You mean' – and his lips and fingers continue calculating – 'around about, at a pinch, approximately, four months? Pregnant? Is this some type of joke, Ziggy? Very funny, *very* funny, ha ha. Four months pregnant. You two are absolute faarking lunatics. Clowns. Zig and Zag.'

Zig and Zag ignore Jules' insults, nod with profundity and hold up an ultrasound photo.

'You are pregnant, Julian. You are pregnant with twins.'

Jules snatches the photo angrily, examines it and faints.

When Jules comes to, his first notion is that perhaps he is dead. A sheet tucks tightly about his body as he again lies corpse-like on his back on the narrow bed. A scientist in a white coat and some floosy in a white coat sit by his bed having a cup of tea and chocolate biscuits, looking pleased and excited.

'Is this the party fundraiser?' Jules asks, his mind peering through a foggy brain at an ambiguous reality. He heard somewhere that there was going to be some kinky stuff this year. Oh yes, is that the same girlie that did Bob's 60th? She was rather good as he recalls. Hang on, what's old Ziggy doing here? 'Ziggy. What are you doing here? Haven't seen you for years. I'm not sure what they're spiking the drinks with this year, but I just had the strangest dream, Ziggy. You were in it. Ye-es, that's right. You told me I was pregnant, actually pregnant. A man pregnant, ha ha, with twins! Ha ha. The prime minister pregnant, ha ha.'

'Mr Pope, please stay calm,' says the stripper in the white coat, placing a sensual hand on Jules' shoulder.

'Ooh that's it, come to Papa,' Jules leers as his hand reaches at a breast nestling somewhere inside her white coat.

She slaps his hand away and steps back.

'Mr Pope! Sir, control yourself. I am Professor of Obstetrics and Gynaecology and this is a matter of immense magnitude, is it not, Ziggy?' she turns to Ziggy for support.

'Yes, indeed it is, Zag, indeed it is,' Ziggy nods, eyeballing Jules. 'That was not a dream, Jules,' Professor Bertram Rudolph Zigwell declares in sober, professional tones. 'You *are* pregnant. Remember this?' He holds up an ultrasound.

Jules sits up feeling woozy and surreal. For now all he can do is play along and hope that he wakes up from this dream soon. Jules examines the scan and keels over.

When Jules comes to, both doctors are standing close to the bed and Ziggy is taking his pulse. Jules says, 'Ziggy I just had the strangest dream.'

'Give it to him, Zag.'

Professor Zagid jabs the PM with an injection. It is the medical equivalent of a sucker punch, and PM Julian Pope is out cold.

An hour later, Jules wakes, pleasantly relaxed.

'I'm pregnant,' he says sensibly to Ziggy who is at his desk rapidly typing.

'Well, that's correct. Now, Julian, how are you feeling?' Ziggy continues typing at a rapid pace, glancing perfunctorily at Jules.

'Well pregnant, of course,' replies Jules. 'With twins.'

'And how pregnant are you? Do you know?' asks Ziggy as his typing becomes more urgent.

'Of course. Sixteen weeks and five days, Ziggy. Why do you ask me these questions? I'm not a faarking moron, I'm the faarking prime minister.'

'Wonderful, *wonderful*.' Ziggy beams as he taps a couple of final keys with a flourish and finally leaves his typing to stand at Jules' bedside. 'While you were sleeping we conducted a consult under hypnosis to help you come to grips with your situation. Which I am very pleased to see has been most successful. We also ran some more tests and had a consult with an expert in transgender medicine–'

'Let me stop you right there,' says Jules, raising an arm with the flat of his hand facing Ziggy in a stop sign. 'I'll take care of this. I don't need to know anything more.' Jules gets up from the bed and bends awkwardly to put on his shoes.

'But, Jules, don't you want to know how this happened? I mean, apparently you do *not* have both sex organs. Although you do have a very healthy and pregnant uterus. You are *not* inter-sex, or bi–'

'That will be quite enough thank you, Ziggy. I'll take it from here.'

'But you don't understand, Julian,' Ziggy pleads. 'I've already started writing you up for the *Medical Journal of Modern Miracles* and we really need to get to the bottom of how this happened for me to finish the article. Protecting your privacy of course, Julian. You may be the ex-prime minister–'

'The *ex*-prime minister?'

'Yes, yes, it happened while you were away with the fairies, but it won't affect our paper for the *Medical Journal of Modern Miracles*, or the pregnancy, if you're, you know, not the prime minister. I mean give it a couple of hours, eh? But look, Julian, about the publication, with my colleagues as co-authors of course, Professor Zagid and the transgender specialist–'

Jules hears nothing more. He is out the door. Slams the door. On his way. 'I'm the ex-prime minister, for faark's sake.'

It is only then that Jules realises he's wearing no trousers.

'Right, that's the dusting, two bathrooms and powder room done.' She manoeuvres the upright vacuum cleaner out of the laundry cupboard, plugs the cord into the wall socket and the engine revs to life. Stopping to adjust her phone music to an old rock 'n' roll classic, she vigorously begins a duet with her vacuum cleaner dance partner. She scoots about with little hops as her bottom wiggles and her shoulders shimmy.

Vacuuming is Carol's favourite. Not only does this vacuum cleaner make a nifty dance partner, but its design and bright colours create an adult-size child's toy, rather than a tool for adult drudgery. Seeing the carpet debris sucked up and whirling inside the clear vacuum container is kind of fun and very satisfying. Carol likes working here. Some clients leave a disgusting mess everywhere and then complain rudely when she can't get through the housekeeping in the time allocated. But not at this job. Carol loves the views across the city from the floor to ceiling windows. She loves the space and, if she's honest, she loves being associated with someone so famous.

Carol pushes open the door of the master bedroom. She stops the vacuum's motor with an expert foot tap and moves to the bedroom window, flinging wide the curtains so sunshine streams in.

'That's better,' she says.

The bed is a hillock of bed clothes and clothing. 'Goodness.' These are *her* clothes. Carol is used to picking up after the messy man of the house, but rarely the mistress. There might be an occasional naughty pair of knickers hiding in some nook or cranny, but that's about it. This is unusual, but nothing Carol hasn't seen before. Carol shrugs and gets back to centre stage in a solo dance, bopping and hopping as she collects and folds the clothes from the bed and puts them away. Then, with a dramatic dancing sweep of her arm, she flings off the doona.

Dancing feet stop. Rocking hips halt. Hands eject earphones. Miniature, tinny musical notes escape into the air around her. Shock and calamity.

'Oh, oh dear. Oh, no.' Carol jumps back. She and Reg can't afford for her to lose this job. What has she done? 'I'm so sorry, excuse me, please, I, I did not know you were here.'

From under tousled brunette hair, a face turns to Carol. A body slowly rises to sitting and props on one arm. Black eyes blink and squint. The mascara-smudged eyes are like one of them big-eyed, long-lashed possums in the park, thinks Carol. So adorable and so vulnerable. Especially 'cause she's as naked as the day she was born. Well, except for that tacky necklace.

Carol's eyes roll around the outer borders of the master bedroom. Anywhere but at the naked contents of the bed. Carol always imagined that someone as sexy and glamorous as Genevieve Parker would sleep in the nude. Unfortunately, she was right.

From the corner of one rolling eye, Carol is aware that Ms Parker is more than bleary-eyed, she's out of it. She must be ill, poor thing. Averting her rolling eyes and her rock and roll moves now more like a limbo, Carol sidles towards the bed and gently pulls the doona up over Genevieve's beautiful naked legs, torso and shoulders. Retreats again.

'There you go, Ms Parker. We can't have you getting a cold now, can we? Can I get you anything Ms Parker? A cup of tea? A toastie? A doctor?'

In the absence of any response at all, Carol decides its best to get things back to a normal footing.

'I'll just get back on with the cleaning then, shall I, Ms Parker?'

*Shall I?* Carol has never spoken the word *shall* in her whole life. A word spoken by queens and people like Genevieve Parker, but not the likes of house cleaner, Carol. This morning the usual rules about who does what, when and where and the usual order of things has been quite upturned. Painful tension slices across Carol's back and into her brain. Get out now, *skedaddle*!

But as Carol turns to the door, heartbreaking sobs fill the room, and she turns back to see tears bubbling out of Genevieve Parker like suds wrung out from a hand-washed delicate. A desperate grief and aloneness fills the room, and concern for this delicate creature settles on Carol's soft, big heart like the white butterfly on the fabric softener label.

'Oh, love, whatever has happened? There, there, sweetie.' Carol sits on the bed, wraps her arms around the poor, lost little girl wrapped in the doona like gumnut baby in a eucalyptus leaf. Carol rocks her to and fro. 'It will be okay.' To and fro. 'Let it all out, sweetie.' To and fro. 'It will all be okay.'

Half an hour later, in the shiny spacious neutrals of Genevieve Parker's kitchen and with the beautiful Genevieve Parker clad in a plush white dressing gown, Carol feels like a coloured threatening to bleed into a white wash and ruin it all. Carol is wearing bright blue trackies and a red t-shirt, both $5 specials. She shouldn't really be here like this, in the home of one of the most beautiful and famous women in the country, and not cleaning. It's all so intimate, far too intimate, and Carol is not cleaning. Yet, here Carol is, patting a manicured hand and riffing on her philosophy of life.

'Life is a rainbow, Ms Parker,' Carol says, 'You only get a rainbow when there's rain *and* sunshine. A beautiful rainbow! All those glorious colours appear like magic and you feel so lucky and happy. But then it's gone, and you're sad. But rainbows come back, sweetie,' says Carol, smiling kindly. 'Sunshine comes back. You've just got to keep an eye out for the rainbow.'

Gen is looking at Carol so intently, that Carol hesitates before answering the boiling kettle. 'Now, where's that teapot?' Carol's eyes dart about the gleaming kitchen counter, everything quite unfamiliar suddenly. Her place in Ms Parker's penthouse, her place in the world, has been turned on its head and Carol hasn't got a clue what a rainbow would have to say about that.

'Oh, here it is.' Carol lifts the teapot from a shelf. Well, Carol can only be herself, she decides. This little girl needs someone to look after her, so Carol is it. 'You know, Ms Parker, having a natter over a cuppa is the way we women have got through troubles for hundreds of years, yes it is.'

Ms Parker blows her nose and says, 'I know just what you mean about rainbows, Carol, and please, call me Gen. My friends call me Gen.' Ms Parker smiles and sniffles sadly.

'Of course, Ms Parker, I mean, Gen. Gen, of course,' Carol says feeling quite chuffed. She's in Genevieve Parker's kitchen, not cleaning, and calling Ms Parker, Gen, because that's what her friends call her. Carol opens one of five glossy white caddies lined up in descending order of size, delivers three spoonfuls into the teapot and pours in the steaming water.

The teapot and cups are made from glass so beautiful that Carol is quietly petrified she might drop them. *How ridiculous,* she scolds herself. Carol has never worried all the other times when she carried out her duties as the efficient, capable home help she is. But Carol finds herself handling the glassware *extra careful* as she carries the pot, and then the cups, to where Genevieve Parker sits on a high stool at the kitchen bench. Struggling to get up onto her stool, Carol anticipates an awkward, if not dangerous, descent when the time comes, not like Gen with her beautiful long legs.

Carol wobbles a little on her tall seat as she twirls the teapot carefully three times in one direction and three times in the other, then pours into the glass cups. A divine scent wafts about the two women: strawberry, nectarine and vanilla.

'Ooh, I could float off to heaven just on the smell of that tea, Gen.' Carol sips. 'Ah, beautiful tea, and these glasses feel real nice to drink out of,' compliments Carol.

'Thanks, Carol. Mother brought them back for me from...' Gen's voice cracks and stops as tears well.

Deep in her chest Carol re-experiences the tremors of Gen's earlier heartbreaking weeping. She re-hears Gen's wrenching words then: *I just wanted to hear that she loves me, but she hates me. My own mother,* my own mother *has hated me since the day I was born – waa...*

'Well, a very beautiful, precious gift then, from your mum,' Carol observes, *extra careful.*

Carol has her own issues where mothers are concerned, and then there is her own tragic journey to becoming, and not becoming, a mum herself. Mothers really are a no-go zone, *a no-go zone.*

*Then again, there's always the exception that makes the rule,* thinks Carol.

'You know, Gen,' says Carol, 'becoming a mum doesn't come natural to every woman, no matter how much the baby is wanted and how well the pregnancy goes and no matter how beautiful the baby is. And you must have been a really beautiful, bonnie babe, Gen.'

Carol looks deeply into Gen's lilac eyes. Even though Carol and Gen are poles apart on any index you can name – glamour, income, intelligence, age – Carol feels a real connection between them. *It's them lilac eyes, or are they more violet? How could any mum not fall in love with the baby that was Gen?* Carol wonders as she finds herself swimming in Gen's eyes. The experience reminds her of when she and Reg had that special trip and swam on the reef. Everything was like another world, another light, different colours, movement, everything. So wonderful, but also a little terrifying too, like some big fish might swim in and eat her. The day begins and the world is one thing, and then something happens and the world is suddenly so much more, like there are all these other worlds no one even knows exist.

'Anyway, Gen,' says Carol as she swims back into Gen's penthouse kitchen, 'childbirth and motherhood can be a frightening shock for some women that they never quite get over. There's always this, this...' Carol struggles to find the right word for this delicate conversation, delicacy not really coming natural to Carol. 'There's always this, this mis-connect for them.' Carol swooshes her two hands across each other like two aeroplanes in a near miss. 'There's this gap between you, like there's an invisible space stopping you feeling close.

'That's got nothing at all to do with anything that the child has ever done wrong. I mean, babies and children are meant to muck up sometimes, aren't they? They're learning, aren't they? So it's got nothing to do with anything you did, Gen. This stuff belongs to the grown up, Gen, not you. This stuff belongs to your mum. But I guess you being the responsible and lovely girl that you are, since you were very young, you might have thought that it was your responsibility to fix it, when maybe it's not yours to fix, Gen?' Carol ends on a question mark and sighs, aware of the slightly frightening fact that Gen has been watching her with deep attention.

'I can see that your mum has hurt you terribly, Gen. I understand that you've always felt that lack, that gap where love should be. But I can also see that either you've had others who loved you real well, or you've somehow worked real hard to overcome your mum's issues, or that your mum' – Carol hesitates to complete the thought – 'your mum has done some things right as well.'

The ensuing silence becomes more than Carol can bear.

'But it's not my place to say really, is it?' Carol grimaces an apology and inhales. As she breathes out, Carol sits up straight and changes tack.

'I reckon your' – Carol picks up the packet from the counter to read the label – 'Posch Organic Muesli' – pops the packet down again – 'goes real well with this tea, Gen, and the strawberries and yoghurt go real nice too.'

Carol does her best to coax Gen to eat from the bowl in front of her, which Carol filled with the highfalutin muesli made from every dried berry and every weird and wonderful high-fibre grain ever grown. And rather than plain old milk to accompany the muesli, Gen has all natural goat's yoghurt. Carol blushes at the thought of her own breakfast this morning of home brand tea and toast with peanut butter.

Watching the sad, beautiful young woman reluctantly spoon up a mouthful and munch, Carol encourages, 'That's the way, Gen. You gotta take good care of you, sweetie, especially when times are tough. Is there anyone you'd like me to call for you, Gen?' Carol raises her eyebrows, but the sad young woman smiles and shakes her head.

'That bloke of yours, Gen?' Carol asks uncertainly. Carol has had some run-ins with that rude and messy man. She's read the stories in the mags too, not that you can always believe those, but Carol has good judgment about people. She always has, and besides, he's far too old for Gen. *She's probably got father issues too, poor love,* Gen guesses. He's not even that good-looking either. *Scowls are always ugly even on a pretty face,* Carol thinks.

Gen shakes her head and Carol is even surer of the young woman's odd relationship with intelligence. Yep, gets *A*s for news anchoring, gorgeousness and niceness. *F*s for choice of men and mothers. He seems like a nasty piece of work and Carol reckons he's nowhere good enough for Gen. What is it with these modern young women? Gen could have anyone she likes. He's not right for you, Gen, Carol wants to say, but men, like mothers, are off limits, *off limits.*

Oh well, in for a penny, in for a pound. Carol looks into Gen's mesmerising eyes.

'Your man has to be able to comfort you, Gen. He has to always encourage you in what *you* want in your life. Otherwise...' Carol's soul is suffused with Gen's soft lavender sadness, as she shakes her head. 'Your special one can always soothe you, Gen, and if they can't, they ain't it. This one, him, he ain't it. He is *not* your special one, Gen. You deserve better.'

What a strange turn of events. Whatever will Reg say? Carol wonders if he'll believe all this when she doesn't even quite believe it herself and she's right here living it. Carol feels like she and Genevieve Parker could be best friends, mother and daughter, even. God knows, with a mum like hers, Gen needs someone in her corner to look out for her. Carol pats Gen's hand again, before wobbling down from the stool.

'I'll leave you to take a shower, but call me if you want to talk, *any time.*' From her pinnie pocket, Carol takes out a pen and one of the cleaning agency's business cards, writes her own personal phone number on it and hands it to Gen. 'Oh, and whatever I haven't got to today, I'll do tomorrow, Ms Parker.'

Gen glides from the stool and holds Carol's hands in her own hands, and Carol's eyes in hers. Carol sees glowing deep violets, lilacs, catmint, lavender, hydrangea... a whole garden of soft purples and blues living in them eyes.

'Thanks, Carol. You've been so kind to me.'

Carol feels her hands squeezed gently as her own simple smile and Gen's spectacular smile meet with warmth in the space between them. Then Gen withdraws her hands and they fly about. 'I hope you have no other clients like me, Carol, or you will be setting up shop as *Doctor* Carol. Although' – Gen tilts her head to one side thoughtfully – 'then I could have Dr Carol on *The LoDown* instead of that mad, vucking Dr Felisberta Freudenfrau.'

Gen's humour is a surprise and a relief to Carol. Laughter bounces and tickles, bringing them both together again in this new and warm human relationship.

'You take care now, Gen. Okay?' says Carol wrapping her arms around the beautiful, lost girl like she was her own daughter.

After Carol's kind counsel, Gen manages to make herself presentable. She has lost track of time and calls Brian to pick her up. Gen needs her composed and reliable driver, Brian. She needs close safe walls, protection from prying eyes and the reassuring murmur of a smooth ride in the sleek, black sedan. She needs a reminder that it is not about her and that there are much larger moves in play. But when Gen's usually smooth ride and usually calm driver arrives, the sedan hiccups and Brian startles: a transient ripple across their usually unflappable surfaces.

As the car and Brian hum along, questions and thoughts roll around Gen's mind and gut like petrified, indigestible crystals. Marbles endlessly crash into each other. Beautiful patterns one moment, ricocheting brutality the next. Shiny and enticing, then chipped, sharp edges stinging and hurting, rattling with questions and threats.

Gen chases one in its dizzying orbit on and on, possessed and obsessed, until another catches her mind and she darts after that one. Is Mother even her mother? Mother has hated her since the moment she was born? If Mother is not her mother then some other woman, her real mother who is meant to love her, hated Gen more? She has never been lovable then? Possibly, maybe, that is an indisputable fact. But should she try to find her real mother? And what about her father. He was not her father? Was that the reason why he...?

Gael loves her. Does he? Gen waggles her finger adorned with the dazzling engagement ring, and reaches for the ruby at her throat with her other hand. She and Gael are just both flawed human beings. So, they belong together. But is she meant to just put up with his put downs and…? Gen's fingertips squeeze the ruby at her throat until they are tattooed with dotted indentations of its setting, and Martha's voice in Gen's mind says, *You are missing the point.*

They reach the underground car park of the glassy-but-not-classy twelve-storey building housing the shabby chic *LoDown* studio. The rear passenger door stands open. Brian's head lowers and he inquires, 'Ms Parker, is everything all right? Gen?'

Gen reaches for Brian's steady hand and alights. She is comforted by Brian and his routine, escorting her to the elevator where he presses the button, waits with her, and when the lift arrives, Brian smiles, nods and says, 'Break a leg, Ms Parker.'

As the elevator smoothly soars to the eleventh floor, Gen is left with the impression that, *break a leg, Ms Parker,* is not at all what Brian said, but she has no idea what his words were.

Gen can remember every word Carol said. Her special one would never hurt her. Her special one needs to be able to soothe her, and Gen would feel better about herself when she is with him, not worse. She would feel loved for just being herself. She would be enough just being who she is. Well then, that is not Gael, not Mother, and not Father? Who is she? Where is she? In her tangle of relationships, she has lost the thread of why she is here at all, but she knows there are bigger things in play.

As Gen steps out of the elevator and walks the corridor, the edges of her awareness see glances and raised eyebrows between co-workers, whispers behind hands. Until, 'Colwyn to the rescue! Come with me, lovey. Just two secs and we'll have you sorted.' Colwyn dismisses curious staff with a flick of his hand through the air like a concert pianist. 'Talk among yourselves. Nothing to see here.' Colwyn wraps his other arm around Gen, and steers her away.

In the confines of Gen's dressing room, Colwyn steps back, places his hands theatrically on his hips, pouts and looks Gen over.

'Hmm, we have tied one on, haven't we, pet. I mean, who are you?!'

'Who am I?' Gen asks with a frown. Looking past Colwyn, she sees her reflection in the mirror and asks again, this time with shock, 'Who am I?'

'Exactly,' agrees Colwyn. 'We're just looking a teensie weensie bit bedraggled this morning.'

The word *bedraggled* may be the kindest that can be said for Gen's appearance, she realises. Her face is clean but sad. Her eyes are red and puffy. A wet ponytail sprouts straight up on top of her head before keeling over to one side. The buttons and button holes of her cashmere cardigan are teamed with wrong partners so she is lopsided at hem and neckline. The fly on her trousers has failed miserably to rise to the occasion. A white court shoe is on her left foot, and a beige court with a slightly higher heel is on her right. And clearly fronting up to the wrong gig at the wrong time, around her neck is a ruby necklace screaming, *crown jewels*.

Gen stands mute and zombie-like. Inside her the question reverberates, Who *am* I? *Who* am I? Who am *I*? Gen's heart beats rapidly, thumping to the rhythm of her question, *Who am I, who am I, who am I*. She perspires.

'My cat doesn't even drop things at my feet that look as bad as you this morning, lovey! Oh, don't cry now, you know I love you.' With a flourish, Colwyn hurriedly snatches a tissue out of the box, dabs at Gen's cheeks and chin, hands the tissue to Gen for her to blow her nose.

Gen feels grateful to be hidden away from her colleagues and horrified to be so completely exposed to another human being. Utterly vulnerable and totally dependent. She is being so un-Genevieve Parker-ish– again. First with Carol, where at least she was at her home. But now with Colwyn? At her workplace?

'I miss school,' Gen says sorrowfully.

'I kno-ow,' replies Colwyn, his voice going up and down as if this is exactly what he expected Gen to say and that he knows exactly what she means.

School for Gen was such a relief, the escape from Mother and from home. School was welcoming and fun. Gen and school was a match made in heaven, a place that loved her intelligence and hard work. A place where she was appreciated and embraced, and her achievements were acknowledged and rewarded. Mother never attended parent-teacher night or concerts or award nights. Gen never told her about them and the teachers never had reason to follow up. Gen joined every club, took part in every sport and musical, and dined on the whole extra-curriculum smorgasbord. She spent all her time at school, then at uni, then at work. Work is now the place where she is good enough just being herself, where her skills are appreciated, and her personal issues are nowhere to be seen. Until now. What has she done?

'I kno-ow, school, right?' Colwyn is saying. 'I *so* miss the old flush-the-faggot-head-down-the-toilet parties, the pop up homophobic graffiti on my locker, the caring cuts from old Mr H. Aah, good times, great times.'

Amidst Gen's self-pitying confusion, shame slaps blush on her cheeks. How horrible for Colwyn.

'Now then, sweetie,' Colwyn says tenderly, taking the sodden tissue from Gen's hand and throwing it expertly into a bin. 'Let's find drop dead gorgeous Genevieve Parker, shall we?' He smiles kindly and looks into Gen's eyes.

Gen returns Colwyn's gaze and relaxes a little. She slips ever so slightly into the perfect skin of Genevieve Parker. Colwyn and Gen go way back and he has never let Gen down. Colwyn is a fixer and she really needs fixing. With a nod, Gen gives Colwyn the okay to do as he sees fit.

'Right, first thing's first, eye drops. Let me tell you, lovey, vampire eyes are not becoming. We don't *do* vampire eyes here, no we don't.' Colwyn produces a small vial. 'Look up. Ooh, aah, is that Hunky

Mickey dancing on the ceiling?' Colwyn stops for a moment with a hand on his hip, a little miffed. 'Oh no, that's Jason, isn't it? Lovely Jason was the one partying on the ceiling, wasn't he? Oh well, he's gor-geous too. Take a good look at that *gor-geous* man on the ceiling now.' Colwyn drops liquid first in one eye, then the other. 'Good girl, that's the way, pet. Have a good blink now.'

A tissue dabs softly under each eye, luring her eyes to close. Relief.

When Gen opens her eyes, Colwyn steps back, looks her over again with a frown, and steps forward to undo her cardigan buttons.

'Let's reacquaint these buttons and button holes *cor-rect-ly*, shall we? There we go.' Colwyn nods approvingly as he steps back again, before one thinking finger pokes a deep dimple of wisdom in his cheek. 'Right-i-o, now, I don't mean to be too familiar, gorgeous girl, but this has to be done.' In one swift action, Colwyn efficiently grabs Gen's fly and pulls it up. 'Of course, my real skill is pulling a zipper down.'

Gen feels the hint of a smile trembling on her lips.

Colwyn steps back again, admiring his handy work and assessing what else needs attention. 'Hmm,' he hums as he leads Gen gently to the swivel chair in front of the large mirror. 'We'll just fix up the tresses a bit, shall we, lovey?' Colwyn says to Gen's reflection as he stands behind her.

He gently removes the ponytail elastic and then, with tickling, soothing fingers, massages Gen's scalp and fluffs her hair with an occasional soft whirr of a hairdryer. Gen's eyes close for several minutes as Colwyn's rippling fingers send a resonating warmth through her whole body.

Colwyn moves around to face her.

'Now, look at me, pet.' Gen opens her eyes obediently but reluctantly. 'That's my girl.' Colwyn alternates between little question mark head tilts and delicate magic finger adjustments to Gen's hair.

'Close,' he orders again as Gen feels a cooling, moisturising balm applied to her face with extra dabs beneath her eyes.

'Gor-geous!' he finally declares and steps aside so Gen sees herself in the mirror. The reflection is most definitely Genevieve Parker and she almost smiles.

'Now, I don't think we'll worry with anything on our eyes, do you, lovey? Would probably end up all dribbled down our face anyway. We are just a smidge fragile this morning, aren't we? I doubt that will be the last of the water works for todaaay?' His voice ends in a squeaky question mark that is a definite statement of fact. He surveys the jars and tubes of creams and potions lined up in front of the mirror. 'Hmm, you know what, sweetie? With your perfect beauty, we don't need anything more at all, except maybe a touch of lippie? There we go!'

A shiny peach toned lipstick streaks across Gen's mouth and sets her whole complexion aglow.

He swivels Gen around away from the mirror, stares at her ruby necklace and smirks.

'Well, the Queen would look quite lovely wearing this to her coronation or what, not! Really? Didn't we agree that red is *not* your colour?' Colwyn stands akimbo and disapproving. 'We really were out of our minds this morning weren't we, lovey? It has to go.'

But as Colwyn reaches for the clasp, Gen grips the ruby firmly, frowns and shakes her head. *Mine*, her brain says. Gen is convinced that the ruby is all that stands between her and oblivion, between Gen and madness. This ruby is Hope. Hope that there can be love and happily ever after. She must never let it go.

'Okay, *okay*, you're the boss, sweetie.' Colwyn steps away with both hands raised in surrender. The standoff is brief. Colwyn's Genevieve Parker appearance check resumes.

'Hmm, well, I guess the different coloured shoe thing *could* become the next fashionista fad,' he says doubtfully. 'Oh, you know, like those big boy tennis players and basketballers all balling around with one shoe side pink and the other black.' Colwyn is shuffling through a shelf of shoes. 'I mean, don't get me wrong, pet, I mean what's not to like? Gorgeous, muscular men in pink!'

Colwyn holds aloft two beige ballet flats. 'Ta-da!' Prince Colwyn kneels and attends to Cinderella Genevieve, chattering on. 'We definitely need flats today, lovey. We need to be grounded and sensible. And aren't they cuuute?'

Taking her hands in his, Colwyn lifts Gen up from the chair. 'Right, gorgeous, powerful Genevieve Parker, who are you?'

Gen looks blankly for a moment then repeats with a questioning rise in her voice at the end, 'Gorgeous, powerful Genevieve Parker?'

'That's right. Who are you?' Colwyn baits like a sports coach.

'Gorgeous, powerful Genevieve Parker,' Gen replies without a question mark.

'Who?'

'Gorgeous, powerful Genevieve Parker.' Gen hears her own voice, smooth and assured. She is determined to get back to everything that matters.

'Yes, you are. Now, go get 'em!'

Colwyn turns Gen towards the door and gives her a slight nudge towards it.

Gen takes two steps and turns back. 'Thanks, Colwyn,' she says sincerely. 'You are a true sweetheart.'

'No, you're the sweetheart, you are. Oh, you know that sentimental stuff sets me off, Gen,' Colwyn says, flapping his fingers at his eyes as they go to water. He shoos her away like a mother bird to its newly flying chick. 'You go get 'em, girl!'

*Thank you, Colwyn,* Gen thinks as she walks the corridor back to where she belongs. *And thank you, Carol.* Maybe she should send Carol a thank you, or give her a bonus, or – oh god, hush money! What has she done? Gen has revealed her deepest darkest secrets to her housekeeper, a relative stranger who will make a fortune from a tell-all scoop.

But Gen's retreating marbles of madness are nudged further

along by a breeze of rationality. Carol has worked for Gen for two years and has had plenty of opportunities to betray Gen's trust. Carol never has. Carol is kind and motherly and very neat and very clean. Gen showed herself to Carol without her usual glamour or competence and, Gen swallows uncomfortably with the thought, without clothes. Carol saw Gen at her most vulnerable – saw far too much of her – but Carol could not have been more lovely. And, she even gets the rainbow thing! Gen feels surprised and grateful all over again.

Still, as Gen reaches the door she must open, doubts linger. She stands looking at the door and pondering that Trust is such a fragile commodity at the best of times. Trust is the foundation for love, work and play. Everything that is worth anything requires trust in the other, and that begins with Mother, *but there was no loving beginning with Mother*, thinks Gen sadly. *Trust is dead*, Gen determines, she can only rely on herself. It is Gen against the world.

Gen opens the door and enters. And there is her team. Her colleagues putting it all together and covering for her. Dissecting the latest news and what it means for tonight's segments, divvying up assignments and crafting Gen's script the way they know she likes it. They stop, her team, and look to her with concern and need. Gen feels a warm glow fill her body and her soul. Is this love?

'Thank you all,' she says professionally, 'for your understanding. Now where are we?'

Gen listens and nods soberly and proudly. Finally she speaks. 'If I may, Trish?' Gen turns her violet eyes to the news director for approval to continue. 'I wondered if we might lead with The Epidemic Killing Women story and expand our coverage.' Gen looks to the producer. 'Teasers through the day. Our nation's shame. We could get a couple in late afternoon. What is killing more than one woman a week? The epidemic cutting women's lives short? What you need to know and what can you do about it? This could be a two-, three-, maybe four-night, hard-hitting story. Interviews could be worked accordingly. Maz with a soft touch, hard stats interview with the researcher. What is her back story? Why did she ask the question? Personal? Professional? If she is good, maybe a live interview with me. Toby, the human face? The story of one woman murdered by her intimate partner. Who she is, what happened, the perpetrator, the family, the process.'

Trish adds, 'Why are the police and courts allowing women to be murdered and allowing men to get off? We need soundbites from the justice minister, police...'

Gen is gorgeous, powerful Genevieve Parker, and is smiling inside. Every last jagged and doubting marble has rattled right out of her.

The top-rating *LoDown* icon takes up her proper place in the limelight. Her quick promos go without a hitch and late edits progress. Soon Gen will present *The LoDown* and reveal the unadulterated truth to her adoring audience.

*Unadulterated truth?* Gen puzzles. What is the unadulterated truth, and why would anyone ever want to know the unadulterated truth? Why did she ever ask Mother for the truth? Her life was better not knowing. Maybe her audience would be better off not knowing all the truths she tells them too.

Gen recognises that one scallywag marble is refracting into a stream of questions. She mentally detours around it and heads for her position in one of the four crucial pillars of any decent democracy: the media. Of course the public must be told the truth. *But*, she demurs, *sometimes the whole truth must wait until the time is right.*

In the spotlight, perfectly unlovable Genevieve Parker prepares to report the truth and keep her own truth secret. Out of the corner of her eye she watches the floor manager's dancing fingers:

Five.

I am Genevieve Parker.

Four.

I am powerful Genevieve Parker.

Three.

I am LoDown's top rating news anchor.

Two.

I am certain.

One.

I am very certain about everything.

Swoosh.

Reg takes a swig from his stubby. Carol takes a sip from her wine glass. After a long day, Carol and Reg are sitting on their neat little couch in their neat little home, enjoying the glamour, the excitement, the highlight of their day: *The LoDown* with Genevieve Parker and Tim Mirren.

'Hmm. Tomorrow night on *The LoDown,* men who get away with murder. The system that is failing our sisters, mothers and daughters.' Gen looks seriously at Carol and Reg before briefly looking down at a piece of paper on her desk that she moves elegantly to one side.

'She really cares doesn't she, Reg?' Carol says turning her blue eyes on Reg. 'All those poor women with men who hurt them, hurt them real bad. And then if the woman tries to leave, she's in even more danger. What's happening to the world, love?'

'I don't know, Cazza,' Reg says sadly.

'And where are they meant to run to? Why isn't there help out there?' Cazza is starting to feel angry.

'Earlier today, *LoDown* reporter, Marion Song, asked the prime minister about the 66 million unanswered calls made in the past year by people desperate to access welfare assistance,' Genevieve Parker says, before putting a hand to her ear and saying, 'Just in. Mr Pope has lost a leadership spill and is now ex-prime minister. Mr Julian

Pope spoke earlier today, as PM, after he completed a 10k bike ride along the beach boulevard.'

'Did Gen say 66 million, Cazza?' asks Reg.

'Yes,' replies Carol. 'No wonder women living with a violent bloke can't get any help, Reg. What is it with some men? Saying what a woman can and can't do with her own life. Deciding whether she lives or dies. How she lives and dies. Even our own prime minister, and I know he's a very busy and important man, Reg, but he hasn't a clue what it's like to be a woman. Because of him women are being forced to have a kid when they've got good bloody reason not to. Women need respect from a man, not punishment. And sometimes...' Carol's voice cracks and her hand involuntarily embraces her belly. 'Sometimes,' she resumes in almost a whisper, 'women need help real bad, Reg.'

'You're right, love,' agrees Reg, quite oblivious to the altered tenor of Carol's emotion. 'It's life or death for women, isn't it, eh? Welfare is not sounding well or fair.'

Carol and Reg watch Julian Pope, clad in lycra in the design of the national flag, and standing on a beach-side boulevard. He leans on an expensive road bike also painted in the flag colours. A matching helmet hangs from a handle bar. The PM's hair is slicked back, thighs and calves muscular. Carol's glance at his crotch is obstructed by a stomach very much front and centre.

Carol says, 'You can't say he's not patriotic though, can you?'

Reg says, 'Blimey, Cazza, he's really put on the puddin'.'

The PM scoffs. 'Sixty-six million? Not correct. Fiddled news. Trumped up truth.' Pope looks directly down *The LoDown* camera to speak with Carol and Reg in their lounge room. 'But what everyone *will* be happy about is that my government has reduced the cost of running our welfare budget by 180%. We now *make* money from single mums, the disabled, and all those other dole bludgers. Now that's money we can use to support our big businesses and our hard-working politicians. That money rightly can go to our nation-building negative-gearers, and everyone who works hard for a living and pays their taxes. Plus we are on track to cut taxes.'

Carol harrumphs.

Reg says, 'I know the PM's gotta rein in the budget somewhere, love, but I reckon he's lost touch with ordinary people and what it's like for people out in the real world. Maybe that's what happens when you've got a cushy million-bucks-a-year job, a mega-bucks pension-for-life and live in a mansion.'

Carol's frown furrows more deeply as her thoughts take a worrying turn.

'I hope I didn't overstep the mark with what I said to Gen. What if she doesn't want me back, Reg? And you know, love, I didn't get the job done, did I? I was chatting with Gen, wasn't I? Didn't get the next job done either. I could be in trouble, Reg. I'm sorry, love. I mean they'll cut my pay. As long as they don't sack me, eh?'

'It'll be all right, Cazza. The dole's just a phone call away,' jokes Reg.

'I'd do it all again though, Reg,' says Carol, ignoring Reg's wit. 'Even if I do lose my job. I couldn't just leave her there all alone. She was in such a bad way. Who knows what she might have done? What sort of mother says such a thing? How can that woman even call herself a mother? My own mum wasn't so great, well, she was a prostitute who preferred a line of drugs better than her daughter, but...' Carol shakes her head angrily.

Gen reappears on the screen.

'The tax office began legal action today to recoup unpaid taxes from five big bludgers, excuse me, big businesses. The unpaid taxes for each runs to hundreds of millions of dollars, and according to Tax Office Chief Mr Frank Hoarder is the first of hundreds of planned legal actions against big bludgers, excuse me again, big corporations.' Gen smiles. 'PM Pope had this to say earlier today.'

'Nah, Gen would never let me get the sack,' Carol states confidently as she watches the PM flipping a leg in the air to dismount his bike and wobble to a stop. Puffing and sweaty, the PM removes his helmet, and takes a swig from his water bottle. His hair is a scarecrow's until his hands smooth it back into the hairdo Carol saw in a previous segment. She has some sense that Time is messing with her and the world is off-balance.

'The world's gone mad, Reg. But Gen's a good person isn't she, love?' says Carol, uninterested in what the PM on the tele is saying. 'I feel real proud of how she has got herself all put back together to do her job so good. I bet she's still hurting underneath, though. She's just real brave and professional. She's just real gorgeous, Reg,' Carol says dreamily. '*My friends call me Gen*, she said to me. *Call me Gen*, she said. To me. I mean today I felt like I was her mum, Reg. It felt nice, you know? I know she's not a little girl, but if you had have seen her, love, broke my heart to see her like that. I'm so glad I was there, so glad I could help that little girl today Reg, and then there we were sitting together, Princess Genevieve and the cleaning lady. Here's Gen this famous, glamorous newsreader, and me? Well.'

'You, my darling,' says Reg looking at Carol, 'you are *my* princess.'

'And you are my prince charming,' Carol reciprocates. They smile and kiss. *Such a beautiful feeling to know you have someone who loves you,* thinks Carol. 'Gen doesn't seem to have anybody who really loves her, Reg. Just that loser boyfriend of hers and that cow of a mother.'

'It'll be all right, Cazza.'

'I just felt so, so sad for her,' says Carol to the tele, her eyes watching but not seeing the ad now on screen. 'And I was furious with her mum. But you're in dangerous waters if you criticise someone's mum. You get nowhere, right? So I told her RidgyDidge,' Carol says now turning to Reg, 'I told that beautiful young woman, "You are a beautiful, young woman, Gen. You are beautiful on the outside and the inside. You are smart and kind. You've done nothing wrong", I said. "Gen," I said, "you deserve to be loved, love. Cherished", I said.

I was a really good mum to her, you know, and all the time, I wanted to tell her, Reg. I so wanted to tell her.'

Heartbreaking sobs ripple through Carol's body.

'Oh, Cazza, come here, love, you soft-hearted, beautiful woman, you.' Reg takes her wine glass and puts it on the side table. Does the same with his stubby. Holds her in his arms. 'It's okay, love, you let it out. It's okay.'

'I – I wanted to tell her. I wanted to tell her so much, Reg.'

'I know love, I know.' Reg rubs her back, rocks her quietly. Carol's special one soothing her.

'My little one would be older than Gen. Probably married now with a couple of kids. Or, maybe a career professional like Gen. Or maybe... But you know Gen's got lots of time, I mean she must only be 30 or so, don't you reckon? But today? It just brought it all back. The 10th of September, 40 years ago, Reg. They scratched that date so deep in my heart, them monsters with claws. Forty years. Can you believe it? And today I just, well, I just wanted to tell Gen about my own precious, beautiful baby. Tell her how the bastards took her away from me. I was just a girl, Reg.'

'I know, love. It's okay, love.'

'No, it's not okay,' Cazza says, pulling away from Reg and surprised by her anger, still, after all these years. She wipes her sleeve over her wet face. 'It's not okay at all.'

'You're right Cazza,' concedes Reg. 'It was bloody wrong, love. It was so bloody awful. It was.' Carol appreciates that Reg is searching hard for the right word. 'Sinful,' he states emphatically, as if the word itself can stamp its foot on the throats of the evil power brokers that thought doing such a thing was okay.

Carol feels vindicated by the word Reg speaks, but cries uncontrollably as emotion dances grotesquely inside her. Humiliation and heartbreak. Helplessness and fury. She was a piece of trash called Carol, and sometimes she still is.

'I was the 14-year-old runaway, Reg, crying out for my own

mother. A child in the agony of childbirth and they pick up my new born baby and never bring her back. I ask, they tell me nothing. I scream, they tell me nothing. Finally they bring in the doctor and he nods to that cow of a charge nurse and she slaps me hard to shut me up and the doctor says, "You're baby died. Just as well, you irresponsible girl. Next time, keep your knees shut", he says, "It's for the best", he says. "You'll get over it", he says.

'And then to hear those nurses talk behind their hands. Thought I was asleep. As if I could sleep. Talking about my baby and how they gave her to that "lovely young couple" next door,' says Carol in a patronising la-de-da voice. 'I mean, back then, what did you do when the doctors accidentally stuff up the birth of such a lovely young *properly married* couple? Stuff it up so badly the baby dies? "Almost lost the mother too", they said. I tell you what they do, they cover their own arses. The doctor tells the nurse to go next door to the teenage slut who's in the shrieking throes of labour. Take her healthy, baby girl, put a tag on the babe's wrist saying she is now Baby Hoity Toity, the property of the lovely young couple next door, and no one is any the wiser.'

With hiccupping sobs, Carol struggles to catch her breath and her words. Reg rocks her in his arms until her tears abate and her breathing calms. Finally she sighs deeply.

'Maybe it was for the best, I don't know, Reg. I was so young. I had no one to help me. I just needed a bit of help, just a bit of kindness. Someone to... Anyway, I'll just never ever really get over it, Reg, and something just sets me off and it's like it happened yesterday.'

Unexpectedly, Reg sits up and reaches for the remote. 'Sorry, love. Gen just said your name, love.'

'What do you mean, love?'

'I'm not sure, but let's just rewind a bit. I mean I might be hearing things or probably some new famous celeb housewife or chef called Carol or... Let's just... Here we go.'

Carol blinks and wipes her eyes, watches the footage. For the briefest moment, Genevieve's eyes are veiled by long lashes as she looks downward to her news desk and casually neatens the pile of already meticulously organized papers in front of her. Then her extraordinarily beautiful eyes look up and into Carol's.

'Here is a special Thank You, to a special someone. Thank you, Carol. The world would be a better place if there were more people like Carol.' Genevieve's gaze and smile hold for a crucial two seconds, an eternity in screen time.

A tear trickles down Carol's cheek.

*OutRageOnLine:*
*GENEVIEVE'S LESBIAN LOVER, CAROL*
*Sign up for girl on girl sex porn today and*
*Receive half price Betcha!*

*Dear Rosie,*

> *I'm uncertain about everything. ~~I can't even write I want to tell you~~*
> *I'm so sorry my darling Rosie.*
> *You are the only one who keeps me going. I can do it for you. I will do it for you.*
> *Love Always*
> *Gen*

# III

# OBSESSION

At 3:11am the next morning, **Gen** is awake again when she should be asleep. She is a mind full of ghosts and a body full of agitation. The bed beside her is empty. Gael and sweet dreams failed to show.

She needs to run. To call Brian at 3:11am for a run is unthinkable, but she needs to run. Just go, she tells herself.

Five minutes later, Gen is on the street in a flow of striding legs and swinging arms. Cross-trainers hit pavement like hammers on wood. Noises and scents hum in the darkness and echo in the quiet emptiness. The rare cab or car passes and an ambiguous figure steps into a delivery van parked at a curb. Random lights blink from buildings and street lamps spotlight Gen's route. Her heart pumps and muscles stretch and loosen. Freedom washes over her skin and through her hair. Gen breathes and feels alive.

Out of nowhere, a black streak roars and screeches, jolts over the gutter onto the footpath ahead. Gen slows. A door flings open. Gen stops. A bundle rolls out, dumped by disembodied hands. The door slams shut and the vehicle reverses, bump, bump onto the road. Deep growl of the engine as it accelerates away.

Gen runs to the bundle. Earthiness hangs in the air and ketones hover. Blood stains on fabric. A white face moans.

'Hang on, help is coming,' Gen says, a quiver threading her gentle voice. Gen unzips her pocket, retrieves her phone and speaks, 'I need you. A backyarder. Hurry, please, *hurry*.' Gen peels off her running jacket, places it over the woman and kneels beside her. 'We'll have you warm in no time,' Gen says shivering in her sports bra and forcing herself to smile. 'It's okay, I'm Gen. I'm here, and help is coming,' says Gen as calmly as she can, and as much to reassure herself as the injured woman. 'It's okay,' Gen says even as her body shakes and her brain says, not okay, *not okay*.

The white van finally pulls up. Wearing white track pants and T, Gen's driver, Brian, opens the rear doors to a similarly track-suited woman and an interior kitted out with ambulance precision. In seconds, the patient is gone, headed for urgent medical care to be delivered with the utmost discretion.

Gen stands on the footpath loose at the knees and heavy in her heart. Light in her head and tight in her gut. Gen knows too much. The world is too much. She breathes in and out and pulls herself tall. Then she runs like she can outrun the spinning planet.

Jules sleeps late the day after the fiasco of his twin pregnancy diagnosis. He breakfasts lazily and, against Nance's advice, he takes a faarking doorstop in his dressing gown, with faarking journos and their faarking stupid questions about faarking stupid world events. Finally showered and dressed for the day, Jules is alone in his office seated at his oak and walnut knee-hole desk, a gift from the high chancellor. Jules taps at his phone and puts it to his ear, only to hear it ring out. He tries again with the same result.

'What the faark kind of country are we living in?' he fumes. Jules is used to others doing the waiting for him. He doesn't wait. He never waits. Too many things are a weight on his mind to wait. He carries the weight of the nation. Deals with the weighty issues that can't wait. Pulls his weight and punches above his weight and throws his weight around. But, 'I do not wait! I'm the prime minister, for faark's sake!'

Even as he hears himself say it, Jules realises he's really not sure if he is still the PM. Politics these days is a banana republic of rapidly changing heads of state, Jules rues. All without bloodshed of course. The country prides itself on its bloodless coups. Opposition coups, cabinet rebellions, party betrayals. All cutting you off at the knees. Stabbing you in the back. Burying a dagger in your heart. Slitting your throat. No blood shed, of course, Jules reminds himself. But it's all so faarking exhausting and disorienting.

'Hang on, no, I'm not the ex-PM, I *am* the prime minister. I'm the prime minister, for faark's sake!' Jules bullies his phone. 'Answer me!' he dares.

On Jules' seventh try, a woman answers in a sing song voice, 'Love Life Help Line.'

Prime Minister Pope clears his throat nervously and pitches his voice as high as he can, 'I'm pregnant and I don't want to be.'

'Right, we can tee up a counselling appointment for you.'

'But I don't need a counsellor. I know I'm not happy and I know what I need. I need a referral to a faarking,' and his squeaking voice gives way to an angry basso whisper, 'abortion clinic.'

'Now madam, I really must insist that you watch your language. We don't use the "A" word here.'

'What do you mean you don't use the "A" word?' Jules bellows, before he remembers he is meant to be speaking like a girl. 'It's the "A" word I want.'

'Well, I'm sorry madam, but you must see a counsellor before anything else can happen.'

'Well, make me the faarking appointment then,' Jules says impatiently.

'Okay, now there is a five week wait to see a counsellor. But in the mean time you can book to have an ultrasound. You need to do that before you can be seen by a counsellor.'

'But you said I need to see the counsellor before anything else, and I've had a faarking ultrasound already.'

'Any ultrasound you have had already will not do. You must go through Saint Mary's Holy Trinity Hospital. I can make an appointment for you if you like?'

'Well make me the faarking appointment then,' Jules replies not yet having worked out what that might mean and his throat burning with the effort of speaking in a high voice.

'Ah, the first available appointment is in seven weeks.'

'But you said–'

'I don't make the rules. Prime Minister Pope's government does, so you can take it up with him. All this is treated very seriously under the Terrorism Act. So, the ultrasound is in seven weeks' time, and before you interrupt again madam, I know it is after the counselling session I made for you, and I know that the legislation stipulates that you must have the ultrasound video with you or you are not eligible for the counselling, so perhaps we'll just pop that counselling session in a bit later shall we?'

Jules' voice roars in all its male PM ferocity, 'But all I want is an abortion, you faarking bitch.'

'Now madam I have asked you nicely to refrain from rude language. I'm afraid if you use the "A" word one more time, I'll have to end this conversation. We don't do the "A" word here. Now, it's all quite simple. You will receive a letter, sent out on the 30th of the month, setting out your options and providing you with relevant phone numbers. That is, once you've had your ultrasound, and after your counselling session, which, I'll just do a rough calculation for you, should be in roughly 18 weeks' time. And madam, I suggest you make an appointment to see someone about your vocal chords. You sound like you might have some throat cysts, or worse.'

Two hours later, Jules pours a glass of whiskey for the archbishop as they both sit together in The Dodge den in matching winged phoenix lounge chairs, a gift from a pharaoh.

'Look, Bell, my ankles are swollen, I'm half the night to the toilet, my blood pressure is skyrocketing, I'm fat as a faarking fart, and the very thought of something growing inside me makes me want to puke. I'm the prime faarking minister for faark's sake.'

Archbishop Bell sips his whiskey appreciatively, coughs and proceeds, 'This is a gift from God, Julian. This is a miracle wrought by His hand.'

'Don't give me that religious crap, Johnnie!' Jules admonishes the Bell. 'This pregnancy is outside the usual rules and you know it.'

'Oh, Julian, no, no, I mean the whiskey. The whiskey is an absolute gift from God. M-Mmm, tasty little drop.'

'For faark's sake, Johnnie, you're not here for the faarking whiskey, you're here for me. I need your help to get rid of this abomination.'

The archbishop frowns and sermonises in his most sonorous voice, 'My son, your pregnancy is a gift from the Lo-ord, a mi-iracle. You have been chosen, Julian. You are the Chosen One and the male Madonna. The Holy Papa Julian and the Holy Mother Mary in one. You may be carrying,' and he pauses for effect, 'Two sons of God.'

'I don't want to be the Holy Papa Julian!' whines Jules. 'And this pregnancy is most definitely the daughters of the devil!' Jules angrily throws his hands up so the entire contents of his glass splashes over his belly, and thumps his glass down on the 400-year old side table given to him by the Queen. He stands up furiously, grasping beneath his ballooning and untucked shirt for his hanky. A giant pair of yellow boxers beams out from unzipped trousers held together at the waist by a chain of nappy pins.

The archbishop seems unfazed, either by Jules' outburst or his pregnancy attire. He stands and deliberately removes the whiskey bottle from Jules' reach, settles back in his chair and pours himself a refill, all the while admonishing Jules, 'You really should not be drinking alcohol, Jules. Are you taking your fruitful folate? Keeping away from sinful shell fish? And all that evil bain-marie food? Are you keeping pure with the right exercises, Jules? You have to look after yourself and your babies, Julian.'

As if Jules is not hurt enough by his friend riding rough shod over his feelings, the Bell cuts Jules off and again seems awfully happy about his predicament.

'Of course!' the Bell exclaims, 'That's the next thing on our agenda, isn't it? The regulation of pregnant women so that they do not smoke, drink or eat anything they should not, do anything they should not, attend all their medical appointments, exercise appropriately, must be in a loving relationship with the father and so on and so forth, with a dob-in-a-preggers-mama hot-line. And for unworthy mothers? Confinement in prison and confiscation of their baby to the home of a God-fearing het-ero-sex-sual couple.'

Jules musters all the self-control he can to reply. 'With all due respect, Bell' – which, as Jules knows more than most, is the preamble to disrespectfully asserting some home truths – 'I'm a faarking man, not a faarking cow!' Jules gets up with some pregnancy-induced difficulty from the winged phoenix chair, glares at the Bell, retrieves his bottle of whiskey and fills another glass for himself.

But the archbishop is not at all deterred.

'Now, now Julian, my dear fellow, pregnancy can make a man a little irrational, don't you know, a little hysterical? It's not unusual to be a little prone to neurosis or a touch of the old psychosis. Let's just look at this rationally like the rational men we are. You and I worked so hard and patiently on our Concatenate Of Conception and Unborn Person Priority amendment to the Terrorism Act. Do you think His Holiness would have even glanced my way if it wasn't for this life work of mine? A little administrator from some far flung country? Why, the Vatican doesn't even know where our nation is in the world, Julian. Might as well be on some other God-forsaken planet. My Vatican mail takes three redirections before it reaches me.' The Bell shakes his head and closes his eyes. 'No, we cannot compromise.' His eyes pop wide open. 'Even for you, Julian. I could sit at the table of the wealthiest, most powerful institution in the world, Julian. I could head the money, *the money*.' A dribble of saliva spills out of the archbishop's mouth and onto the drinking glass before he quaffs God's miracle of a whiskey.

Jules' turns around like a dog chasing its tail, sensing the answer must be somewhere just out of sight. After two turns, and feeling a little giddy, Jules stops only to find himself exactly back where he began.

'Stop that nonsense, Julian, and stop that racket!' bellows the Bell, his face scrunching grotesquely as Jules' teeth grind metallic filling on metallic filling. 'Pull yourself together man. You and I, we did this, inch by inch, step by step. The mandatory Medi-con counselling. The mandatory around-sound, magnified, 3-D ultrasound and the prescribed information about the baby's soul from conception. The fires of hell for abortion sinners and abortion's appalling dangers. The compulsory pathway via the Love Life Help Line. Upping the accreditation criteria for abortion clinics and hospitals till they had to be palaces and most of 'em had to shut down. And the way we swatted that ghastly medication abortifacient away with a little argy bargy trade war, it was just,' tears appear in the Bell's eyes, 'so, so inspirational, Julian. I, you, we were magnificent.

'But our absolute stroke of genius, Julian? Abortion as an act of terrorism. I mean your mob love nothing more than a *de*-regulated, free-range and dog-eat-dog market. But just say the word *terrorism* and everyone's on board with legislating and enforcing, detaining and imprisoning. This is the first time in living history, women will outnumber men in our prisons and in the mortality stats. That is something to be proud of Julian. And our population growth has been outstanding. Go forth and multiply. And we are. None of this overpopulate and perish crap. We, the money men, know we need growth, Julian, *growth*.' The archbishop stares at Jules' belly, 'Growth is all that matters. God won't let us down. You can't go shaky at the knees now, Julian.'

Shaky at the knees is exactly how Jules feels. He drops into his chair as if admitting defeat. 'Of course, all that rings a bell. We *were* there with bells on. But hell's bells, Bell, none of this is ringing my bell anymore, *none of it*!'

'Look, Julian, just man up. You are our *piece de resistance*, Julian. You are a miracle. You must love your babies, Julian. Just love your faarking babies!' With a leer Johnnie Bell adds, 'You and I can make a nice little nest egg out of this first pregnant man in the world gig, Jules, and twins to boot.'

Alone again in The Dodge den, Jules moans, 'I won't be saved by the Bell then,' and sculls what's left in his crystal tumbler of whiskey.

Jules' roly-poly pregnant body is strewn on a modern objet d'art leather sofa, a present from a new hip world leader. Jules feels so rattled after his meeting with Johnnie Bell that he can't keep his self-talk on the inside of his head. Instead he talks to himself out loud, ranting and raving.

'The Bell can be such a faarking dingdong sometimes. No one gets it, gets this. I can *not* have a baby, let alone two. I will *not* have a baby, let alone two. They're not even bloody babies for god's sake. All this is some outrageous mistake. Those twin *its* are faarking leeches and wouldn't even exist without me.'

Jules belches loudly as his sculled whiskey collides with his pregnant tummy.

'It's my body to do as I faarking well please, and this is not pleasing me or my body. *I did not ask for this!*'

Jules paces back and forth over the rug presented to him by a hard-line imam. 'Right, that's it, I'm going to the top. Sam!' he yells out to his advisor. 'Get me the Pope!'

Ninety minutes and a couple more whiskeys later, Jules reclines on the modern *objet d'art* sofa. Electronic buds are in his ears, and on his belly balances a screen. Jules stares into the other world and says with an alcoholic slur, 'Yes, yes, get me the Pope. *Si si,* I am Prime Minister Julian Pope. Well, *si si*, okay, I am the ex-prime minister, but just give it a couple of hours. Yes, yes, I mean *si, si.*'

On Jules' screen, blobs of colour appear then disappear as he waits. Finally Jules hears impatient chatter and yelling, the sound of feet in silk slippers padding towards him. A nostril appears on screen then splodges of fingers block the view, before finally Jules can see a forehead and crimson zucchetto at the bottom of the screen. The rest of the screen is taken up with a vast ceiling painted with a magnificent work of art. Jules peers at what looks like a naked man cavorting on the Pope's hat, before refocusing on the matters at hand.

'Ah, Most Holy Father. *Si,* Your Holiness. *Si,* Pope. *Non, non,* I know you are the Pope. I am Julian Pope. Well, no, I'm not trying to cut in on your turf Holy Father. *Non, non,* Please, I need your divine intervention, and failing that,' because Jules has never really believed all that crap about the Pope being God, 'I need a reprieve, an *excusa,* Most Holy Father. I need a *get-out-of-hell-free* card.' Jules nods, shakes his head, nods, and says, 'I have a friend with a most unusual problem, Your Holiness.'

The zucchetto bounces up and down and the Pope's laughter is so loud that Jules' jumps and removes an ear bud.

'*Si, si,*' says Jules to the bouncing hat, 'I know the *I-have-a-friend* is one of the oldest in the book, Your Holiness. *Non, non,* of course I would never lie to you, Most Holy Father.' Jules decides to elevate his credibility by speaking Italian. With a lilting cadence, he begs, '*Per favore, per favore, Santissimo Papa.*'

An Italian voice booms into Jules' ears and Jules apologises profusely.

'*Scusi, scusi. Ah, Santissimo Padre, Padre.*' Jules takes his hanky out of his pocket and mops his sweat-beaded brow. '*L'uomo, si? L'uomo e e...*' Although Jules can bluff his way through many situations, conversing in Italian is not one. '*L'uomo e e bambino. L'uomo e e prega-to. E e preggers-a.*'

Finally giving up, Jules says, 'Look a man is faarking pregnant! He looks like he's eaten,' and Jules again speaks melodically, accenting the last syllable, 'gela-*to*, piz-*za*, pas-*ta* and the tower of Pi-*sa*.'

The Pope laughs so much that Jules actually catches a glimpse of his eyebrows as well as a hand raised to steady his hat.

'*Mi sta prendendo in giro.* Now you pulla de udder leg!'

When the laughter dies down, Jules tries again.

'*Non, Non.* I am not pulling your leg. *Non, non*, Most Holy Father. *Si*, it is true – true and medically verified. But it is not natural, a man being pregnant. It is an abomination Most Holy Father. It is not *Come Dio Comanda*. This man, this *l'uomo*, he needs a Holy Pardon to, to, become a man once again.'

Jules listens, putting his hand to his earpiece, his face squirming as if in pain.

'Yes of course, Most Holy Father, an abortion is a sin. If it is a pregnant woman, of course. But a pregnant man? Surely–' Jules listens and grimaces. 'I don't see what an *ippocampo* has to do with it Most Holy Father. *Si Si*. The seahorse. *Si*.' Jules shakes his head and rolls his eyes incredulously and internally rants, *I am not a faarking sea horse. Do I look like a faarking sea horse?* 'Non non, it is not a miracle, well, maybe it is, Your Holiness, but it's not God's miracle, it's the faarking Devil's.'

Jules listens intently, suddenly aware that his face is betraying his every emotion. Jules internally rants, *you can't hide a faarking thing,* and briefly pines for the days of old-school, *incognito* phone calls. He pulls himself together and nods at the screen with a grave expression. Internally, he placates himself with witty wordplay: *Face-to-face is no way to face off with a Pope who won't take him at face value*, decides Jules. He wants to face the other way because everything's gone face-about and he doesn't know how he can face up to this problem without losing face and becoming a faceless man. *Now, about face*, he commands himself, *and end this faarking thing.*

Jules hasn't a clue what the Pope is saying but he knows it's not good. 'Oh, *si*, if that is your final word. *Come Dio Comanda*, Most Holy Father. *Ciao.*' Jules slams the link shut and yells, 'Sam!'

'You'll have to speak with Natalie Scott-Boyer,' Sam responds calmly five minutes later in response to Jules explaining his *I-have-a-friend* problem.

'It's a delicate, faarking matter, Sam,' and now Sam's best advice is to consort with the enemy? 'Scott-Boyer's a communist, feminist greenie. She was Opposition leader, and she's a *woman.*' The last is spat out with such derision, the adviser cops a splash of spittle on her cheek. As far as Jules is concerned his adviser is far too nonchalant about this whole faarking catastrophe.

Undeterred, Sam retorts, 'I'm a woman, too, Julian. Scott-Boyer is the only parleymentarian to be pregnant during her term and manage it, so she can help your friend manage anything.'

'But my friend doesn't want to be pregnant. She can't be pregnant. She doesn't want to know how to *go on* being pregnant, Sam. She needs to know how to *stop* being pregnant. She wants to become *un*-pregnant.'

'Sorry, Mr Pope. I am unable to assist in that case,' Sam says with firm formality.

'Right, that's it. Sam! Get me Deborah Freer – no, no, she's lost her marbles, hasn't she? Jesus Christ, where's a bra-burning, man-hating, femo, lesbo, abortion-loving subversive when you need one? I've got it. Sam!' yells Jules again, 'get me Maxine Badlands on the phone.'

'I'm sorry sir, you'll have to phone her yourself,' Sam replies a little snootily. 'I'm tapping her contact details to you now.' Sam's nails tap rapidly. 'I'm afraid that is all I can do for your friend. I really have to leave now. Remember, Mr Pope? I'm delivering a Chastity

& Christianity in schools workshop this afternoon, as part of your inaugural teens program: Spirituality, Love & Just Say No?'

Early evening, Detective Senior Sergeant Jimmy Park lounges on the couch in his sparsely decorated apartment. He sucks on a beer and scolds the reflection of himself in the lifeless TV.

'You're getting fat, Jimmy. Fat, unfit and old.' The odour of stale beer, takeaway and pongy socks drifts in a malaise about him. Jimmy's marooned.

His thumb presses buttons on the remote and the tele flutters into life. Jimmy keeps the TV on mute as he channel surfs and feels sorry for himself and a little ashamed. What a lazy bastard he's become. Jimmy used to work out hard. His kinaesthetic sense of his six-pack and biceps, quads and calves, gave him energy and pride. But that was then.

Jimmy stops his thumb push-ups on the remote.

'Hello Genevieve Parker,' he serenades. 'You are the most beautiful woman on the planet by a mile,' he flirts. 'And I guess,' he adds, with a sigh that whispers disappointment, 'you'd be the highest of high maintenance. Being a goddess can't come easy.'

Loneliness swallows Jimmy whole. He realises he's staring at *LoDown* footage of a beached whale. Right now, Jimmy feels just like a stranded whale lolling and dying on his couch.

Jimmy met a whale once. Waves had carelessly sent it somersaulting like a toilet roll unravelling in the surf. It landed dense and immovable, lifting a fin in a flopping flap, a drowning swimmer signalling to life guards, Help, I'm dying here. With others, Jimmy waded in, arms like oars, cold water dragging on his legs. His feet planted in the sucking sand, Jimmy's flat palms pressed the rubbery flanks covered in scars and barnacles. He smelt its acrid fishiness. From buckets and eskies, the whale-saving crew doused the cranky hull of a prehistoric submarine to cries of, 'Keep her hydrated!'

A column of spray spewed from its spout, soaking Jimmy in early morning fish markets, farts and halitosis. Cries of disgust and laughter, duck-diving to wash off whale breath and snot amid cries of, 'She's breathing okay.'

Jimmy gazed into the ancient eye misplaced below the horizon of its mouth. In that ocular portal into creation, Jimmy saw the wisdom of brutality and kindness, sadness and joy. He found it terrifying and exhilarating. The whale gave Jimmy a sense of his own mammalian ancestry stretching back down the eons. He half expected a diaphanous sprite would eventually emerge from the scarred blubber chrysalis, like a surfer peeling off the skin of her wetsuit to stand on the sand, all bronze curves and blonde tresses.

Water lapped at Jimmy's throat and he trod water as high tide came to the rescue, and a swell lifted up both rescuers and whale. She was on her way. Cheers and tears, hugs and high-fives. Exhausted, Jimmy floated on his back and gazed down the length of himself – his boardies billowing over goose-bumped legs, his toes poking out of the sea – and then out to the horizon and the fading disturbance of whitewash caused by the magnificent creature. Jimmy's body rocked and shivered in the nodding water, his heart thumped and his soul sang.

Then, magic. Jimmy's whale breached. Her majestic body leapt and twirled above the sea, plunged and vanished. A cloud of water and mist hovered. Her huge tail appeared and waved back and forth.

'Thank you for my life, Jimmy Park.' Jimmy's whale saluted. 'See you in another world.' And she was gone, heading to eternity. Jimmy had never felt so alive.

As Jimmy lazes dishevelled on the couch, ancient whale magic flutters inside him. He is a good-looking macho detective senior sergeant and he's going all gooey eyes over a whale and Genevieve Parker.

Jimmy turns up the volume and Genevieve Parker tells him, 'Climate change disaster has hit the world. One thousand dead, two million homeless as islanders evacuate their homes in the wake of rising sea levels.'

Her voice continues as visual footage captures waves lapping at small houses, aid workers carrying children, islanders clutching a pathetic cache of possessions. They stand in thigh-high water, cram into naval rubber duckies or set out to sea in primitive leaking, creaking boats tossed about in the ocean like corks.

'God, what a tragedy,' Jimmy tells Genevieve.

Her velvet voice-over replies, 'Experts agree this is a tragedy for this once beautiful island nation and for the world. International aid workers began the long and difficult task of relocating an entire nation when rising sea waters surged. Islanders are taking measures into their own desperate hands, fleeing in small boats to other countries, including our own.' Genevieve's beautiful face fills the screen, her eyes glistening. '*The LoDown*'s Marion Song caught up with the PM at the gates of The Dodge this morning. This is Mr Pope's response to this unfolding tragedy.'

'Here we go,' says Jimmy, taking a gulp of beer.

PM Pope appears unshaven and in his dressing gown.

'Good golly, Miss Molly,' says Jimmy out loud. 'I don't feel like such a slob now, do I, Mr Prime Minister-in-his-dressing-gown?'

'Haven't they heard of swimming lessons?' the PM thunders. 'In this world, you have to make your own luck. Life wasn't meant to be easy. You have to work at it. The world's got too many people as it is, hasn't it? This is God's way of clearing the logjam and washing away the dead wood. I say leave these kinds of things to God.'

A voice from the invisible cluster of journalists asks, 'Have we sent a contingent of aid workers to the disaster, Mr Pope?'

'Are you stark raving mad? My precious money and resources are needed for my people. Bugger the international program. My government stands for projects that benefit *us,* like the fabulous

Addon coal mine. That's capitalism at its best, right there. My government is giving over a billion dollars to a corporate crook, er, giant to come and rape, ah, ravage, ah raid, I know it's an R word, ah... oh, anyway, rip the guts out of our land for themselves – and us, of course. Thirty-two jobs will be created. Thirty-two! And Addon has promised to bring in one thousand of its own workers using our magnificent 666 slavery, er, work visa scheme.'

Jimmy shakes his head at the PM.

'You are losin' it, mate. Losin' your mind and losin' our world.'

'Mr Pope, *Mr Pope*. What about the impact of the Addon mine on the Great Reef, surrounding national forests, First Nations cultural heritage and world heritage-listed landmarks? And isn't it true that 500 different species of aquatic and land animals will be endangered and the whole area will be an eyesore for centuries to come?'

Pope ignores the question.

'What about our closest neighbour, Mr Pope?'

'What about it?' the PM retorts gruffly.

'Well, their islands are being gradually submerged too and they have been building up their already impressive military and naval force–'

'Let me stop you right there, girlie,' says Pope, propping his chin on his chest in an elder statesmen stamp of admonishment, 'I have a wonderful relationship with that fine leader. I was chatting to Betsy just the other day and she was saying that the creeping sea level is a boon for their economy, an absolute boon. Such talk of invasion is irresponsible and incorrect, Missie. I'll be over there this weekend for the World Trade Forum. Betsy and I will be discussing serious matters at the WTF. And let me make my final comment quite clear; I believe in God, only idiots believe in science.' Julian Pope turns on his slippered heels and is gone.

'What do you think of our science-denying leader then, Gen?' Jimmy asks Genevieve on the tele.

'Thousands of eminent climate scientists from around the world protested today against world leaders' climate change negligence and inaction,' she replies, 'They demand that politicians act on the expert scientific evidence.'

Genevieve's stunning eyes reach right into Jimmy's soul and her voice tickles his ears.

'For Prime Minister Pope, it seems that science is only good for gall bladder or coal extraction.'

'Good one, Gen. And that's how you nail it in front of the camera,' Jimmy says, still ruing his own embarrassing TV interview at the front of Koroskovas. 'I don't know how you cope with our crackpot PM or this bullshit every day. You must have to work out every day to stay sane, Gen,' says Jimmy.

She answers with a glint in her eye, 'For those of you wanting to see a real workout, A-Pop boy band, Sooper Neo, arrived this morning. Toby Green reports.'

Music blares and seven young men in straight visored baseball caps and baggy pants, bop and leap in Sooper Neo's urban hip hop brand. Jimmy puts down his beer and stands up. His feet kick away the dross of his lounge room floor to clear a space and his body jangles with the rhythm. Suddenly, his legs alternate in sharp bending side steps, synchronising with precise flag-signalling arm formations. Jimmy's torso undulates like he's just swallowed the music's sound waves, before his legs cross tightly and his feet pirouette. Fingers run along an imaginary cap's brim. Jimmy is slick and cool. He dives to the ground, his body bouncing in rolling waves.

'Oh yeah. I've still got it!' A one-arm push up and a cap rim salute, and Jimmy rolls to his back and flips up onto his feet – almost. 'Eee-yow!' Slick style lands in a shemozzle on the floor, both hands gripping one leg around the back of his thigh. Jimmy's done his hammy.

Ten minutes later, *The LoDown* is a background blur as Jimmy stands in his undies with an ice pack secured to his thigh by a few metres of cling wrap. He stares despondently into his fridge. He hasn't torn the hammy, he reckons, just strained it. What was he thinking? Reckoned he could just pick up where he left off with all those A-Pop moves? But it was, what, almost 10 years since he danced, and that last time was just an A-Pop break-out at Ruby's 30th. What was he thinking?

But he'd do it again. Yeah, he would. A-pop makes him feel alive. He's still got it – until he didn't and it wasn't. His hamstring squeezes the carefree joy out of him like he's a wet towel, squeezes him till he's dry and ragged. Now the hammy's numb. Emptiness digs its icy fingernails into him and looks in the fridge with hungry eyes. Jimmy needs filling up with something, anything. His fridge used to be full of fresh vegies and fruit, lean meat and protein shakes. Now it's empty, except for beer and half a dried up red capsicum, or that could be a piece of tomato, Jimmy concedes.

'I guess it'll be takeaway tonight,' he mutters to himself, 'again.'

He pulls out another stubby and lets go of the fridge door. Slow reluctant closure and sudden extinguishment of light. Even Jimmy's fridge has got the blues.

'What the fuck are you doing with your life, mate?' Jimmy's coming up to his 38th birthday and what's he got going for him? Yeah, he's got a mortgage and he's saving because he doesn't spend it on anything. 'You can corroborate that, can't you?' he tosses back at the fridge as he hobbles towards the loneliness of the couch and TV.

'You're talking crap, mate,' he says out loud to himself irritably as he watches the beautiful Genevieve Parker. She probably has a personal trainer every day. What a great job that would be: Gen's personal trainer. Maybe he could apply. Jimmy's bod is still in pretty good shape, only a smidge out of shape really, and don't forget the hair. Yeah, he's got the hair. Jimmy could do it.

Who's he kidding? Who has time for physical discipline now? His fitness is AWOL with his gym membership. They eloped together on his watch. 'Healthy Diet' absconded as well to be their marital witness. Jimmy is the jilted groom, left with his skinny fat – the slightest flabbiness around his middle, shamefully taunting his slim genes and defying his heritage of hard work and discipline. Well, maybe he should do a few pushups and sit-ups. He could start right now, right this minute.

'Shame about the hammy,' Jimmy says out loud and burps. He settles in for a night on the couch. With each sip from his stubby of beer, he feels like one of his creased shirts being smoothed out by a steam iron. Hot and crinkled with crankiness, then soothing sighs and relief, 'Ah.' Jimmy drinks in the beer and he drinks in the stunning Genevieve.

Jimmy gets down on hands and knees and crawls up close to the screen. He peers intently and frowns at the TV screen. He zeros in on Genevieve Parker's breasts. Jimmy scrounges his phone out of his pocket, takes a few quick snaps of Genevieve Parker's cleavage, and re-pockets the phone.

'What the fuck, Jimmy?!' he says.

Peeling the cling-wrapped ice pack from his thigh, Jimmy searches the room with his eyes. He's still moving awkwardly, but the leg is feeling not too bad. He reckons he can tell, even inside that empty numbness. A pongy odour wafts up as he gingerly rescues his socks from under the couch, turns them right side out and pulls them onto his bony feet. He picks up his trousers, gets one leg in, but falls backwards onto the couch when he puts weight on his bung leg. He completes the trousers and stands in his pongy socked feet, holding one shoe and impatiently surveying the floor for the other shoe. His socks and undies are yesterday's. He desperately needs to get a load of washing on, but it isn't looking like tonight will be the night.

Maybe he should get a housekeeper in again. He had one once. Like a magic elf she was. Karen? No, Carol? Yeah, Capable Carol. Once a week he walked out the door, leaving behind an appalling mess that amassed like garbage at the tip. He'd return that evening with everything tidy and sparkling, the fridge filled with meals for the week. After work, he had a home waiting for him, ready to care for him. But eventually, somehow, it all lapsed. He was interstate on a case for a while and when he returned, he thought he could do it on his own. How hard could it be?

'This is how hard, Jimmy,' he says out loud to himself. Things are getting way out of control on the home front. He uses up all his neat freak nous at work. His note-taking? Meticulous. Filing? Accurate. Diary? Pedantic. Interviews? Planned, efficient and effective.

As Jimmy continues to look under newspapers and furniture for his missing shoe, he speaks sternly to himself, 'But on the home front, Jimmy?' He knows he needs a personality change or a housekeeper. He might have Carol's phone contact somewhere.

Jimmy trips over last night's fish and chips wrappers, next to the night-before-that's containers and the stubby he drank a moment ago. He stubs his toe on a hardness that should not be there.

'Got ya!' Jimmy sits and puts his shoes on and hand-checks the phone bulge in his pocket. He grabs his keys and jacket (which are surprisingly where they should be) and loops his jacket over one arm. As he heads out the door, his hand busily taps at his phone to locate the address of the TV station, his mind ticking over. It's the break they need. Genevieve Parker, you gem.

Maxine Badlands hasn't answered his calls. Jules slouches miserably on the camel hair sofa, a gift from a sultana. He flips on the television looming large on the wall opposite him like a pair of wrap-around sunglasses for The Dodge. He watches *The LoDown*, and presses mute. It's how he likes Genevieve Parker best. Well, all women, in fact.

'Ah, Genevieve Parker, you naughty girl.' Jules' hand steals inside his pants for a quick wank.

Just as his eyes are crossing, his body heaving and saliva dribbling from his mouth, Jules' phone rings. He steals a glance at the caller ID.

'Faark!' withdraws his sticky hand and answers his phone.

'Max*eene*,' charms Pope, putting the phone on speaker and laying it beside him on the camel hair sofa as he wriggles to get his hanky out to tidy himself up, 'How are you? Been too long, Maxine. You are one of the most impressive and passionate women in the House, and–'

'I'm the only woman in the House, Jules,' Maxine responds curtly. 'You saw to that.'

Jules' charm slides right off Maxine Badlands like water off a duck's back. Make that a dyke's back. Jules is fleetingly buoyed by his duck-dyke cleverness. Faarking dyke, lesbo, femo greenie! Exactly who he needs. Jules straightens himself finally and holds his phone in his hand and resumes in polite statesman style, 'Yes, well, that may be, but Maxine, I am appealing to you as a colleague and your prime minister.'

'Actually Jules, one hour ago you were the prime minister. Now you are the ex-PM. But who the fuck cares anymore? Jules, I am doing you the kindness of getting back to you about your 66 phone messages.'

'Thank you, Maxine.'

'So, what's so urgent? What do you want, Jules?'

'Well, ah, I wish to appeal to you as one human being to another–'

'Jules, you are the devil incarnate,' Maxine states bluntly.

'Yes, well, I'm sure we can put our differences aside. Agree to disagree type thing. All part of mankind, er, the same human family, er, ladykind and, er, human, you know you girls too, of course.'

'Yeah, I get it, Jules. Your feminist consciousness-raising is truly impressive. Now get on with it,' Maxine says.

'I need to speak with you about a most sensitive matter, Maxine. Er, where is one to begin...?'

'For fuck's sake, do not begin at the beginning. I do not have all night, Jules. Just get to the point.'

'Ahem, I need to know, Maxine, ahem, how to go about getting,' Pope cups his hand around the phone and whispers, 'an abortion.'

'Didn't quite hear that Prime Minister. You what?'

'I need to know how to, you know, get...' and he whispers again, 'get... access an abortion.'

'Jules, you really need to speak up.'

'Abortion!' he yells so that he gives himself a fright with the abrasiveness of the harsh, ghastly, Godless, femo, lesbo word.

'Oh, do you now, Jules? One of your daughters done the naughty without proper protection? Oh, that's right, you religious nutters believe contraception is the work of the devil. A woman's place, hey, Jules? But not if it's one of your own?'

'Look, come on Max-*ee*n, *Maxee*,' he wheedles, smiling broadly into the phone. 'I know you girls have a black market out there, an abortion network, you know, an underground.' His smile crumbles into desperate pleading, 'I need it, Maxine, *I need it*. Help me, Maxine.'

'Well, if you're determined to break the law, Jules, I suggest you visit Her Majesty's prison, oh, and those being kept at her Majesty's pleasure too in the psych ward. Because of you and yours, you'll find all the abortion doctors there.'

'Maxeen, ple-ease, can't we work something out, surely?'

'What are you prepared to put on the table, Jules? Because it will have to be big.'

'Well, I see now that perhaps I was a little hasty. I understand that access to safe effective and timely contraception and abortion is necessary if girls are to fully participate in society, and–'

'Cut the crap, Jules. Just 'cause you can parrot my own words back at me about *the girls,* doesn't mean you get it.'

'Oh, but I do get it, Maxine, I do. It is one's own body. One must have control over one's own body to have control over one's own life. I'm a person, Maxine. A pregnancy isn't a person. I'm the person. I'm the living, breathing human being. I am. I am, Maxine. Help me!'

There is silence on the other end of the phone. 'Maxine?'

'In that case, Jules, one easy and only path for you to take.

Immediately rescind your Terrorism amendment, The Concatenate Of Conception and Unborn Person Priority – we *girls* call that *the COC(k)UPP*.'

'But that could take years, Maxine, with all the leadership upheaval and the Senate wackos. The Bell and I spent years stacking the parleyment with God-fearing, anti-abortion zealots in every nook and cranny of parleyment, in every party, every independent–'

Jules hears the sharp clunk of the phone disconnecting.

'Nance!' Jules hollers in panic. He's tried everything and everyone, except Nance. Nance is his only hope. He paces back and forth on the llama wool rug, a gift from a royal oman, and whispers to himself, 'Oh faarking hell! I can't tell Nance, she'll think I'm absolutely mad, and she'll be no help what so ever. A woman who's had five girls? She'll be all gooey, gooey, clucky, clucky.'

But when Nance appears, Jules crumples in her presence.

'Oh your home, Jules. I thought you were out. I was just knitting and half-watching *The LoDown* in the small lounge and – Oh, Jules, whatever is the matter? You haven't lost the PM-ship again, have you? Or have you just got it back? Really, either situation might bring you to–'

'Nance, I saw the doc this morning. It's not good news.'

'Not good news? No. Is it...? It's not...?'

'I'm afraid it is Nance. Four months.'

'What? Four months?! Surely not.' Nance's eyes open wide and pool with tears. 'We need a second opinion. You can't–'

'Nance,' interrupts Jules a little impatiently and still pacing intermittently, 'I've already had a second opinion. Dr Zigwell got in Dr Zagid on the spot and she took a look too. Zig was white as a ghost. Zag was red as the devil.'

'But four months, Jules,' says Nance shadowing Jules pacing. 'Surely there's something someone can do.'

Jules stops. Nance stops.

'Look, Nance, there's nothing anyone can do. I've tried the official hot lines. I've reached out to leftie femo lesbos about the underground network they think I don't know about. I've spoken to the Bell, and I've spoken to the Pope.'

'What *are* you talking about, dear?' asks Nance looking puzzled.

'It's quite obvious, Nance. I'm pregnant. I'm a man who's pregnant.'

'You're pregnant *and* have cancer?' Nance frowns, then suddenly looks enlivened, 'Oh, it's brain cancer, is it? I thought as much. That would explain a thing or two, Jules. Sit down, darling.' She sits on the camel hair sofa and pats it with her hand to invite Jules to sit too.

Jules ignores the invitation and speaks as if Nance is the leader of the opposition. 'Nance, let me put this as simply as I can.'

'That would be helpful, dear.'

'I do *not* have cancer.'

'Oh,' says Nance with a hint of disappointment.

'I am, however, pregnant, four months pregnant, with twins.'

'Oh,' says Nance brightening. 'I think, Jules, that you've just confirmed that your cancer *is* brain cancer. I'll make us a nice cup of tea, dear, and then call that nice Crisis Assessment and Treatment squad for the psychiatrically challenged, dear.'

Nance heads for the kitchen, her voice floating in the air behind her in a cloud full of gravitas, so heavy it lands in a puddle on Jules' shiny patent leather shoes, 'I wonder if the CAT team is on the same number as the terrorist dark ops group. I did like that lovely young T-DOG that dropped in by parachute that day the lefties had that beautiful love-in sitting in our garden. All those beautiful flowers strewn about. Mind you the tear gas spoilt all that. I don't think our current situation calls for tear gas...'

Jules shakes his shoe to get rid of the messy puddle and flops into the sofa. He jiggles his left leg, which is crossed and cross. Jules is all cross bones again. He's in the cross fire and cross-stitched up. He has been double-crossed. Cross his heart and cross his fingers, if he can just be rid of this pregnancy.

Jules' wordplay makes not a dent in his dark mood and he desperately tries to control his cross impatience as he watches Nance carry in the Wedgewood teapot and teacups on an ornate gold tray, a present from an emperor. She places the tray on the coffee table, a gift from a presido, and sits down next to Jules on the sofa with her knees and ankles together and her frock spread across her lap. Nance twirls the pot three times clockwise and three times anti-clockwise, pours into the cups in a stutter-step manner, and places one steaming cup in front of Jules and the other in front of herself.

Jules ignores the cup of tea and silently hands her a memory stick and a black and white photo. Jules knows Nance will have to believe him once she sees it.

Nance looks curiously at the stick in the palm of her hand, then turns the photo this way and that. 'What is this, dear? It's an ultrasound photo *in utero*, dear,' Nance answers her own question as Jules knew she would. 'An ultrasound of *in utero* twins.'

Jules nods feeling he's admitting to a crime.

'In white along the bottom is, let's see, the date, gestation details, and – What's your name doing on this ultrasound, Jules?' Nance doesn't wait for a response but resumes her searching gaze of the photo. She stands up to bring the photo towards a sharpening light, 'And this is unusual in this type of ultrasound. A man's genitalia, and there's a little kink in the penis, just like – oh.'

'You see Nance, it's me.' Jules stands too. 'Me, with twin faarking foetuses inside me.'

They both stare at Prime Minister Julian Pope's ultrasound with the kink and the twin pregnancy. 'So, Nance? What can I do?' Jules beseeches his wife whose brain is frightening but apparently extraordinarily cluey.

'It's probably photo-cropped. You know, two ultrasounds merged, overlapped. Do you think they can do that? One of you and one of some pregnant woman,' ponders Nance, 'but then there should be two sets of sex organs and–'

'It's not faarking photo-cropped, woman!' yells Jules. 'I went to see Ziggy, yesterday morning. You know, my old mate, eminent Professor Bertram Rudolph-if-you-don't-mind Zigwell.'

Nance sways a little and drops to the sofa in a befuddled, unlady-like manner with her legs splayed and frock dishevelled. Her head lolls and her eyes glaze over in that frightening cogitating dreaming she does. But maybe his little brainiac might finally come up with a solution, *the* solution, Jules hopes. He waits and pins his hopes on his wife's scary, girly brainiac brain, like a femo, lesbo pins an *Abortion On Demand Now* button to her bra-less, hairy chest.

At last, Nance speaks. 'Seahorses,' she says.

'Oh for faark's sake, Nance, I copped all that from the Pope. What the faark do sea horses have to do with anything?' This is not what Jules expects or needs from his wife. Where are her arms wrapped around him? Nance taking control and knowing just what to do? Arranging everything so Jules can slip out of this body and this mess and back to his normal, wonderful life and his superior, beautiful body? 'Why aren't you fixing this Nance instead of going on about seahorses?' Jules demands.

'Ah, great minds, Jules. His Most Holy Holiness also went to the *cavalluccio marino*. The *ippocampo*. The seahorse.'

'What the faark, Nance!' shrieks Jules, feeling even more enraged as Nance purposely flaunts her brilliant credentials in the Italian language and marine biology. Just kick a man when he's down next time. 'Faark! Faark! Faark!'

'That's enough, Jules. Sit down and I'll tell you all,' Nance says in her best rendition of a bossy school ma'am.

Suitably chastened, Jules sits meekly and listens. What choice does he have? Nance is his only hope.

'The potbelly seahorse, Jules, is one of the only species where the male has the babies. Now some might say that there is also the sea dragon and the midwife toad and they would be right of course.'

Jules rolls his eyes and sighs.

Nance continues unfazed.

'But the male *sea dragon* carries the fertilised eggs under his tail, and the *midwife toad* carries them on his back before wrapping them around his legs for protection from predators. Whereas, the seahorse,' Nance breaks into lilting Italian again, 'the male *cavalluccio marino*, the *ippocampo*, woos the female with a dance. *She* deposits her eggs in his brood pouch in his stomach, *he* adds his sperm, *she* swims off and has nothing more to do with him – clearly an intelligent species I rather think,' muses Nance, 'and *he* carries the fertilised eggs embedded in his pouch wall that becomes surrounded by all this spongy tissue.

'He can be carrying a thousand embryos, so, well, you should just see the size of the poor little fellow's tummy, Jules. The usually slim-line male seahorse ends up looking like one of those seagulls down at the foreshore who have stuffed themselves with hot chips and bread.' Nance laughs at her own clever description, while Jules frowns and fumes. 'And so, in your case, Jules, *not* the sea dragon and *not* the midwife toad. Santissimo Padre is correct. Most definitely, you are the seahorse,' Nance finishes and looks squarely at Jules' potbelly.

'Fasc-in-ating, Nance!' Jules says sarcastically. 'How the faark does that help? For faark's sake, woman! I'm not a faarking seahorse, or an overstuffed seagull, I'm a man. I'm the Prime Faarking Minister!'

'Well, actually dear, it is quite possible that what I heard on the tele is that you're the *ex*-Prime Minister. I'll check on the removalists' boxes, will I?' Nance begins to rise but stops midway between sitting and standing, 'Or should I just wait a couple of hours?'

'Nance! Forget the faarking boxes! What am I going to do?'

'Well, dear,' Nance settles back into the sofa and calmly takes a sip of tea. 'You're right of course, Jules, seahorses do not explain this at all. How? How?' Nance bites her bottom lip and her eyes search the ceiling as if the answer might be written there.

'Look, Nance, I don't give a flying faark *how,* I just want it fixed.

I want this twin thing out of me. I want to be me – my adored-and-envied-by-the-masses *me*, Nance.' Jules' eyes plead with his wife.

'But, dear,' Nance says hesitantly, 'it's still a precious child, isn't it, dear? Two in fact. I mean, since you befriended the archbishop, that's all I seem to hear, dear. You're all about protecting the precious unborn, the unborn children, a person from the moment of conception. Even though I must say, dear, that we really have no idea when that moment is and if one does take that argument to its logical conclusion, then perhaps we should be grieving every menstrual discharge of eggs and every masturbated sperm, dear. Banning vasectomies too, and even you had one of those, dear, remember?'

Jules blinks. Now is not the time to revisit his reasons for finally undergoing that particularly dark ops operation. How the faark can he be pregnant? What sort of faarking idiot of a God is presiding over this bullshit? *Christ, maybe God is a woman after all*, Jules thinks.

'Anyway,' Nance is saying, 'I thought that as far as you're concerned, even the earliest, tiniest, even the most pre-embryonic pregnancy is the most innocent and most precious of all persons. Once a woman is pregnant, well, what she wants, or needs, or might suffer is irrelevant. I mean she must continue her pregnancy. It is a gift from God that cannot be re-gifted or given back or unwrapped at an inappropriate time, so-to-speak. The pregnant person must sacrifice whatever is necessary to sacrifice, dear, to make sure the precious unborn is born.

Jules blinks again.

'Your pregnancy, dear, is two precious infants, and the vessel is, well, you. You are just the vehicle, if you like. You are just a womb, dear, a uterus. You have no say. You are unimportant in the scheme of things, aren't you?' Nance pauses.

Jules mouth opens then closes. He is a seahorse transitioning to a guppy fish.

Nance continues, 'Or are you saying, dear, that the already-born person that we call a woman is *less* precious than the unborn person, but the already-born person we call a man is *more* precious than the unborn person? But surely it doesn't matter what, or who, the precious infant is gift wrapped in? Or is it just *your* person that is more precious, dear? Does this have anything to do with Adam and Eve, dear? You know, for aeons women have been paying a horrendous price for one little bite from an apple.'

Jules feels dizzy and muddled. His body shakes off seahorses, seagulls and guppy fish. Jules musters all the intelligence and control he can. He is the ex-prime minister, for faark's sake. He stands and looks down on Nance. His voice rings out in an oration worthy of a standing ovation in the House.

'Nance, I speak to you this evening as a humble man, yes, a humble man. But clearly a great man too, Mr Speaker. You know there is a proper order of things, Mr Speaker. A pregnant man is, as I said to the Pope, just this afternoon – the Pope and I, as state and spiritual leaders, are very close. We go way back of course, and, Mr Speaker, I said to the Pope, my dear friend the Pope, Mr Speaker, and he agreed, yes he agreed, Mr Speaker, that, Mr Speaker, a pregnant man, Mr Speaker, is indeed an abomination, *an abomination*. I mean men do not get pregnant, do they, Mr Speaker? Men can't get pregnant, can they?'

'Well I think you're rather the living proof that men can, dear,' interjects Nance from the opposition benches.

'Order, *order*,' Jules says in a loud, basso voice. 'Who will govern, Mr Speaker, if men are off having babies? I mean, this is just wrong, isn't it? It's unnatural, Mr Speaker, and...' Jules drops his belly and his bundle. He is an old sack of words laced up with hiccups and sniffles, and so he sits back down.

'I-I don't know how you can say such a hurtful thing, Nance, that what I want or need or what I might have to suffer, what I am already suffering, doesn't matter. How can you say such a thing? I mean this is torture, Nance. To force me to continue on in this way. To force me to get more pregnant every day! And then what about, oh my God, the labour, Nance! Yes, torture, Nance. You can't torture the PM, Nance. You can't torture me!'

'Of course not, dear,' Nance consoles patting his hand.

'I don't want to be put on the rack, Nance. I don't want to be pregnant! I don't want to be an abomination. I'm not an abomination am I, Nance? Am I?'

'No, dear, of course you're not,' Nance coos, putting her arm around him. Then she proclaims, 'You're the faarking PM for faark's sake, Jules. Well, give it an hour.'

'Yes I am, aren't I,' Jules sniffles and smiles.

'And of course seahorses are of no help, dear, but the *how* you got pregnant might lead us to how to fix it.'

'But who would know, Nance? I'm not going back to Zig and Zag, those two clowns.' Jules pouts and thumps his fist on his thigh, which hurt rather too much, but not being one to break stride in the middle of a tirade, Jules bravely keeps right on. 'Utter faarking clowns! Both of 'em happy, ecstatic, about my faarking awful predicament. Raving on about their fame and fortune and the prestigious faarking Journal of faarking Miracles, and using some of those rude, queer scx-sual words, Nance, that make me feel quite faint just thinking about them. Doc Roberts has been a complete and utter farce too. Nance! You must fix this, *fix me*!'

By the time Detective Senior Sergeant Jimmy Park arrives at *The LoDown* studios, he has shown his ID and repeated the same mantra three times, 'Detective Senior Sergeant Park, here to speak with Genevieve Parker about an ongoing investigation.'

The woman looks down a list of names on her phone and frowns. Her outfit has danced out of a 1950s musical: green satin pedal pushers, sneakers, a t-shirt tied at its bottom edge to reveal her bare midriff, bright crimson lips, and she occasionally flicks her blonde fringe from her forehead while her short pony tail bounces. Jimmy keeps expecting her to break into a jitterbug.

'I'm Sandy by the way,' she says as she checks and re-checks her phone with much theatrical frowning and face-pulling.

'Of course you are. Like Danny and Sandy,' Jimmy hears himself say smoothly recalling the movie.

'Why, yeah, like wow!' and the wrinkling 40-year old consternation of her face transforms into a brilliant 30-year old smile. 'You're, like, a fan, or something, hey?' she sparkles. 'Me too! So, like, you like–'

Jimmy swots away a 'like' punctuation mark to interrupt and get back to the task at hand.

'Yeah, I'm a big fan,' Jimmy smiles his most adoring smile. 'Now, if I can just speak with Ms Genevieve Parker, I might have time to watch that movie tonight,' and Jimmy winks.

Sandy blushes and titters before recovering to her version of professional mode.

'No probs, Detective,' she says brightly with only a touch of flirtation, 'Please follow me.' Sandy sets off confidently and wordlessly, focused on reaching her destination somewhere through a warren of corridors.

Jimmy follows along, caught up in his head with dreams of gems and Genevieve Parker. Shown to a seat in front of a bank of mirrors, Jimmy sits down obediently. A young woman with a stud in her nose, three earrings in each ear, a sloppy joe baring one shoulder, and wearing cut off shorts and cowboy boots, flaps a hairdresser's gown over his head, lands it professionally across his lap and sprays a cloud of water around his hair. Like a beautifully synchronised dance, a young man wearing a wide-necked white t-shirt under red braces clipped to loosely draping tartan trousers and feet clad in red sandals, begins mopping Jimmy's face with a small moist cotton pad.

'Hi lovey, I'm Colwyn. We'll just wipe away the dregs of the day, shall we?' he says brightly. 'We'll have you looking *go-or-*geous in no time.'

'What?' Gorgeous in no time? Where the hell is he? Jimmy finally realises where he is, and waves them both off in an attempt to stand. 'No, no mate, I'm here to question Genevieve Parker.'

'Ooh, I don't think you've got that quite right, sweetie,' Colwyn demurs pursing his lips, raising his eyebrows, lowering his chin and standing back with one hand on his hip. 'It's Genevieve who asks the questions on this show.' Colwyn stares at Jimmy curiously as if he is just the last of many ignoramuses he's had to deal with today.

Jimmy flails around with his arms trying to get himself out of the back-to-front cape. His voice emanates from under the material, 'I am a police detective here on official business. I'm here to speak with Genevieve Parker. Off camera.'

'Ooh, all right big boy,' Colwyn giggles delightedly, helping pull the police officer free. 'Wires crossed, but no need for knickers in a knot. Come and have a seat in the Green Room. I'll go check with Dinah.'

Jimmy follows Colwyn's swaying shoulders and hips. What the hell has he got himself into?

'Feel free to have a bite to eat, drink, coffee, me?' laughs Colwyn coyly as he shows Jimmy to a seat in a comfy lounge room.

Jimmy maintains his serious detective mien. He is hot on a trail. Tick, tick goes his mind. Jimmy is on it.

Tap, tap goes Colwyn's soft rebuke. 'Lighten up sunshine.'

*Ouch*, grimaces Jimmy watching Colwyn's figure retreat into the warren of corridors as the lilt of Colwyn's voice trails behind, 'Di-naah. Di-naah.'

Genevieve Parker puts her hand to her ear with dramatic gravitas. 'Breaking news. We take you to our award-winning, roving crime reporter, Tim Merrin, live at Koroskovas, the scene of a violent jewellery heist, just days ago.'

'Ooh,' Carol trills as she tucks her feet under her and snuggles into Reg. 'Come on, Tim, what's going on, love?' There is an awkward delay as the footage shows Tim Merrin wearing a heavy jacket, jiggling up and down in the cold, blowing his red nose with a hanky and tucking his hands in his arm pits.

'Poor love,' says Carol watching roving-crime-reporter-and-live Tim Merrin wait for a cross that has already happened.

'What a duffer,' says Reg.

Once Tim realises his time has already come, he clasps his hands at his waist and begins. 'Well, Genny-er-vieve. I am standing outside iconic Koroskova's Jewellery Emporium where just days ago *The LoDown* reported exclusively that 60-year-old Mrs Koroskova, who lives on the premises, was brutally forced to open the safe by violent criminals.'

'I understand that there are dramatic new details, Tim, known only to *The LoDown*. What can you tell us, Tim?'

'Well Genevieve, there has been a disturbing and dramatic turn of events,' Tim enthuses. 'Hours ago, *The LoDown* received *exclusive* footage of the heist taken by a passer-by on his mobile phone.'

Carol listens to Tim as if Tim is the one snuggled with her on the couch, 'We'll roll that footage for you now and I'll walk our viewers through it.' *But really just for you, Carol,* she hears Tim whisper.

Carol and Reg watch the mobile phone footage while Tim's voice commentates, 'You see here the perpetrators, clad head to foot in black, enter the premises, situated on a corner block. Let's fast forward to the perps' exit, here. Police are already using the latest in police identification technology to narrow down suspects, but if we zoom in on the background, here,' Tim's voice takes the viewers by the hand and leads them to a grey splodge suddenly highlighted by an illuminating white halo. 'And slow this down,' continues Tim as the video progresses frame by frame in a slow staccato. 'You can make out a figure running from the rear of the jewellery shop and across the road.'

Slow motion limbs pump across the dimly lit road before the footage returns to normal speed. The lens turns around to the person shooting the footage, now $1000 richer for it, to reveal a bulbous nose sprouting two pimples, a mouth of crooked smiling teeth and stage whispering, 'Fucking awesome bro!'

Tim's face reappears and he says, 'Police are keen to speak with the background figure who may be an unwitting witness to the crime. And, of course Genevieve, it's pretty clear that the person in question is completely starkers.'

'Bloody hell, love, jewel thieves and nudie rudie joggers. This'll be turned into a Talk Fest-cum-six-part-Crime Noir series all right,' says Reg to Cazza.

Carol doesn't hear Reg. She's staring at Tim's handsome face, his eyes dancing with twinkling delight and the word 'starkers' still playing about his beautiful kissable mouth.

Gen gives a curious smirk and her eyes twinkle with fun.

'Thank you for that unusual update, Tim. In another matter,' says Gen, becoming serious, 'I understand, Tim, that police have asked *The LoDown* for assistance in a missing person case.'

'Yes, Genevieve,' Tim's voice says as the photo of a woman appears. 'Twenty-nine-year old Eva Larsson was last seen yesterday morning and has not been seen since, Genny-er-vieve. Police hold grave fears for her wellbeing and are keen to speak with Eva or anyone who saw Eva yesterday or today. Back to you, Genevieve.'

Gen can do nothing but look down the lens of the camera wide-eyed, unblinking and silent. She free-falls into the heavy grey of her early morning run. The rusted brown of the blood. The bruised purple of a pregnant woman with nowhere to turn. The black evil of God's men. A woman's face bleached of colour. The face of Eva Larsson.

'Go to an ad. Now!' the director roars.

Genevieve Parker's audience has already forgiven and forgotten the previous *glitch in transmission*. A small hiccup, nothing to do with perfect Genevieve Parker. After the ad break, she is back in all her gorgeousness telling Carol and Reg, 'In the wake of recent *LoDown* stories on the epidemic of women killed by their intimate partners, *LoDown* now brings you two death tolls for women.'

Carol and Reg look silently at the screen where two lines, one purple and one green, angle upwards on a graph whose vertical axis is labelled 'Deaths', and horizontal axis is marked with the months of the year.

'The green line indicates that 94 women have been killed by their current or former intimate partner in the first six months of this year,' Gen's voice says. 'Last year at the same time, 65 women had been murdered by their current or former partner.

'The purple line indicates that over the same period, since the Pope government made abortion an act of terrorism, 240 women have died from illegal abortions. Last year at the same time, zero women had died from abortion.'

Genevieve reappears on the small tele in the neat lounge room to conclude, 'The graph does not, of course, include the thousands of women hospitalised with serious injuries from both these forms of violence against women.'

Carol and Reg are transfixed by Genevieve Parker who says, 'The women we love are dying needlessly. You can join *The LoDown* campaign on our website, or protest to Prime Minister Julian Pope directly using the address now on screen.'

Carol is stunned by the horrifying power of God, and shamed by the horrifying cruelty and stupidity of men.

'And now, the weather with Fairley Fine,' smiles Genevieve Parker.

Jimmy is fed up with waiting in the Green Room. He wanders down a corridor, and there she is: the strikingly beautiful Genevieve Parker gliding towards him in slow motion and emanating a rainbow aura. Jimmy blinks to clear his dreamy vision and shakes his head to recalibrate his hair and brain to professional mode and recapture his cool.

'Ms Parker?' he says in his deepest, manliest voice.

She stops, stiffens and says, 'Dinah?'

'Apologies, I didn't mean to startle you, it's just–'

'Security!' she yells, taking a step back. 'Do not come any closer. Security!'

Jimmy takes a step back too, raising his arms as if she has a gun aimed at his heart. Jimmy makes quite a show of slowly lowering one hand to reach inside his jacket and retrieve his police ID. Detective Senior Sergeant Jimmy Park is in control and calm.

On the other side of his skin, Jimmy's face is astonished. That was one hell of a reaction, completely uncalled for, puzzles Jimmy, with thoughts dodging and skidding through his brain. Maybe this unwashed detective thing's gone too far? Maybe he's more freaky derro than professional detective these days? Maybe he's lost his cool Jimmy charm, even if he does still have the hair? Maybe it's not him, it's her? Is she high maintenance and highly strung? Or something more serious like post traumatic response? He guesses he is 188 cm and 85 kg, and she's what, 168 cm and 55 kg? Yep, he's terrified her.

Way to go Jimmy. Poor Jimmy already feels like a heel and he hasn't even asked one question. Her fragility is unexpected and somehow endearing.

Colwyn appears at Gen's side, wraps an arm around her and eyeballs Jimmy.

'Oh, you've met the hunky Detective Senior Sergeant Park, have you? Yes, he gave me quite a shiver too.'

Colwyn looks at Jimmy, lifts his chin and proceeds defiantly.

'Now look here, Mr Big Boy Detective, Ms Parker has had a long, trying day and you can–'

'No, no,' Ms Parker interrupts, gently shrugging off Colwyn's protective arm and words.

Jimmy can see she has already reset her alarm. Under her intense gaze, Jimmy feels a rush of embarrassment he hasn't felt since he was in primary school and proposed to Molly Davidson with a 50 cent ring from the local milk bar.

'It's fine, Colwyn, thank you. You have better things to do. Thanks, Colwyn,' she smiles reassuringly, shooing him with an elegant hand.

As Jimmy watches Colwyn reluctantly walk away, checking back over his shoulder as he goes, Jimmy feels a stab of envy in his chest and a stodgy humble pie in his gut. Colwyn earnt her smile, Jimmy made her recoil. Yep, the Molly Davidson humiliation all over again.

'Well, Detective, er, I have quite forgotten your name.'

'Park,' Jimmy replies helpfully as he notices that Jimmy Park and Genevieve Parker are just two little letters, an *e* and an *r,* away from sharing the same name, in holy matrimony, till death do us part.

'Detective Park?'

'Yes, er, that's me. I am the hunky Mr Big Boy Detective Senior Sergeant Jimmy Park,' Jimmy says, crumpling inside. *Did he really just say that?*

She tilts her gorgeous head and politely ignores his foolishness.

'Detective Park, what's this about?'

Her eyes are the stars weaving purple silk into the clouds of a setting sky. Her eyes are the heavens whispering an invitation to fall into its soft lavender pillows. Her eyes, *her eyes*. Jimmy is falling, falling head over heels. Jimmy swallows and clears his throat. He's quite forgotten why he's even there.

'Ms Parker, I, I...' He lowers his eyes, and the reason is right there staring him in the face: a superb, one-of-a-kind 12.25 carat pear-cut ruby in a gold, ragged halo setting of 22 0.8 carat diamonds and diamond-encrusted peg bail, suspended from a 24-carat gold Figarucci anchor chain necklace. Genevieve Parker may be a gem, but it's the gem around her neck that he's here for.

Detective Senior Sergeant Jimmy Park has learnt his jewellery lessons well. Every case he works is like taking intensive language lessons. Jimmy rapidly learns the concepts and new jargon of whatever case he's on, and that peculiar knowledge ultimately snares the perps and makes Jimmy a more interesting human being.

The stolen car syndicates case means Jimmy can mix it with the best of luxury car mechanics and collectors. The rare stamp collection theft means philately is a routine part of his conversational repartee. The way tiny pieces of old paper can be worth so much, and how human error can add dollar value, like when some guy incorrectly engraved the words, *Post Office*, instead of, *Post Paid*. One hundred of them sent out before the mistake was discovered, each one now worth almost a million dollars.

The sex slavery case, well, that was one case Jimmy wished he hadn't been assigned. Language and ideas were turned on their heads in ways that made Jimmy feel disgusted for being a man. Jimmy discovered a global, multi-billion dollar business, maybe the biggest legitimised criminal enterprise in living history, with links to money laundering, porn, paedophilia and terrorism, all propped up by all those Tom, Dick and Harrys who don't want to know any better.

So far with Jimmy's latest case, a jewellery heist, his team is nowhere. The most they know is that the usual suspects are not involved. There are clues to the perps, but they keep leading nowhere. They may be new on the scene, smart, no loose ends, but maybe, just maybe, too cocky for their own good.

This little ruby and diamond piece staring him in the face at *The LoDown* studios is an X-marks-the-spot treasure trove to Jimmy. He is certain the ruby around Genevieve Parker's beautiful neck is *the* ruby. Pretty sure, well, he needs to examine it a bit closer. It might not be it, but, no, he is sure this is the ruby necklace with the long history of gracing the necks of princesses and queens, sultanas and duchesses, Hollywood icons and filthy rich nobodies. When it was stolen, Koroskovas was the go-between in a deal that would have seen the necklace worn by yet another outrageously wealthy woman. Now there is political interference from powerful people abroad and the whole case could become a minefield if they don't solve it quickly. Luckily, the media has not yet cottoned on to this heist being anything other than a rather brutal jewellery robbery.

Jimmy is impressed with his eye for jewellery and his jewellery lingo, even if he does say so himself. And to spot stolen property when he isn't even really looking? To spot it on the tele when Genevieve Parker is competing for his gaze? Detective Senior Sergeant Jimmy Park is in awe of himself. Detective Park is on the case.

'Ms Parker, is there somewhere we can speak more privately? I have some questions for you in relation to an ongoing criminal investigation.'

'Now is not a good time,' Genevieve Parker replies, shaking her head and avoiding eye contact.

'Ms Parker,' Jimmy says quite tenderly, 'I understand that your day has been a long one, but time is of the essence in any criminal investigation, and I must insist–'

'Look, Detective,' Ms Parker interrupts rather irritably now, 'I know nothing about any crimes. You can arrange a time with Dinah on your way out. I can*not* speak with you now and I'm *not* sorry.' Genevieve turns to leave.

And that is when Jimmy makes his first mistake. His hand reaches out to prevent her leaving and grips her shoulder. She automatically counters with a sweeping left arm and a stinging right-cross to his face. Caught completely off guard and stung by the hurt, both to his flesh and his dignity, Jimmy says under his breath, 'Now I am really pissed off, lady, and I don't care who you are.'

That is when Jimmy makes his second mistake.

'You have just assaulted a police officer, Ms Parker,' Jimmy observes plainly, as in one smooth move, he secures Drop Dead Gorgeous Genevieve Parker's drop dead gorgeous wrists in cold metal rings, snap.

*OutRageOnLine:*
*GENEVIEVE IN KINKY HANDCUFF GIG.*
*Exclusive pics HERE.*
*Free dildo and cuffs*
*With first BETCHA! bet.*

'Full name?'

'Genevieve Natalie Parker.'

'Date of birth?'

Genevieve Natalie Parker, date of birth unknown, sits opposite Detective Senior Sergeant Jimmy Park at a table in a police interrogation room. Her hands are no longer handcuffed. She sits straight and attentive. Her voice is *that* voice, that silky newsreader voice, but a little on the shirty side, Jimmy reckons. Fair enough.

Two Art Deco Fire-Rose cut 2.0 carat transparent amethyst eyes watch Jimmy intensely. Her eyes are even more stunning in person than on the tele. *She* is even more stunning in person. Yet much tinier than Jimmy expected, even fragile. He feels the urge to wrap his arms around her, gently, and make everything all right. He feels guilt and shame spotlight his pathetic violence. *Handcuffs, Jimmy? Really?* He had to go the handcuffs? He takes a breath. *Be smooth, Jimmy,* he counsels himself. Detective Jimmy Park gives his most professional don't-mess-with-me look and raises an eyebrow with just the right amount of friendly question mark,

'Date of birth?'

'Tenth of September.'

'Tenth of September. A Virgo, eh? That explains a bit,' he adds quietly with a touch of humour to put her at ease. Yeah, that'll win him some brownie points. 'Year?'

Jimmy watches a red rash appear on Genevieve's chest and creep up her slender neck. Eyelashes twitch then settle as she inhales sharply.

'I refuse to answer on the grounds it may incriminate me,' she says.

Jimmy raises an eyebrow and decides to give her a break. *It's another world this show biz world,* he guesses, all glitz and trash mag gossip completely out of touch with reality. He lets it slide. He's Mr Nice Guy. He can access it in seconds later.

'Ms Parker, I have advised you of your rights and you have declined legal representation, is that correct?'

'Yes, there's no need for lawyers. I think this has just been a misunderstanding, Detective, and I sincerely apologise about, ah, that,' and she points to the right side of his face where the skin is already purpling. 'It probably could do with some ice,' she adds with concern. *Or maybe she's just rubbing salt into his humiliating wound,* thinks Jimmy.

'Yes, well,' Jimmy stumbles, tenderness protesting as his hand touches the spot, 'that is some right hook you have. You must work out? Martial arts? Boxing?'

'Both. But I would never, *never* have hit a police officer if I'd been in my right mind. Oh, I mean, not that I *wasn't* in my right mind, I'm not *crazy.*' She shakes her head vigorously and grimaces as if the very idea is a joke. 'It's just stalkers are the most horrible part of my job. Not that you're a stalker of course.' She shakes her head again and half-smiles apologetically. 'Of course you're not. But it had been a *very* long day and when you appeared I didn't have a clue who you were and so, of course, my fight response can just take over and I know I cover it well, but to be truthful it does take some time to settle, and when you grabbed my shoulder, well, it was just a reflex action. I was preserving my own life, you know?' There is a pleading in her eyes. 'I'm really, *really* sorry. I'm so *very sorry*. Oh.' Genevieve Parker's shoulders drop and her eyes fill with tears.

That's definitely not news anchor style, Jimmy observes. Genevieve Parker is definitely rattled by all this, and why wouldn't she be?

'Maybe we should call a truce,' says Jimmy quite touched by her remorse and with a new appreciation of her circumstances. 'I could charge you, you could sue me,' he sings like the words are nothing more than a nursery rhyme. 'Usually crims are the only ones who clock me like that, and my actions were a reflex too. I'm happy to put all that to one side if you are, Ms Parker.'

'So, I can go?' Genevieve begins to stand.

'Look, I really would appreciate some help with this,' Jimmy says knowing he's made it clear his answer is *no*. 'It shouldn't take long,' he adds to put a positive spin on it.

Genevieve nods once and resumes her seat.

Jimmy looks down at his file and says, 'Ms Parker, you are assisting police with the investigation into the armed robbery at Koroskova's Jewellery Emporium on–'

'Aa-rr-mm.'

Genevieve's high pitched intake of breath is odd and unexpected. Her whole demeanour and visage unexpectedly relax and, is that a smile? Before Jimmy can process exactly what this change signifies, Genevieve Parker says with a tone and facial expression of surprise and relief that extends all the way to the ends of her fluttering eyelashes, 'I'm not sure how I can help you with that, Detective. I know only what we've reported about the robbery on *The LoDown*. If this is about the recent phone footage, the one with the, the nudie run witness, I guess you'd call it, I understand that Tim Mirren alerted the police as soon as it came into his possession and he has been nothing but cooperative.'

'Yes, yes, of course,' nods Jimmy before continuing gravely. 'No, that is not the issue, Ms Parker. The issue is the exquisite item around your,' *exquisite*, Jimmy inserts to himself, 'neck.'

A delicate, manicured hand reaches for the ruby and diamond pendant. Violet eyes widen.

'Would you please tell me where you got the necklace, Ms Parker?'

'It was a gift,' she says frowning and looking down.

'What were the circumstances of the gift, Ms Parker?'

'My fiancé gave it to me the morning before yesterday.'

'Two days ago. Time exactly?'

'Ah, well, um, 4:02, ah, 4:04 am?' She looks somewhat confused.

'Ah, a smidge after 4 o'clock, then,' Jimmy clarifies, 'In the morning?'

'The morning.'

'Okay, so around 4 *am*? Have I got that right?'

'Yes.'

Four *am*? Jimmy wonders. What better time to give a gift of love than at 4 am when most law abiding people are snoring their heads off. Maybe Jimmy just doesn't understand the celebrity lifestyle.

'Can you tell me about that, please.'

'Tell you about it?'

Jimmy notes the interviewee is blushing.

'Yes, tell me about it.' Jimmy notes she is shifting uncomfortably.

'Well, my fiancé, Gael, my fiancé,' she suddenly breaks into a half-smile, 'we're getting married in the spring, a beautiful spring wedding.'

Jimmy watches her magnificent eyes sparkle briefly before filling with sadness. *How the hell did she get mixed up with this guy?* Jimmy wonders. She's in *La La Land* if she reckons that wedding is still going ahead. Poor kid, she comes across all confident, and she must be smart, but... Jimmy nods encouragement for Genevieve Parker to continue answering his question.

'When my fiancé came home, to my, our, to my penthouse, he woke me up to give this to me. He placed it around my neck and then we, ah, to express most beautiful sentiments. The ruby symbolises our true love, our hearts as one. Diamonds of course symbolise *Forever*. You know how it is,' she finishes quite brusquely.

But Jimmy does not know how it is at all. Not his style. Not since his rejected school kid proposal to Molly Davidson. Not Jimmy's style at all.

'Really, awfully sweet,' she is saying as if she is puzzling through a problem. 'So like him, *just* like him, to make such a grand gesture. I mean it was by way of an apology as well, of course.'

'Of course,' repeats Jimmy for no real reason he can think of.

'We had a misunderstanding the night before and he was sorry and ah, I guess I was sorry, and ah, his apologies are always,' she hesitates, 'always so romantic.'

*Always? How often do they have misunderstandings exactly?* Jimmy guesses as often as they have make-up sex. He wants that unpleasant thought out of his head. He needs to focus on the job at hand. Jimmy makes sure his face gives away nothing.

'Your fiancé's full name please?'

'Well, I'm sure there's a logical explanation. I–'

'Ms Parker, please, just answer the question.'

'Gael Pierre Saucisse,' she says despairingly.

'Saucisse? Gael Pierre the sausage, eh? And he has been quite the sausage, hasn't he? What does he do for a living, Ms Parker?' Jimmy asks.

'Gael is an entrepreneur and consultant.'

'Of course he is,' Jimmy says a little sarcastically, and immediately regrets his remark given Genevieve's sad expression. Still this is classic stuff.

Jimmy is feeling more certain that this Gael Saucisse is behind the Koroskova job and maybe others. At the very least this bloke would've purchased the item from a fence who could then lead Jimmy to the perps. But the exorbitant price tag on this little beauty says otherwise, even if Gael does consort with the likes of celebrity highflyer and moneyed-up Genevieve Parker. Plus there's the sheer cocky arrogance of the bastard, knowing he would be hiding it in plain sight around the neck of the most beautiful, most watched woman on the box.

No more mucking around, Jimmy means business. He stands, blows into surgical gloves and pulls them onto his hands.

'Ms Parker, I must ask you,' Jimmy hesitates as one of his fingers detours into the wrong glove finger and he struggles to manoeuvre it out and into the correct one. The plastic screeches like an orchestra tuning up. Jimmy glances down at the goddess witnessing his artless accessorising and colour rises to his cheeks. The orchestral cacophony continues.

Finally success, phew.

'Ms Parker, I must ask you to relinquish the item, which is evidence in an ongoing investigation.'

'No!' She clasps the necklace at her chest as if her life depends on it.

*Bloody hell, step back, Jimmy,* Jimmy commands himself. Do not touch her without warning. His cheek throbs where she clocked him earlier and he really should've put ice on it already. Jimmy suddenly has an ugly thought: maybe she's in on it. She's hamming it up to cover her own involvement.

But his heart softens as a tear traces a path down her cheek and she begins to sob quietly. Smooth, cool, in charge Detective Jimmy Park knows he is a heartless bastard. He knows the gorgeous Genevieve Parker is just an innocent. She's a love-sick stooge in this whole thing. He nudges a box of tissues towards her and speaks kindly, 'I understand that this is all unexpected and difficult, Ms Parker, but I'm afraid...'

Genevieve plucks a tissue from the box, dabs at her face delicately and then blows her nose.

Jimmy moves behind her and says gently, 'Would you mind? Could you lift your hair up at the back please, Ms Parker. I'm just going to undo the clasp. Is that okay with you, Ms Parker?'

She nods and bows her head as Jimmy's plastic encased fingers stumble with the clasp against the warmth of her skin. He momentarily surrenders to the fresh scent of her hair, the pulse at her neck, while his own heart thump-thumps. *Be smooth, Jimmy,* Jimmy coaches himself, *just another routine interview.* The golden thread unclasps and he manoeuvres the two ends of the golden chain to the front. All good. He's cool.

'Ow,' she says.

'Oh, ah, sorry about that, ah...' He's just hit her in the head with his elbow. *What an idiot,* Jimmy scolds himself. His big mitts are built to take strong marks of the footy, or strongarm bad guys, not this delicate fine motor shit.

'Oh, shit!' he curses as one end of the golden thread slips from the grasp of the pinched thumb and forefinger of his right hand, and the line of gold hangs vertically off his left. The glistening pendant slips and is lost to the floor.

They both reach urgently for the jewel and their heads clash.

'Ow, sorry,' she says.

'You sit. I'll get it,' says Jimmy.

'Where is it?' she panics.

They both scour the floor on hands and knees.

'Got it!' says Jimmy with relief as his gloved hand falls, snap, just as a small perfectly manicured hand beats him to the priceless symbol of love between Gael the sausage and Drop Dead Gorgeous Genevieve Parker. A jolt sizzles through him as he looks at his hand on top of her hand, like he has captured the rarest and most beautiful butterfly in the world. His eyes follow the curve of her hand to her wrist, shoulder, neck, her adorable face now with a smile, an inch away from his own. The smooth, cool, bungling detective's eyes meet those of the most beautiful woman on the planet. He and she. Alone together. In a bubble on planet earth.

Her smile evaporates and she wriggles her hand free to gracefully stand.

Jimmy lifts himself and his dicky hammy from the floor with a grunt, in awe that he was just gifted one of the wonders of the world: Genevieve Parker's smile.

But when Jimmy reaches his feet, she stands before him rigid and a little snooty. Yeah, he'd call that a snooty expression. She offers her hand, palm up, and solemnly gives up the jewel. 'Detective,' she says.

'Thank you, Ms Parker,' Jimmy says professionally, his gloved fingers brushing her small hand as he takes the jewel.

Back to business then. They sit once more and Jimmy examines the necklace and is sure, *absolutely* confident in his assessment. To have an item like this in his hands is thrilling. He glances up to see her watching his every move.

'Red really doesn't do me any favours,' she says. 'But Gael doesn't really pay attention to those things. It's very beautiful, I suppose, and the symbolism... Do you think it looks like something the Queen would wear?'

Jimmy looks up, stifles a grin and notes that Genevieve Parker suddenly looks quite unimpressed with the item that's been the centre of so much fuss. But Jimmy reckons beautiful doesn't come close to what this jewel is, and beautiful doesn't come close to what Genevieve Parker is. The stark décor and harsh lighting of the interview room suit neither jewel. Both the necklace and Genevieve Parker should be surrounded by classic luxury. Jimmy wants to place the necklace into a velvet-lined, handcrafted antique jewellery box. He wants to take Genevieve Parker away with him to a secluded, lavish paradise.

Jimmy deposits the jewel into an evidence bag, seals and tags it, and removes his gloves with a professional smack of plastic.

Genevieve Parker startles at the sound and Jimmy again wonders about her fragility. But he has a job to do. *Get on with it, Jimmy*.

'Where were you on the morning of the Koroskova robbery, Ms Parker?

'Ah, at home in bed until 6 am when I got up and went to work.'

'And where was Mr Saucisse?'

'Beside me,' she replies then blinks several times and amends her statement, 'I didn't hear him come to bed, but when I woke at 3:11 am he was there. When I woke at 6 am, he was not.'

'That's a very precise time window, Ms Parker,' observes Jimmy quite puzzled at how often Genevieve Parker seems to be awake at such hours.

'I have a time piece beside the bed and I have a tendency to wake at that time, usually just for a few minutes,' she says uncertainly, 'or longer.'

Jimmy tilts his head quizzically and she responds, 'Hmm, some years ago I received a phone call at that time about a family event, a catastrophe really.' Her chin tremors.

'I'm sorry, Ms Parker,' says Jimmy gently, feeling like a heel. He knows up close and personal the catastrophic events that happen at ungodly hours.

'If I'm going to wake in the night, it's always at that time. I guess there are some things you just don't really ever get over.'

'You're right,' says Jimmy, lost in her sad eyes.

She smiles briefly, then turns deathly pale.

'I'm feeling a little unwell.' Genevieve topples sideways out of the chair. Detective Senior Sergeant Jimmy Park's strong arms catch her. Jimmy hasn't moved that fast since, since... Jimmy has never moved that fast. Jimmy Park is in love.

The smell of sweat, fresh cedar, old man's clothes. A deep voice, a kind voice. 'Are you okay? Ms Parker? Genevieve?'

Gen feels finger tips brushing her hair from her forehead. The soft padding of a suit jacket bunched under her head. The cool hardness of the floor beneath her body. Blurs of movement slowly sharpen. A shirt sleeve smooths over a muscular bicep. Dark eyebrows ask questions above chocolate eyes.

'Just as well I caught you, or you would have one hell of a headache.'

'I do have one hell of a headache.' Is that her voice? Her brain answers, *yes*. Her ears and head believe it's an anonymous echo coming to her down a dark tunnel.

'Have a little water, you're probably dehydrated being under those bright studio lights. I probably stuffed up your usual post work routine, sorry.'

The brash detective looks quite sheepish and concerned. He cradles her head upwards to the mug of water and brushes her chin with a finger where the water spills. A sob catches in her throat. She just wants to go home.

'I think we better get you home, Ms Parker.'

'Yes, yes,' Gen agrees and begins to get to her feet. Her head spins and nausea bolts. 'I think, I'm going to–'

The detective has the metal bin in place in the nick of time. His cool hands lift her hair from her face as she vomits. He gives her a tissue when she's done and gently sits her back in her chair. He squats down at her feet, his suit trousers straining against his thighs. Perhaps he thinks she's going to throw up again. She shivers and dizzies. She refuses to throw up again. She refuses to faint again.

He looks directly into her eyes. 'How about taking a couple of deep breaths,' he says. 'We wouldn't want you fainting again, or... Deep breaths. In 2 – 3 – 4. Out 2 – 3 – 4. In...'

Holding onto his eyes and his words, Gen copies his slow

breathing. His dark eyes contain a flash of yellow like a honeycomb mousse centre in 80% pure cocoa dark chocolate. She's just thrown up and is still feeling quite unwell, but there is always something deliciously comforting about chocolate.

Relief rushes through her again. Her abortion underground secrets are safe. This has been nothing, *nothing* at all. Except for the end of her happy-ever-after. Except for the end of Love. How could she be so stupid? How could Gael be such a bastard? But she will get through this and continue on towards her end goal. Will she? Her arrest, her association with Gael, on top of all her on-air gaffes of late? This might mean the end of her career and the end of the only thing that really matters. Of all the things to happen.

Anger roils up from her gut and morphs into hatred at her throat. *Men! Selfish, cruel bastards and this detective is just one more. This bumbling, demanding detective. Oh, is he all right?*

The detective stands up uneasily, wincing with pain and rubbing the back of his leg and Gen experiences a twinge of concern for the ignorant, bungling detective with the 80% cocoa eyes, cool hands and nicely muscled physique. Gen's hand unconsciously reaches for the empty space at her throat. *You cannot keep mentally deleting the tough stuff,* says Martha. *You pride yourself on telling others the important truths. But what do you tell yourself?*

And it is all so clear. The truth. And all so confusing. That same truth. Why does the truth always have to hurt so much? Why is the truth always so awful? Why is there no nice truth, *none*? Why does she spend so much of her day making sure everybody knows the truth, when she is incapable of coping with her own horrible personal truths. Mother, Rosie, Gael. Her fiancé is nothing but a criminal, a jewel thief. Clearly the truth will not set her free. She has been trapped in a relationship with Gael that has been nothing but lies. Gen has been played for a fool and deserves everything she has coming to her. 'Which won't include what he owes me,' she whispers.

'What, Ms Parker?' asks the detective, who is sitting back in his chair.

Gen's shoulders collapse.

'I thought he was working crazy hours to set up his latest business venture,' Gen says mournfully, not caring a jot what this detective thinks of her, as she continues processing her own pathetic truth. 'I was trying to be the supportive, understanding girlfriend and then the supportive, understanding fiancée. He was always concerned with big things, more important things than me. His money was always tied up. I paid for everything; I loaned him money.'

'How much have you loaned him, Ms Parker?'

*That is the total you have handed over to him,* Gen hears her accountant say, *for absolutely no security, no return, and nothing in writing. You must say no, Gen.*

'Two hundred and fifty,' says Gen. The detective's quizzical look tells her she has not explained herself properly.

'Thousand,' adds Gen, '$250,000.'

The detective whistles air through puckered lips.

'Okay, let's just park that one for now,' he says.

Gen feels ashamed and ridiculous. She just wants to go home, curl up in bed and never wake up again.

'We really should get you home and into bed,' says the detective. 'Ah, into bed to, ah, rest, in bed and, ah, get better, recover. Let's get you home, Ms Parker,' he says, bumbling again. 'At some stage we'll speak further, but I'll arrange for uniforms to drive you home and you can provide them with a recent photo of Gael Saucisse. Police will be stationed outside your apartment throughout the night. You can rest easy, you're safe.'

Safe? Just what Gen needs: police watching her every move. How can you be an active member of the abortion underground with police watching you? Surely they won't bug her phone, will they? Gen sighs before deciding that Brian will know what to do. Everything will be okay.

'Ms Parker?'

Gen is feeling dizzy again and would rather like the detective to stop talking now, *please.*

'I'll stop talking in a sec,' he says, 'but, there's one last little thing and I hate to ask you this Ms Parker, but...'

'Detective,' Gen interrupts, exhaustion and anger seeping through her bones and her brain, 'You and I have shared some extraordinary intimacies tonight. I could not feel more humiliated than if you had handcuffed and arrested me. Oh, that's right, you did. Tick. Or if it all were captured on cameras and uploaded and I am now a laughing stock for the whole world to see. Tick. Or if I had fainted into your arms. Tick. Or if you had held my hair back while I vomited. Tick. Or witnessed my romantic humiliation. Tick. Tick. Tick. So please, call me Gen, and I will call you?' she looks for a name tag, peers into his face. She has made him look sheepish again. But is that a smile? How can he smile?

'Jimmy,' the detective says.

'Jimmy. Well, Jimmy, fuck it,' Gen says, suddenly aware of all her shame, anger and exhaustion transposing, like alchemy, into a reckless familiarity. 'Ask. A. Way,' she says defiantly. Gen is released from worry and from worrying about the worst that can happen. All of this is quite freeing, this not giving a fuck.

Jimmy clears his throat.

'Yeah, well, as I was saying, ah, Gen,' Jimmy says, gentler again now. 'And, ah, Gen, I hate to ask you this after, you know, everything.'

'Go on,' Gen commands because it seems he is waiting for some sort of permission, and his gauche fawning is most unbecoming, though perhaps a fraction endearing, and really quite hilarious. Gen's mouth twitches as she stifles a giggle.

'Yeah, sorry. I, ah, I, Gen, just one more thing.'

'Go on,' Gen commands again, a giggle playing on her lips, merriment in her eyes, and an exhausted hysterical laughter threatening to overwhelm her.

'I need you to hand over the engagement ring too.'

Gen grips the massive baguette on her ring finger, the dazzling diamond symbol and promise of true love and happy-ever-after.

'You are kidding?' she says. 'He gave me this months ago. Surely, surely...' Gen looks intently at the most beautiful ring in the world, the only truth she ever had with Gael. She eyeballs the heartless detective Jimmy. She refuses to cry in front of this horrible man. Under no circumstances. Never, ever, will she cry, *never ever*.

'Waah,' she wails. But Gen's noisy grief is not enough to blot out her final humiliating indignity at the hands of the rude, clumsy Jimmy with the beautiful couverture chocolate eyes, the gentle hands and the lean, muscular body.

'Sorry, Gen,' he says. 'that 18-carat diamond ring on your finger is known as the Iceberg Beauty and is worth somewhere in the vicinity of $5 million.'

*Dear Rosie,*

*I am so sorry. I have put everything in jeopardy. All the plans. All my work. Everything I was doing to set things right by you.*

Tears wet Gen's face. Raindrops wet the penthouse window. Gen's world wells and heaves. Everything – inside, outside – is fractal.

*I love you*
*Forgive me*
*Love*
*Gen*

IV

# CHAOS

More than a week later, at 7 am, *The LoDown* anchor, Genevieve Parker, is at her day spa. In a private room, Gen lies under a soft towel, a revitalising mask on her face and two attendants polishing and priming. She revels in the serenity of burbling water, chortling birds and rainforest scents. She revels in the fact that she got away with it.

Gen's enforced time off was communicated to her by the *big boys* via text. Gen tapped back, *hard*. She secured a commuted sentence: 'Four weeks, take a holiday, and get some fucking help.'

Gen wasted no time. She spent three adventurous days in a glorious neighbouring country where myriad wonders awaited around every corner. One of those wonders was no bigger than a one carat diamond, but these days was far more valuable. Brian accompanied Gen as her cameraman. They travelled with impressive equipment, all of it bogus, all of it housing an array of empty lead-lined compartments. On her return, airport security couldn't get enough of Gen. They posed for Brian as he filmed for Gen's fabulous *LoDown* story about fearless border security, and then just waved them through with all that equipment and the thousands of concealed abortifacient tablets. Tiny life-savers escaped on the first leg of their smuggled journey to deliver desperate women from crisis pregnancies.

Gen could hardly believe she had the nerve to be so brazen, so reckless. The exhaustion that followed ebbed, as a thrilling wish to do it all again rose up on a terrifying tide of paranoia. But here and now, Gen relishes the win and the relief. She feels proud of her escape and the 'fuck you' to the entitled white men clenching their self-righteous egos while women die, like Eva Larsson, tossed from a van like a bag of garbage.

Joining the criminal class by successfully smuggling an illicit substance is not all that Gen has been up to. Contrary to Martha's advice, Gen has been editing and deleting. Breakfast with Mother? Never happened. Exposing herself in all her naked and vulnerable glory to her housekeeper? Deleted. Assaulting a police detective? Handcuffed? Jimmy Park? Just a dream, ah, nightmare. Fiancé and jewellery thief Gael? Shredded. Penthouse security? Upgraded.

As Gen is pampered and teeters on sleep, her phone buzzes. She drags herself back to the real world to check who's interrupting her Me time. Gen picks up and sits up immediately. Her spa treatment can wait. One of her well-placed sources, Maxine Badlands, gets straight to the point, anticipating Gen's part in the conversation so that Gen merely has to listen.

'Gen, I had a very strange phone call with the PM. Not Bull, Bull's the ex-PM now. No, I'm talking about Pope, PM Julian Pope. I had a weird phone call with Julian Pope a week ago. Yes, I know they're usually weird, but this one was out-there weird. I decided to sleep on it, mull it over for a few days, do a bit of digging. I got nowhere, but look, there's just something not quite right. Yeah I know, *not quite right* is Pope's go to, but I just could not shake it.

'So look, Gen, what do you know about the ex-PM? I mean the PM, Pope and a problem pregnancy? In his family? A mistress? Or, and well I know this might sound completely nuts, but it was the way he spoke, the things he said, so I know this is the last thing you'd ever expect to hear from me or anyone else for that matter, but I'll just ask the question, Gen, and you can do the leg work, you know, do your thing. Is Pope pregnant? Is it possible? Yes, I said pregnant. P. R. E. G. N. A. N. T. Pregnant. Is he a closet trans? Is he a woman? Is he from another planet? I mean we've all thought that from time to time, haven't we, Gen? Gen?'

'Mr Pope! Mr Pope!'

*Do they have to be so faarking loud?* Jules grimaces at the media throng. He has woken with a hangover like none he's ever experienced before, like a post-partying-all-night-trans-ocean-flight-jet-lag-hangover ramped up to the max.

What else could he expect after a night of sleep so deep and dreams so vivid, that he tossed and turned and woke startled in a cold sweat, as if he'd been sleeping in the fires of Hell, to rush to the toilet for a wee for the umpteenth time. Plus, he could feel the tender bruising on his calves and ribs where Nance had nudged and pushed to roll him over to shut down his snoring. Confounded woman, where's her sympathy, her self-sacrifice? Neglect, that's what it is, *neglect,* Jules fumes. Faark this faarking pregnancy.

Surrounded and blinking in the hot whiteness of lights and thrusting microphones, Prime Minister Julian Pope pulls out a hanky from his trousers and mops sweat from his brow. On this mild morning, the media hounds catch the PM returning from an hour's power walk through the expansive and palatial green lawns surrounding Parleyment House. Well, in fact, 10 minutes into his hour power walk, Jules sat down on a bench for a good half-hour and pondered the weighty problems of the world, which, of course, meant the weighty problems of himself, which meant the weighty problem of his pregnancy. His detail helped him back to the media scrum so, an hour's powerwalk it was.

Usually, when Jules power walks he wears nothing but his runners and his trademark silk shorts emblazoned with the national flag. His toned upper body is a thing of beauty, and the wiggle of his power walk is sexy. Why not share himself with the masses? Politically, the PM bare-chested and leggy is better than any other photo op or statement. Jules knows his fit and pleasing body showcases his masculinity and everyman gutsiness and houses his acute, moral mind. His body provides him with the vigour and stamina to dedicate himself to ruling. Jules does not consider his pride to be conceit or vanity; these things are just indisputable truths.

So what if lately he's been covering himself up? Absence makes the heart grow fonder. Let 'em hunger to see his iron man bod. He'll be back. But meanwhile, Jules' power walk garb has to be a large t-shirt, also in the nation's colours, stretching over his stomach. Nance suggested he wear the tee so he could still wear his usual running shorts with their now far-too-small waist slung under his belly. Good old Nance, it works a treat.

Now Jules sniffs the scent of power and begins to relish the journos hankering for his attention with their surging bodies and screeching questions. Yes, what a wonderful ambush. This is the argy-bargy he was made for. Jules smiles charmingly. Bring it on, people, you adoring morons. They can't get enough of him. He's the Prime Minister, for faark's sake! Jules is the fit, athletic PM the country adores. He decides to make the media throng wait, while he enjoys a drink from his water bottle. Jules draws out his power over the pack by taking his time between mouthfuls of water, to survey his domain.

As the media grows impatient with the PM's leisurely drinking and surveying, Jules falls in love with this place, and with himself, all over again. Nestled on a hill of rolling green lawn and overlooking the nation's most famous lake, his seat of power is a modern brutalist cathedral with its spire stretching up to heaven, from man to God. It is a sacred site of democracy, representing and welcoming all peoples. It is also home to *The Bully*, the Terrorism Act-enshrined bulwark. This secure iron fence, with turreted armed guards dotted around it like charms on a bracelet, encircles the seat of free speech and democracy to ensure the security of the nation's leaders, and to keep out any of the threatening riff raff. Completed at a time when Jules' nemesis, Mr Tommy Bull, held the Prime Ministership, it was christened, *The Bully,* in a moving ceremony of shredded ribbon, smashed champagne bottle and guardian salvos.

Jules breathes in the air about him with great satisfaction. Yes, he loves this place. The rush of post powerwalk endorphins in his system means he's feeling, what exactly? Yes, happy, that's what that emotion is, *happiness*. He has not felt that for months. He's actually doing very well. Maxi-Mum effort with close to opti-Mum outcome and mini-Mum fuss, especially given certain matters best kept Mum about. Despite his intolerable circumstances, Jules enjoys an endorphin-driven chuckle to himself at his pithy punning about his horrendous secret about which he is keeping mum.

Jules is suddenly aware that he is sweating and puffing in a most un-macho way, in front of all these journos. Abruptly, he feels, well, Jules is not sure what this emotion is. Emotions after all are weak girlie germie things. He has a fleeting memory of holding his mother's hand, being presented to the teacher at the kinder door. Shy, that's it, self-conscious. How faarking pathetic.

One of Jules' detail proffers a towel, also in the colours of the nation's flag. Jules takes the towel and drapes it over his shoulder to further veil his girth. Faark, this stomach is spoiling his media pack love-ins. The veneer of his charming smile chips and peels, revealing its cheap and nasty underside in a snarl. Why are they so close? He can't breathe.

'Move back you faarkwits!' he booms.

He's standing here like some pathetic daisy in the middle of swarming bees, all these bastard bees just waiting to sting and suck the sap right out of him. They've bee-lined for him. And here he is with a bee in his bonnet when he's the bee's knees. This whole thing is a load of beeswax. The daisy PM struggles to stand erect and the PM's security detail shoos the buzzing journalists back.

*They're not still going on about the budget are they?* thinks Jules gloomily. He points to his old mate, Bill Bolton, from *The Morning Star*. Bill's only ever concerned with foreign affairs, 'Yes, Bill?'

'Mr Pope, what can you tell us about the latest reports coming out of the world's oil belt?'

Jules hasn't a clue what the latest reports are. He was sick of the whole shemozzle months ago.

'A basket case,' he says, before recovering with diplomatic clichés, 'We are of course working closely with the alliance using diplomatic sanctions and working behind the scenes to bring a peaceful resolution to this appalling situation.'

'No, Mr Pope,' Bill follows up. 'I mean the reports that since The United Straits of Anarchy has bowed out, there has been a successful negotiation of peace and–'

'Genevieve, *Genevieve* Parker,' interrupts Jules as he spies a delightful and surprising little bee. She can suck his daisy stamen any time. 'Welcome, go ahead, *go ahead*, Miss Parker.' Jules' whole being exudes charm and lust. How he's missed drop dead gorgeous Genevieve. She's been stuck behind that news desk under hot studio lights for far too long, *far too long*. Come to papa.

As a distraction from his own woes, Jules spent a few moments this morning looking up Genevieve Parker online and laughing his head off at the footage. In the reverse chronological order that is the online world, Jules viewed the most recent Genevieve drama first, and worked his way forward to the past. Genevieve's handcuffed arrest, Genevieve gone goofy at the helm of *The LoD*own, inebriated and stumbling around in the city in the early hours, blurting a raspberry at her audience and dropping a solid *faark* on national prime time television.

Word has it, Jules reminds himself, that she's spent the last week having a holiday, when actually Genevieve Parker is TV royalty thrown off the throne. You throw a tantie, girlie, and they throw the book at you, throw you aside and here you are a throwback to old times. But good times, so he'll throw her a bone. Don't want to throw the baby out with the bathwater. Although, in Jules' case, that's exactly what he wants. But just look at her, faarking Gorgeous Genevieve Parker. Who cares if she's lost her mind, she hasn't lost her looks, and her loss is his gain. How lovely to see her back roving about in the sunshine and with a full TV film crew too. Lovely.

Jules can see Genevieve's presence seems to be as much a surprise to the other journos too. Surely, they would've all heard loud whispers about the bosses' impatience with Genevieve Parker's emotional instability and plans to send her packing. Jules watches the press posse crane its neck to see her and tilt its ears to hear her, whispering and giggling as they look up and down from notepads and equipment. She's a disgraced has-been who's cut in on their turf.

'Mr Pope,' Genevieve begins in her sexy voice.

'Please, Genevieve, call me Julian,' Jules says smarmily as he catches sight of a beautiful pubic mass hovering above him. No, just one of those black fluffy microphones.

Genevieve begins again in a manner that means she means business, 'Mr Pope.'

Jules sees Genevieve Parker's formality with his own stern teeth clench and raises the ante by pushing his chest out and unsuccessfully sucking his stomach in.

'Mr Pope, is it true that you are pregnant?'

All eyes look to Genevieve, eyebrows rising and falling. Smirks appear on the media faces with accompanying chuckles of disbelief, whispers and clearly audible remarks, 'Did she just say what I think she said? What did she say? She really is off her rocker. Is this a joke? What's Genevieve been smokin'? The same stuff as that Freudenfrau nutter. Genevieve Parker really has lost it.'

As the focus returns to Jules, he feels a horrified expression scoot across his face in a split second, before a sweep of politician polish paints over a gleaming smile.

'Genny, my dear, you've noticed a certain spreading of my physique, have you? I guess all's fair in love and politics,' he leers. 'Although perhaps you've hit a little below the belt this time, Miss Parker.'

The assembled journalists laugh loudly in relief and Jules smugly knows he has them back eating out of his hand. Except for Genevieve Parker, whose visage remains dialled to serious, her left eye with a hint of a twitch, like a bee's threatening micro-movement.

'As you all know,' Jules says with a cheeky twinkle in his eye, 'I am usually a dashing and fit specimen of a man.' The journos titter admiringly. 'But certain medication, following my cholecystectomy, has this rather cumbersome side effect. Plus, and I know all you girls especially understand this, I did rather enjoy my French baguettes at the Paris summit last month, ha ha.'

The whole gathering joins in laughing, except for Genevieve Parker, who pitches her voice even lower and throws it even higher, over the scrum.

'Mr Pope, Julian.'

Her voice lands slap bang in Jules' face like a wet cream pie. And Jules can think of so many better things to be doing with Genevieve Parker and a wet cream pie. Jules smiles, unable to take his eyes off her. She is one tasty piece of crumpet and an eye-full of arm candy. A scrumptious honey bun and one hot dish. Jules tummy growls. He suddenly feels very hungry.

'Mr Pope,' Genevieve Parker persists. 'I have it on good authority, sir, that you are pregnant.'

The surrounding journalists laugh derisively, yell mild abuse at Genevieve. Jules shakes his head and smiles patronisingly as if he is finding this little exchange highly amusing, if a little tedious.

'In fact, Prime Minister, I have here a recording of your recent ultrasound showing that you are more than four months pregnant,' Genevieve waves a disc in the air, 'and a little undersized.'

Jules blinks. His hands unconsciously cradle his belly. Too late, Jules recognises his preggers hand-wrap. Realises with horror that the jig is up. Knows that they know. Knows that somehow, some way, they know that Genevieve Drop Dead Gorgeous Parker is right.

'Mr Pope! *Mr Pope!* How long was this in the planning, Prime Minister? Was it planned? What is the ETA? Who is the mother, Mr Pope? Or are their two fathers? Jules? *Jules! Jules! Jules*! How do you feel? What are your plans? Jules!' The stinging buzzing media swarm of worker drones fire barbs so deep, Jules feels he is being crucified. Genevieve Parker stands resplendent as their queen bee, holding Jules' terrified gaze in the world of her self-satisfied violet eyes.

The vomit comes unexpectedly. Explodes over the rolling green parleymentary lawns. Splatters on a few journalist shoes. Pongs caustically on the breeze. The media scrum is forced onto its back foot, hopping quickly out of the way, expletives and 'eews' and 'yuks' and disgust all over its mass sickened face.

Jules wipes the back of his hand across the puke at his mouth. He and his security detail make a hot shoe shuffle escape to the parleymentary doors.

Shut out. Closed in. Silence and sanctuary, at last.

'Who the faark let that mob past *The Bully*?' Jules explodes moments later in his parleymentary office.

'You asked they be let in, Prime Minister,' Sam replies politely.

'Well, hmm, who the faark tipped them off?' Jules fumes to Sam, while phones ring loudly and the world wide web weaves its wicked filigree of deceit, truth and lies: Jules and his pregnancy go pandemic. Worldwide, headlines and cruel pics scream from the dailies and rant from radio shock jocks. They blare from screens and tinkle from watches. Taunt from phones and dominate every rabbit hole of cyberspace. Julian Pope makes an international splash that could drown his political career. He makes headlines he never, *ever* wanted to make:

*WHO POKED POPE?*
*POPE STAYS MUM*
*POPE'S PREGNANCY PACKAGE*
*POPE'S PREGNANT PAUSE & PUKE*
*POPE'S MIRACULOUS CONCEPTION*
*PM STANDS FOR PREGGERS MIRACLE*
*POPE TO BE POP – OR MUM?*
*NON BINARY GROUPS REJOICE*
*OutRageOnLine: CRASHED*

'How can someone breach my confidential and private medical information, Sam?'

'Well, Prime Minister, remember that showdown with the states when your government refused to fund the health systems to update the digital security of personal health information? Well–'

'I don't want an explanation, Sam, I want answers! I want the head on a plate of whoever leaked my confidential information. Whoever he is will be hanged, drawn and quartered, you hear me?!' booms Jules, 'And since when do journalists call me Jules, damn it! Calling me Jules is vulgar familiarity. What's happened to respect for the office? I want it put out that they call me Mr Prime Minister, er, Mr ex-Prime Minister, or Mr Pope or I'll call the feds on each and every one of them and put them away. I put it in the new terrorism laws about insulting the PM, didn't I? I'll jail the lot of 'em.

'Now get on to Genevieve Parker. Tell her it's an exclusive. I'll only talk to Genevieve. Book it in after the WTF trip. I'm not going to let that bitch stop me from my moment in the WTF limelight. Do the deal with Genevieve. I'm going to faark the living daylights out of that faarking bimbo and take her down!'

'Welcome, to this mo-*ost* prestigious world gala event. I am Sir

Rodney Felix III and I shall be your host during this exclusive live coverage of the World Trade Forum, coming from one of the world's most beautiful island nations.' Sir Rodney flashes a brilliant smile, before panning footage of a grand beachside resort fills screens around the world.

One of those screens, an old fashioned television, is being watched closely by the Queen of Great Brexit.

'It is after all a world event, the WTF, and One does laark a good acronym, eh, champs?' the Queen confides to her 18 dogs variously nestled at her feet or lounging next to her on the 19th century drop arm club sofa upholstered in Wilhelmina Morris handcrafted fabric. The Queen speaks the Queen's English in the correct way, which is to say, in a way no one else in the world speaks it. The round vowels are extravagantly plump, especially the *O*, except, of course, on those unpredictable occasions when Her Majesty gives them a drawn out, nasal twang. The straight vowel, the *I*, often takes on an *Ar* sound, as if it feels it is missing out on all the fun.

'One must do One's best to save the free world after all, and the rest,' the Queen instructs the dogs, while her hands labour proficiently with knitting needles and wool. The lemon knit amassing in her lap eventually will transform into a matinee jacket for the newest great-grandchild *royale*.

Knowing how comforting and enjoyable the dogs find her regal conversation, Her Majesty nods, smiles all round and explains, 'One's good friend, Betsy, is hosting, and One does love seeing One's grandson Wiggins on the world stage. One has a piv-otal time to get One's good media coverage for One's monarchy. He is still the most handsome and cleverest of them all, after all.' Since Katerina's demise during her sadly-ended seventh pregnancy, the Queen has been concerned that Wiggins find a new focus. 'Well he does have the heirs, even if he has lost Katerina. She really was a high-spirited and fertile mare that one. One did laark her, a great deal.'

One of the dogs barks in agreement, before they all join in cheering the high-spirited fertile and now dead one.

'Yes, *yes*. One knows you all laarked her too. Hush now, it couldn't be helped, could it?' She looks seriously at her moving fingers and rues the moving finger writing such a tragic chapter.

'Anyway,' her Majesty says brightly, 'having writ, One must move on. One is glad that Wiggins has taken all six of the children with him. One does hope that seeing the pregnant Prime Minister will not be too difficult for he and the children.'

The Queen rests the knitting in her lap and complains, 'What a ri-dic-ulous state of affairs. That colony still can't even stand on its own two feet? Why has it not declared independence yet? One is still their queen, for faark's sake.' Her Majesty sighs. 'The Great in Great Brexit is not great at all, sometimes,' she rues, sighing quite mournfully. 'Now, a man pregnant! Harrumph. And no less a man than a prime minister. What hope! Good luck with that one, Betsy. Still, chin up, champs,' the Queen beams at her canine minions who obediently tilt their little heads up to her. 'One will see that prince ride in on his magnificent stallion. One cannot possibly miss that.'

The Queen excitedly click-clacks her knitting needles as Sir Rodney Felix III's dulcet baritone voice informs her Majesty, 'We are coming live from the glorious Munnidownthudrayn Casino set on one of the world's most beautiful beaches.'

'Aah, no one has as much style as Sir Rodney,' admires the Queen as she feels quite affected by the pageantry of the occasion.

Sir Rodney's voiceover ecstatically and grandly enlightens the Queen about the various dignitaries and greetings being shown in the live-as-it-happens footage, 'The president of the host nation, come on down! Hear the crowd go wild for the host leader.'

'Hello, Betsy,' toodles the Queen, waving at the royal tele. 'One does like that embroidered top and the hat, but the skirt? What were you thinking Betsy? One has told you before.' Softening, her Majesty admits, 'It is hard to find good fashion advisers I suppose. One must not judge when One's friends do not have the fashion machinery One has at the palace. The only one One could not get to toe the line, ugh, those toes, was Gertie. She was never one of us, of course, came from common stock, so what can One expect?'

'A-and, Prime Minister, Mr Tonyee Bull!' Sir Rodney enthuses. 'Oh, one moment, a late correction, I do apologise to our viewers. A-and Prime Minister, Mr Juliaan Poop!'

Moments later, Sir Rodney whispers gravely, as if he's sharing a tantalising secret, 'Soon, these two formidable leaders will formally greet each other. It is a moment pregnant with hope.'

'That's better, Sir Rodney,' the Queen says, approving of his more subdued tone. 'You have been just a little too upbeat. One even wondered if you were introducing contestants in that new political reality TV show, *Public Lies, Private Parties*, One thinks it is called. But no, I can see from the scenery and dignitaries that it is just Sir Rodney getting a little over-excited. One always does love a gala event like this one, Sir Rodney, but do settle petal,' the queen advises Sir Rodney on the tele.

The Queen wiggles her toes, cosily covered in silk slippers, and shifts her eyes to Prime Minister Julian Poop. A shiver thrills painfully down her spine. Her royal mouth curls in distaste. Ever since Prime Minister Kissing put his arm around the royal person at an official function, her Royal Majesty suffers traumatic re-triggering of the brutal assault. When *The Kissing Incident* occurred, the Queen froze into a smiling statue of a queen and a trauma-infused, autopilot completion of her duties. One still feels pride in the fact that her robotic performance was so well carried out that no one suspected a thing. Not one of her subjects was any the wiser. No one even noticed.

'Appaarently, One carried Oneself with such aplomb. Then this twerp of a man, Poop, look at him dears,' directing her dogs with a flurry of fingers towards the TV, 'took it upon himself to do the same and touch the Royal Person. Horrid. Outraageous. One has a good mind to add Oneself to #MeToo.' The Queen shivers and shakes herself from head to toe to remove the dreadful memory from her mind and body.

'And now champs, the man is pregnant. Yes, you heard me correctly. That man is pregnant, 20 weeks apparently. Of course, it could all be a scam. I mean One's subjects over there are all from criminal stock, except for those who were already there before One's kingdom invaded. But why would One choose to hoodwink One in that way? Pregnant? Obviously champs, the man's an idiot.'

The Queen becomes enthralled again with lovely Sir Rodney's soothing commentary, 'And here they are, moving towards each other. The host country's president and Prime Minister Julian Poop. The two nations have a long and productive friendship since the geological parting of the land mass millions of years ago. You can see their delightful and genuine camaraderie in the way the two great leaders smile and extend their hands–'

The broadcaster's sepia voice stops abruptly.

Her Majesty looks up from her knitting, from which One has just then deigned to notice a dropped stitch. What has stopped Sir Rodney in his stylish and soothing tracks? And there it is, Prime Minister Poop standing over the genteel Betsy who is flat on her back, legs splayed, hat fallen over her face. The Queen watches agog as four men in army uniform tackle Julian Poop to the ground. The screen goes to snow followed by an announcement that regular viewing will re-commence as soon as possible.

'Oh Betsy, my dear, what happened? An assassination attempt? Oh, my God! Why did it have to be Betsy?' The Queen begins to tremble, raving to her dogs, 'When the world would be so much better off if that obnoxious upstart, Julian Poop, had been taken out instead. But no, they save him, while poor Betsy, poor Bets, Bet, Be, B, B.' The Queen dissolves into tears. 'What is One meant to do?

'Well firstly, One must behave in a queenly manner,' the Queen advises Oneself, recovering her composure with a regal snort. 'One must look on the bright side and think, yes, *think*. Maybe Betsy is intact. After all One's eyes were not on the screen at the very moment when... where is that gadget thingummyjig?'

One searches the sofa for the handset. One pulls one from behind a cushion, presses a button, 'Not that one,' and One tosses it aside. One finds another on the floor, presses a button, 'Not that one either,' and One exasperatedly pronounces, 'Must One really have so many whizzers for one old TV? Where is the farking thing!'

Finally One hunts round under the royal bottom, feels the rigid stick of a gizmo, momentarily thinks of other things, but happily discovers it is the whizzer One wants and One presses the button. Her Majesty exhales a sigh of relief as the TV picture begins to rewind, and the Queen snaps it to *Play*, impatiently waiting for one of the presidents to get back to his position.

'Here it is, *here it is*.' One glues One's eyes to the screen. 'Yes, all looking lovely, except for that skirt. I have told her. Coming closer, hands to meet, no! What just happened?!'

The Queen of Great Brexit flutters her short eyelashes like a lady bug taking flight and rewinds and replays in slow motion several times, until she is absolutely certain. 'Oh, Betsy! What the fark were you thinking? No, no, noo! One needs a cuppa. *Get me a cup of tea this instant!*'

Fifteen minutes later the Queen is settled in her comfiest chair, an accompaniment to the 19th century drop arm sofa, and sips freshly brewed Great Brexit Breakfast tea from a royal bone china King Luigi V cup-and-saucer, and resumes her education of the pups. Beside her on the Frederic XIV side table is a silver salver of shortbread biscuits bought from the local supermarket. Several of the dogs eye the shortbreads off enviously. Her canine minions are more strewn about her than earlier, as if they are bedraggled balls of wool upturned from her knitting bag.

'Well, One has had quite a fright hasn't One? Yes, a little calming tonic is definitely called for, champs.' Her Majesty reaches into the Ardine maroon handbag anchored on One's arm and withdraws a small bottle of Glenfiddle 40-year old single malt whiskey. One unscrews the lid, pours a little into One's tea, begins to recap the bottle, but stops and thinks better of it. One adds a touch more whiskey to the cup before secreting the bottle back in One's handbag. Clearly satisfied with the calming tonic provided by the most expensive whiskey in the world, One's eyes sparkle and One's lips smile, 'Aah, that's better. *That* hits the spot nicely.'

Biting into one of the shortbread biscuits, the Queen shares her optimism with the dogs.

'One is sure that Betsy will be just fine, *fine*. She is a strong lassie after all and weighs as much as One's award-winning bulls. Yes, Betsy will be just fine.'

The mellow inner glow from her whiskey-spiked tea is nicely softening the One's concern for One's dear friend, when the Queen experiences a ghastly epiphany.

'Ye gads! No! Betsy and that PM Poop? Why, he is made of muscle. All those macho poses in hard hats and figure-hugging, crotch-hugging cycling attire, and those rudie nudie boxers. Scandalous. And I heard that he holds press conferences in night wear! Well, what can One expect from such a downundies nation,' she tells the dogs. 'But oh, my dear Betsy, that must have hurt.'

The Queen phones the royal secretary to arrange medical updates about Betsy every hour and to organise the royal florist to deliver a forest of flora to One's dear friend. Still feeling quite morose, the whiskey bottle makes another appearance with another splash or two or five into One's tea. The royal accent slurs and stumbles.

'Oh, Beltsly dear. What were you finking. Not the belly pat. Not the preggie leggie belly pat. Never de belly blaat!'

The Queen slumps in her favourite club chair, eyes crossing then closing. A throaty snore from Her Majesty is the signal for the dogs to dance and leap. Their small tongues lick the Queen's face, her Fairisle cashmere jumper and her Hoppy Coops tweed skirt: shortbread crumbs and whiskey drops, slippety slurp.

'In breaking news,' Genevieve Parker tells Carol and Reg, 'travelling overseas as the first pregnant man, Prime Minister Pope attended the What The Fu – ah, the PM attended the WTF at the Munnidownthudrayn Casino. Things did not go quite as planned. Tim Mirren has the latest.'

'Oh look, love, Tim's gone on a holiday to the Munnidownthudrayn Casino,' says Carol. 'Doesn't he look lovely standing there on the beach? He looks a bit hot, though, poor thing. A shame he couldn't be in his bathers and cool off with a little dip. Do you think he might...'

Carol's mind savours the fantasy of Tim Mirren in his bathers. Boardies, Carol rather fancies, the sexy kind where the waist band is slung low to show off his six pack smoothly curving into his abs, smoothly curving into his groin muscles smoothly curving into...

'Yes, Genevieve. Today, president and host of the WTF greeted our Prime Minister, Julian Pope, with a preggy belly pat. Instead of the more common hand shake, she chose to place her hand on the ex, er, Prime, er, Mr Pope's pregnant stomach, Genevieve, and pat.

'In an apparent reflex action – and as our viewers all know, Mr Pope's vast sporting experience and fitness means he has excellent reflexes, Mr Pope knocked away the offending arm with a kung fu sweeping motion, and then landed a sharp jab to Betsy's face.' Tim's arms and feet move like a prize boxer as he enthusiastically demonstrates how the PM took down the president. It was all over in less than a second, Genevieve,' puffs Tim gleefully. 'Let's roll that footage.'

Carol and Reg peer at the screen and watch the action on repeat alternating between normal and slow motion speeds. Tim reappears.

'We understand that Prime Minister Pope,' Tim tells Carol and

Reg, 'is sitting in a prison cell awaiting charges of terrorism. Back to you, Genevieve.'

Carol looks at Reg whose eyebrows have raised as high as her own. Carol is worried by Genevieve Parker's frowning.

'Hmm,' but as the lovely girl that she is, Gen quickly provides Carol and Reg with a tantalising alternative, 'I'm sure our expecting prime minister will be home soon,' Genevieve Parker smiles. 'When he is, tune in for my world exclusive, live, tell-all interview with Julian Pope, the Prime Minister and the world's first pregnant man.'

'There you go, love,' says Reg, 'nothing to worry about. Gen says so. You carry the world's problems on those gorgeous shoulders of yours, don't you, love, eh? Come on, then, maybe a warm bath? A foot massage?' With a twinkle in his eye, Reg adds, 'Then I think *I'll* be quite relaxed.'

'Oh, you!' Carol shoves him playfully and laughs. 'Come on, you old thing. Let's have a shower together. I love you, you know.'

'And I love you.'

Thirty-six hours later, PM Julian Pope stands at the top of the embarkation stairs of his VIP jet, his arms and hands nestled on top of his baby bump. Cameras flash and media buzz. Jules descends from the aircraft, finally reaching his home turf. He extends his arms and bends towards the ground.

'He's going to kiss the tarmac,' he hears one of the waiting journos say, as shutters flutter.

But there is no majestic touching of lips to *terra firma*. PM Julian Pope topples and flounders on the tarmac like a bug on its back, legs and arms flailing in disarray above him. He manages to roll onto his hands and knees.

'Faark off, I've got it,' Jules yells as he swats away an aide, before leaning heavily on her strength to rise. Finally stiffly erect, red in the face and working to settle his puffing, Jules straightens his jacket and tie and marches fiercely past the waiting huddle of reporters cursing to himself, 'Baby bump, my arse.' Jules is meant to be having a bumper of a year with lots of bump and grind and here he is bumper to bumper with faarking journos on a road with more bumps and bumf in it than the House on budget night. He's so bummed, he's ready to bump himself off.

'Faarking baby bump my arse.'

The clamour of media questions triggers a headache.

'How do you feel Jules? Did the authorities treat you well? Did you have a preggers hissy fit, Jules? Is the baby okay? Does this mean war with our island neighbour, Jules?'

PM Julian Pope reaches his waiting car, manoeuvres his bottom towards the open door and slides awkwardly inside.

Once arrived at his beloved Dodge, Jules deflates like a bullet-riddled rubber ducky and collapses into his wife's loving arms.

'It's so good to be home, Nance.'

'There, *there*, dear. You're home now. You're home safe and sound, my little schnookems, sweetie pie.'

Jules begins to sob.

'Nance, it was awful. Those thugs put their faarking filthy hands on me, Nance, *me*, the prime minister, and they dragged me off and kept me under lock and key for more than a day, Nance. You have no idea how unkempt and tiny the place was, Nance. I never want to be under house arrest in a four star hotel room ever again.'

In Nance's arms, Jules gags like a toad with the hiccups.

'And Nance, I, hic-hic, I wet my pants, Nance, *me*, the prime minister, wet my pants. All the shock and this faarking pregnancy, hic-hic, wet my pants, hic.'

Nance wops him hard on the back three times and sympathises, 'Oh you poor dear,' and squeezes him even tighter. Jules' gag reflex shuts down. He feels his gut relax and soften and he farts loudly. Yes,

Nance has always known when he needs a thump or a cuddle. Thank God for Nance.

But Jules feels an uncharacteristic aloneness, a tremendous distance from any other human being, even Nance. It's this faarking ballooning belly. It gets in the way. There's no rubbing the cucumber up against the tomato anymore. No more of that little incidental excitement. And it's all because of this twin thing growing inside him. What a mess. What an international incident.

'I'm a broken man, Nance. Now I know what war service and torture is like. I'm a war hero with PTSD, Nance.'

'Oh dear, come sit down and I'll make you a nice cup of tea and you can tell me all about it from the beginning.' Nance leads him slowly to the rather cheap and nasty couch embroidered with golfing motifs and given to him by the golf-mad President of the United Straits of Anarchy.

'I'd rather a whiskey, Nance, neat, a double. And don't you dare make any comment about drinking during pregnancy.'

'Of course not, dear,' Nance obliges, going to the bar and pouring a whiskey, a double. Then she pours one for herself, a double. Jules has never known Nance to drink whiskey before. Things must be really faarking bad.

'Now tell me all,' Nance says with far too much voyeuristic pleasure for Jules' liking.

'It was all going so well, Nance. I mean besides the farting and heart burn, and the back pain and leg aches and...'

Four hand pats from Nance tells Jules she gets it, she understands, she's been there. And she's a little bit impatient with him. Move on, those hand pats say, get on with it.

But he can't get on with it. How can he after all this? He can't just run with it. He's like a beached whale run aground with this runaway pregnancy. And the faarking thing is just meant to run its course? He can't even make a run for it. The faarking thing would still be running neck and neck with him, making him feel run down and his body fluids all runny and he's sure he's running a temperature and he just wants to run for cover and never run for office again, and everything is running amok, and… Jules' breathing becomes panicked and his head feels like it might explode. He's losing it, going mad, like a girlie girl hysterical neurotic panic attack thingy.

Next thing Jules knows, he's looking goggle-eyed over a paper bag held over his nose and mouth by Nance.

'In and out,' Nance tells him. 'Breathe, that's it my schnookems, sweetie pie, that's the way. You're okay now, just breathe.' Nance grimaces in a kindred spirit kind of way.

As Jules continues to breathe into the paper bag, he guesses they are kindred spirits: kindred spirits in this bizarre, un-Godly experience. He had no idea what Nance went through to have their five girls.

'In and out,' chants Nance.

But then, that's what women are made for, aren't they? Jules recalibrates, to serve men by being faarked, procreating and raising the little bastards.

'I-in and o-out.'

That's what all those ghastly girlie germs are for. Jules doesn't have ghastly girlie germs. He's a man, not a madam. What a faarking madcap muddle at the WTF. He's mad as hell about that, and this. He's madly mad about it all. When he should have been sipping on madeira and listening to exotic madrigals, they put him in some madhouse like he has mad cow disease or he's some madman who thinks he's the Madonna. Jesus faarking Christ! When the whole Madonna thing is what the faarking Pope says, not Jules. Jules is not a Madonna. He's not a madam. He's not, *he's not*.

'I'm not!' Jules knocks the paper bag away angrily as his stomach tumble-turns in disgust and the hiccupping toad revives. Nance pounds him on the back and the toad hops away. Jules quaffs from his whiskey, feels its fingers of warmth tickle through him and resumes his narration.

'So, everything was going well, Nance, *exceptionally well*. The hotel suite was plush and lovely with little gifts on arrival.' It was the first time Jules had ever knocked back the usual welcoming sex kittens, but in his unusual state he just didn't feel like it. 'I had time to get in a quick power walk to promote my brand. I was looking forward to my special award ceremony, Nance.' He looks at his wife like a child let loose in a lolly shop but removed empty-handed for rude behaviour. 'To think, in front of all the world, the president of our closest neighbour and the WTF host was going to award me the Meritorious Medal for my role as Minister for Women's International Affairs. It would have been a hoot. But then it all went to faarking hell.'

'I understand, dear. Go on, dear,' Nance soothes and encourages.

'It was just a reflex really,' Jules says hanging his head with shame. 'But when her hand reached out to my belly, *my* belly, and when she actually touched my belly, *my* belly, I, I,' Jules becomes highly animated, 'I was just overtaken with a roaring fury. This ferocious, fiery, God-fearing dragon erupted inside me and –'

'I know exactly what you mean,' Nance interrupts coolly. 'When I was pregnant, all five times, I used to hate the way my body was commandeered by everyone else. My body became public property for any Tom, Dick and Harry, and any Marjorie, Lulu and Gertrude, to just touch whenever they wanted. I wasn't a person anymore. I was just a thing for others' curiosity, *an incubator*. I mean, the questions, the impertinent, derogatory questions and comments and advice and–'

Jules stops Nance in her tracks with a disapproving look.

'Sorry, dear, back to you. Your story, your time,' Nance concedes.

'Thank you, Nance,' Jules says snootily. 'I've been through a farking awful time and this is about *me,* and faark!' Jules startles in panic. 'I've got that faarking interview with that faarking bimbo Genevieve Parker in a couple of days. I know I suggested it, but that was then and now is now. I don't want to do it, Nance. I can't do it.

I just want to curl up in bed and never come out. I want everyone to leave me alone, *just leave me alone*. I'm a broken man, Nance, a broken, pregnant man,' Jules weeps.

Jules looks up miserably at Nance. He looks to her for replenishment and his eyes fix on her bosoms and suckle on the milk of her breast – metaphorically speaking, of course. Jules always found Nance's breast-feeding of the infants rather a turn-off. Women's breasts are made for men's pleasure, not for some primitive, disgusting display of motherhood. Each time, the whole having-a-baby-and-breast-feeding thing quite put him off being able to enjoy the female form for a while. Thank God he always had some work excuse not to make it to the delivery room until all that horrible women's business was over. If he'd seen that, he might never have faarked again! Well, not Nance anyway. Now, here he is, pregnant. He can't stand it, can't tolerate it, can't, can't.

'*Can't*,' he says, spittle dribbling from his mouth, rheum sludge covering his upper lip and his face wet with sticky tears. 'I'm disgusting, Nance, I'm an abomination,' he sobs.

Nance grasps his shoulders firmly.

'Eyes at me, Julian,' she demands. 'Julian Jesus Pope, *eyes, at, me.*'

Julian Jesus Pope looks into his wife's fierce gaze and feels a jolt. There is a fervour there he has never seen before. Yes, she can be enthusiastic at times, even gets a touch of that maddening girlie hysteria, but this look? Nance has never looked so focussed and determined. She seems so evangelical, *it's quite sexy,* thinks Jules. And frightening as hell.

'You are the first pregnant PM this country has had, Jules. You could have been the first in the modern world if that PM in the country across the ditch hadn't beaten you to it. But you cannot let her show you up, Jules. You must be seen to be on top of all this. You must get out there, with the people. *You* are the PM. So what if there are rumblings in the party room about challenging you for the leadership?'

'Are there?' Jules face crumples in disappointment, then in pain as Nance digs her finger nails into his shoulders and continues on urgently.

'Jules, since the news of your pregnancy broke, this is the longest stint you've had in the PM's seat. You've baffled them, Jules, you've outplayed them. Your hard right religious cronies don't want to oust you because it's not a good God-fearing look to oust a pregnant Madonna miracle man from the PM-ship. And your ever so slightly tilted to the loony tunes left colleagues look across the ocean at the cool, pregnant woman PM, and reckon you are the man for the times, Jules. No one can challenge you, for now. But you must get out there and be your magnificent self. You must convince and lead the nation, Jules. So you *will* do that interview. You will do it and you will do it marvellously. We have a couple of days to prepare and you will be ready. You are Prime Minister Julian Pope, and you'll show them all.'

Jules feels his mood lifting on the words of Nance's God-given, inspirational pep talk. Onward Christian soldiers! He is ready to fight to the death. He is the man of the moment. He is PM Julian Jesus Pope, a man of action and a man of destiny. Jules can do anything!

'Now dear, I've got your pyjamas warming by the fire and the hot water bottle in the bed,' Nance coddles. 'You go and have a nice hot bath, dear, then pop into bed. I'll come and tuck you in. You'll be right as rain in the morning.'

A couple of days later, and just a hop, skip and a jump from Julian Pope's beloved bath in The Dodge, a penthouse doorbell buzzes. Gen leaves her prepping, for her world exclusive interview with the first pregnant man, and peers at the small inter-comb screen conveying the face of the visitor waiting expectantly downstairs.

*No, not that face,* she thinks, ambivalence surging and her hand reaching for her bare throat. 'No, *no*,' Gen says under her breath, refusing to acknowledge the person's buzzing request as she watches her visitor neaten and preen and push the buzzer again. 'No, never, *never*,' says Gen.

Gen moves back to her work, but the buzzer sounds again and again. Gen returns to the inter-comb to see the frowning, mouthing insistence of the person now. 'Oh God, this is not going away,' says Gen. 'And, great, now I'm talking to myself.'

*Buzz.*

'A sign of stress, perhaps?'

*Buzz buzz.*

'Or a good thing. My sessions with Martha have made me comfortable saying out loud whatever is on my mind.'

*Buzz buzz.*

'Or, all three.'

*Buzz buzz buzz.*

'No, not going away, *not going away*.' Gen punches the button she is averse to press.

'Hi, Genevieve darling. Just thought I'd pop in. You haven't been answering my calls. I think there's something wrong with our connection, darling.'

*She's finally got something right*, thinks Gen.

'Might be my phone or yours, or both. I'll just come on up.'

'I'm busy.'

'Too busy for your own mother, Genevieve?'

'Are you?'

'Am I what, darling?

'My mother?'

'What on earth do you mean? What is going on with you Genevieve? You've been avoiding me for weeks now and–'

No, Gen cannot face it. With a simple finger motion Gen makes that face and voice disappear. Magic and relief. Gen is at the controls; she is in control.

*Buzz buzz. Buzz buzz.* On and on, again and again, annoying and headache-inducing.

Gen stops the incessant buzz with her magic finger and orders, 'You must leave, Mother.'

'Well I'm not leaving, darling,' Mother replies petulantly, 'until you tell me what is going on.'

'I'm calling security, Mother,' Gen says.

'Oh for goodness sake, Genevieve, don't get all drama queen on me. All I ask is for five minutes.'

Gen does the maths: one security guard plus one mad woman equals a thousand headlines: *Genevieve Family Feud, Genevieve Arrests Mum, Genevieve the Bitch.* No, not a workable solution. Feeling anything but in control, Gen presses the button with her anything but magical finger.

A moment later, Gen watches the elevator doors open and Mother make her entrance in neat red slacks, beige jacket and a red purse slung over her shoulder. Mother's presence, as always, is abrasively overwhelming. Gen feels too soft and invisible in her blue jeans, pastel pink cashmere jumper and ballet flats.

Sashaying past Gen towards the lounge, Mother complains bitterly, 'Whatever is wrong with you, Genevieve?'

'And there you have it,' Gen replies, trailing behind and feeling both discarded and belligerent. 'You have no clue what you have said to me, what you have done to me, *everything* you've put me through.'

Mother cocks her head slightly and raises her eyebrows in pleasant, angelic query.

But Gen is not falling for it.

'My birth story, Mother,' Gen says plainly. 'The one where you said I was not your child, but a pig, a pig belonging to another sow.' *Do not cry*, Gen commands herself, taking a slow breath and reminding herself that she is gorgeous, powerful Genevieve Parker. 'I cannot deal with this now, Mother. I have the career coup of a life time and I must prepare.'

Gen extends a hand towards the elevator indicating the exit she wishes Mother to use. 'Now.'

Mother ignores Gen's wishes completely.

'Oh darling, not that PM pregnancy thing, again! A woman gets pregnant and it's all business as usual and suck it up sunshine. But a man gets pregnant and oh, isn't he amazing, and the whole world stops for *him* and bows down to *him*.' Mother leans casually towards a vase of roses and smells their fragrance indulgently. She flips her hair and continues with some vehemence, 'Besides you could do that interview standing on your head, Genevieve. That bastard rake, Julian Pope, is no match for you.'

Does Mother know she has just paid Gen a compliment? Still it's little more than a lukewarm ray of hope from a dying sun and Gen reminds herself that Mother's compliments are always backhanders, *no exceptions*. That ray of hope will turn into a nasty lightning bolt. *Why is Mother always so exhausting?* Gen sits down on the couch and holds a cushion to her chest protectively as she despises herself for being defeated, *already*.

'Listen to me please, Genevieve, *listen to me, please*.'

There is an unusual pathetic pleading quality to Mother's demand. As Mother looks down upon Gen, Gen reluctantly looks up at Mother. Mother's red lips are softer. Her eyes do not flit about, but look directly into Gen's, and Gen sees panic and sadness in them before they, and Mother, veer away to pace back and forth on the carpet in front of her.

'Okay, now look, Genevieve. Well, er, ah...'

Mother struggles and her voice falters. Struggles and falters? Gen is aware that something quite out of the ordinary dynamic is at play.

Mother clears her throat and looks up from the carpet.

'Genevieve.' Mother returns her gaze to the carpet, takes a breath, looks up at Gen again, and continues to pace. 'All that birth story rubbish. All that, look, what I told you, it's not true. Well, not in the way you think. I guess now I just have to tell you straight up, *the truth* without any sugar coating. There's no avoiding it now. I don't like this truth, Genevieve, I don't like to ever think of it. I don't like to admit it to myself, let alone to anyone else, especially to you. It is something to keep secret because it reflects so very badly on me. But you have cornered me, and so, here it is.'

'So, the last truth was fine because it only reflected badly on me, the rejected runt of the litter? Just as long as the truth does not reflect badly on you, Mother?' Genevieve is amazed at her own audacity, calling out Mother's narcissism like that. How freeing. How terrifying.

Mother continues to pace back and forth and gaze back and forth from the beige carpet to Gen.

'The truth is, Genevieve.' Mother paces some more, stands still, and stares at Gen. 'The truth is.' She paces again, stops again and looks into Gen's expectant eyes. 'The truth is, I had post-natal depression, *P-N-D*. There you are, are you happy now? Me, your mother, was a nut case. Now you know that your mother is a mad woman, and back then, well, women with PND either stayed quiet and festered alone, or let it all hang out and were thrown in the mad house. I mean, doctors knew nothing back then, *nothing*.'

Mother resumes pacing, her energy bouncing and rattling the purse hanging at her hip.

'I'm not proud of it, Genevieve, but I caught it from another woman on the ward. I know, *I know*, psychiatric illnesses are not contagious.' Mother throws her arms about and shakes her head. 'Well, that's what they say, but in my experience they are as contagious as the common cold. You just need to be a bit under the weather, corralled with some utter nut job and *wham*, it catches you, and that's exactly how I caught PND. I caught it from another mother on the ward.'

Mother plops disconsolately onto the couch beside Genevieve.

'I was in a four-bed, can you believe it? Private rooms were as scarce as a ticket for a TayTay concert. Anyway, this new mother was just a little teenager, and back in those days, bad things could happen to little teenage girls having babies. Now I come to think of it, bad things could happen to ordinary married mothers like me, too. Everything I told you before is absolutely true: me being knocked out and the last person to see you. And now I think about it, after seeing your *LoDown* stories on the abuse of women, I expect that poor girl was a victim of exactly that, and then she was abused all over again by the hospital.'

'You saw those?'

'What, darling?'

'The stories on intimate partner violence.'

'Well of course, darling. I watch your show every night, well not *every* night. With my social calendar sometimes I have to record it or catch up online, watch it at a later time. But of course I watch you on the box. You are my daughter, for heaven's sake.'

'But you never told me that before,' Gen says feeling quite shocked in a rather nice way. Then she hears herself say words simply, without even one tear drop and certainly not with the torrent that fell when she first said the words with Martha, 'You have never been proud of me, Mother.'

'Don't be ridiculous, Genevieve.' Mother stands up indignantly and waves her arms about. 'Of course I'm proud of you. Of course I am. What sort of mother do you take me for, Genevieve, *really*.' Mother shoos the very idea away with her long nails to the same *La La Land* that the previous grungy cafe breakfast conversation confetti landed in.

'But you never told me you were proud of me, *never*.' Gen is perplexed and her brain cannot compute what this conversation is about, nor where it is heading.

'Of course I never told you. With all your talents and beauty, the worst thing I could have done was to go all gooey gooey *you're-amazing*, like those reality show parents with their *my-child-is-the-best-thing-since-sliced-bread, follow-your-dream-because-you-can-do-anything-*

*you-are-soo-amazing,*' Mother mocks. 'With all your focus and talent, darling, that was the last thing you needed to hear. I didn't want you going all narcissistic and big-headed and becoming a selfish pain-in-the-arse like your father, did I?

'Now where was I?' Mother scans the carpet and paces anew. 'That's right, on the maternity ward, with this poor girl screaming and wailing for her baby. She was screaming that they took away her baby, *stole it,* that they gave her baby to some nicely married woman whose baby had died. The poor girl was so distressed, as you would be of course, *so distressed,* you can't imagine. Her distress and her story was *contagious.* I think it was all my empathy, darling. Back then I had too much empathy. You won't find me with too much empathy these days. I learnt my lesson. Empathy is dangerous, darling, terrifying. All because of my empathy, I caught what she had and I almost became her, you see. Not that I was an unmarried teenager, but my mind started going round and round and round, darling.' Mother rolls her head in circles in sync with her words so that Gen feels rather dizzy.

Mother blinks and looks at Gen urgently.

'What if they had taken my baby away too and the one they gave me was the wrong one? How could I trust them? How could I ever trust them?'

Mother resumes pacing and telling her story. 'So I convinced myself that I was on the ward where babies were taken away, and my baby was not really mine. You' – Mother stands still and stares with terror in her eyes at Genevieve – 'you were not really mine. It was like being an extra in a sci-fi, darling, *ee-ah, ee-ah,* twilight zone, paranoid stuff.'

Mother crumples into the couch beside Gen again, as if letting go of everything she has held on to so tightly for so long. Her tone is philosophical, almost carefree, as she admits, 'I was stark raving mad, Genevieve. And to be honest, although I thought I was looking forward to being a mother, the real thing was so much more terrifying, and I really, well, I just lost it, didn't I? I was out of my mind for a time and sometimes it trips me up again, you know? Even to this day, I sometimes ponder it all, I ponder you.' Mother takes Gen's hand in hers. 'I slip into that fog of distrust and madness.'

Mother's pointer finger traces around and around Gen's palm. *Round and round the garden like a teddy bear*, Gen hears her mother's voice sing.

'I mean I don't really understand how I ended up with someone like you,' Mother says smiling. 'It's a miracle really, isn't it? Look at you with your stunning looks, your amazing brain, I mean, *look at you*. You are amazing.'

*One step, two step, tickly under there.*

'You know I always felt a bit intimidated by you,' Mother confesses as Gen feels the warm softness of Mother's hand holding her own. *This is the way the ladies ride: trot, trot, trot.*

'Intimidated by your beauty, intelligence and energy. Even when you were a baby, your violet eyes were just stunning, and they still are. You are, *stunning*.'

*This is the way the gentlemen ride: gallopy trot, gallopy trot, gallopy trot.* Gen's violet eyes are wide with the surprise of love and welling tears.

'You are nothing like me, darling, or your father, thank God and God rest his soul. But let's be honest, I'm no Rhodes scholar, I have a mind like a sieve. My looks are mediocre, although I can still be quite eye-catching with my conscientious grooming and good taste, darling, but you, *you* are beauty personified. You didn't get that from me and you didn't get your brains from me either.'

*A B C D E F G*, sings mother in Gen's memories, *H I J K L M N O P, Q R S, T U V, W X, Y AND Z.*

Mother sighs and says, 'I'm afraid the only thing you got from me was your appalling taste in men. Don't look at me like that, Genevieve, you know that's true. We're not lucky with men, you and me. We couldn't pick a good man if God popped him down at our feet with a sign on his chest saying, *I am a good one*. The timing of your father's death was, well, it was very inconvenient, wasn't it? A blessed relief in some ways, but in others...'

*Now I know my A B C, next time won't you sing with me*, Gen hears Mother finish the song, while Mother looks at Gen intently, deeply: a connection with Mother.

'I'm so sorry that the only thing you got from me was a load of shitty relationships, darling, I really am. I'm so sorry, Genevieve, that I went mad. I'm sorry that I was a mad, bad mother, *I'm so sorry I did that to you*.' Mother sobs and pulls a freshly ironed hankie from her purse to mop up her face, stows it up her sleeve. She holds Gen's hands and looks directly and steadily into Gen's eyes again. 'Genevieve, I have lost one daughter, I cannot lose another. *I cannot lose you, Genevieve*. I love you; you know I do. You're my only child, Genevieve. Rosie... I mean we all must take our share of the blame for Rosie, beautiful, gorgeous Rosie.'

Mother sobs and Gen's eyes flood with tears too.

'When Rosalie came along so naturally, a normal birth, with me so normal too, well, I felt reclaimed and complete. I was besotted with Rosie. I know I spoiled her, gave all my attention to her, but in a weird way that was the making of you. You settled down and you became ambitious, at the little age of five. You were always trying to impress me by being excellent at school, sport, manners, and well, everything. I never had to worry about you, Genevieve, not you. You didn't need me; you don't need me. You were, you are, perfect.'

Mother smiles at Gen through her tears and Gen finally speaks sadly and sincerely.

'But I'm not perfect, Mother. I've never been perfect. I've had too much hurt and confusion. I've felt too much rejection. I've always needed you, Mother, needed your love. I was always so sure you didn't love me. I could feel deep down that you didn't want me. Daddy didn't want me either. He didn't love me, either. He left so suddenly, with no goodbye or hug, no smile or even a farewell glance or a note, *nothing.*'

'Oh Genevieve, darling, your father had his faults, I can tell you, but he adored you. He had no choice in the matter, did he? He was literally stopped dead in his tracks by a heart attack the doctors said was like an earthquake that was off the scale, darling. Of course he didn't want to die. Of course he didn't want to leave you. Of course he loved you, darling.'

'But, the day Daddy died, I was particularly naughty and wilful. Daddy sent me to my room and I hated him. I hated him so much I wished he were dead, and then, well, he was, so it was my fault. I killed Daddy.'

Gen suddenly hears the absurdity of that construction, as if she had super powers as a child, and yet... Gen gives her words an adult gloss, 'I mean, it was the stress of having a child like me that killed him.'

'Genevieve, how could you possibly think that your father's death was your fault? You were four years old darling. Why didn't you tell me this was what you thought? You've thought this for all these years? Oh, darling, your father died because he was born with a defective heart, and would never see a doctor about anything. He died because he drank too much and the only exercise he did was in the bed of another woman who ended up with your father dead on top of her.'

'Really?' Gen had no idea about any of this and her brain is frankly not up to the job of processing all this new information. Her shock turns suddenly into an incredible sadness for her mother. 'I'm so sorry, Mother.'

'No, you have nothing to be sorry for, Genevieve, *nothing.* You were the apple of his eye. Your father adored you; he just was a rather damaged human being. His death should not sentence you to the penitence of trying to recreate a relationship with your father by hooking up with all these charming, but *older,*' Mother shakes her head like a ghost has run his chilly fingers down her spine, 'far too old, Genevieve, useless boyfriends.'

This is more shocking news to Gen, who had no idea that her mother harboured such opinions about the men in her life.

'Why don't you break the pattern, darling? Choose someone completely different. Here's an idea, go for a *younger* man, darling, and don't fall for the charming ones, it's a trap, darling. You think I haven't noticed your bruises? Here you are professionally calling out violence against women, while you've been living with that two-faced, cruel bastard. Do not, Genevieve, ever stay with a man who hurts you, darling. Do not get all swept away and be living together after two weeks. Do not become me, darling. I mean I was trying to ensure a father for you girls, but really I just made everything worse with my *desperado* choice of men. You may or may not remember I was heavily pregnant with Rosalie at the time of your father's death. I guess after everything else I've exposed about myself, it's plain to you that at the time I was quite vulnerable.'

'Rosalie,' says Gen and sighs. 'Rosie left too. Why did she have to leave us, *leave me*?'

Gen feels Mother's fingers brush Gen's hair gently from her face and softly wipe tears from her cheeks. A lavender lullaby cloud settles around Gen and Mother as she glimpses new meanings of the losses and misunderstandings of her life, the love that is hers and the release that can come from knowing.

'I think I understand a little more now, Mother. It's important to me to hear how it was for you and how I was for you. To have you say sorry to me and tell me that you do love me.'

Mother nods her head sorrowfully. 'I know it will take some time, Genevieve.'

'Yes, it will, but this is a start, *it's a start*.'

Mother smiles and they hug, not in one of those brisk, meaningless social ritual hugs accompanied by air kisses, but a warm embrace between two beings connected in authentic emotional intimacy.

Gen exists in the present and the past and the future with her mother for the first time in her life.

But all embraces must end. All connection must be broken except for the invisible cord of love that vibrates between humans even when they are apart. Gen and her mother separate slowly before Gen sees her mother stiffen physically and mentally to face the outside world.

'I best be off.'

They walk together to the penthouse elevator. Mother pauses and her eyes and words are penetrating, 'I want you to get him, Genevieve. I want you to nail that bastard, Julian Pope, for all the world to see. You will do that for me won't you, darling?'

'Exactly what I plan to do, Mother.'

'Bail was refused, Gen,' Jimmy says. 'No brainer really, given the extent of the evidence against him and the links to other violent crimes. He's a clear flight risk–'

Unexpectedly she hugs him. Jimmy feels her fragility, and her curves, and wishes the embrace would never end.

She steps back blushing.

'Sorry, *sorry*. Ah, no, actually, I'm *not* sorry, no, *not* sorry, I'm just so grateful. It's been such a nightmare, let alone everything else.'

*Be professional*, he counsels himself. He's really gotta watch he doesn't step over that line. Jimmy's eyes make a circuit of the glamorous penthouse. She's way out of his league.

But Gen has been on his mind. He knows he could have just phoned, but here he is, in her penthouse, where uniforms drove her after the interview from heaven. The interview from hell. In the days afterwards, Jimmy's mind reviewed his smoothly professional interview until it looked anything but. Jimmy's embarrassing gaffes jumped out at him one after another, and a brain button got stuck replaying them over and over again, magnifying them in his mind, until he felt ashamed and foolish. What was he thinking? And what is he doing in Genevieve Parker's penthouse?

'Mm, of course. Detective Senior Sergeant Jimmy Park is always at your service,' Jimmy says, cringing as he hears his own words.

It's a fine line between stalking a woman and going to her home when a phone call would do. A fine line between stalking and an accidentally-on-purpose meeting. Even the scarlet-lipped lady who passed him in the foyer looked him up and down and assessed him suspiciously. Then, if Jimmy heard right, the woman said, *A man like you should be shot.* Yep, stalker written all over him. Or, she might have said, *A man like you is worth a shot.* What the hell does that mean? What is Jimmy doing?

'With our legal system,' Jimmy says, 'you never know when there'll be some legal technicality that jeopardises plain common sense and the safety of others. You never really know 'til it's done. But now that part's done, bail refused and he's staying behind bars. You've had quite a time of it, haven't you?' Jimmy adds sympathetically.

Jimmy just wanted to see her. He just wants to spend time with her. Gen's been making him crazy, even when he knows he isn't her type. Scrolling through old media reports told him that. He even found an old newspaper report of a debating award Gen won when she was 15. Yep, fine line between stalking and a little romantically motivated reconnaissance and creepy scrolling investigating.

'It's such a relief,' she says with a big sigh. 'Of course it has all been heart-breaking and I have been furious at myself and at him. Someone like Gael just sneaks up on you, lies and scams you really, and before you know it you're trapped in that lie, but you can't see it. Then afterwards, you just feel so stupid. How could I be so stupid?' For a moment she eyeballs Jimmy with desperation, before relaxing her shoulders and smiling, 'But now I feel I can breathe again, so, thank you.'

'You're welcome,' says Jimmy returning the smile. 'Anyway, I just wanted to let you know as soon as possible that Gael Saucisse is locked up and won't be coming anywhere near you.'

Jimmy thought if he saw her again, it would bang on the head any of his romantic ambitions. He can be a crazy bastard sometimes. Seeing her would make the fantasy return to reality and plain old Jimmy Park normality. Seeing her would make it completely clear and out of the question, so he could leave it alone, or have it leave him alone or whatever this is. It would be a test, and if he failed, that would be that and he'd push through. He'd move on and get over himself. But now here he is still hoping, *hoping* for the opposite. You never know your luck 'til you test it, Jimmy reckons.

'Unfortunately your jewellery, the engagement ring and the necklace, will be returned to the rightful owners.'

So what if he's not one of those charming, old-enough-to-be-her-father types that she always picks. Maybe that's a good thing. Maybe after her latest love-life debacle, even someone like Genevieve Parker might look for something different. Exactly, Jimmy decides. Gen doesn't need a guy with money, she's got that covered. Gen doesn't need a guy who's into the social scene, she's already got that. She sure doesn't need some grey-haired bastard who treats her bad, she's had that. *His apologies are always so romantic,* Gen's voice replays in Jimmy's head. Okay, so Jimmy's a scraggy, social misfit, a not-Caucasian guy, not rich, has never laid anything but a loving hand on any girlfriend and he lives by a code called Good Manners, well that and Justice. He fits the bill perfectly then. He could be the next Mr Genevieve Parker.

'Of course,' Gen says pleasantly, 'Back to their rightful owners.'

Who is he kidding? Jimmy has waited until he has a plausible pretext to see her, cleaned himself up and is now looking down the barrel of a big fail, a big only-in-your-dreams *fail.* It's just she's so perfectly imperfect for him.

Jimmy is suddenly aware that a silence is becoming awkward.

'All righty then, I can see you're busy. I hear you have a big interview this week. I'm sure you're all over it, it'll go great. But I better be on my way and let you do whatever it is you have to do.'

'Thanks, yes,' she says.

As they walk to the penthouse lift, they both begin to speak at the same time. Jimmy smiles with embarrassment, 'Sorry, after you, Gen.'

'No, *no*, you first, Jimmy,' Genevieve says.

'Well, Gen, I just want to apologise.'

'Apologise?'

Oh God, her eyes, her mesmerising, deadly *eyes*. Jimmy is falling, *falling. You idiot*, Jimmy scolds himself. *Get on with it, say it.*

'Yeah, I want to apologise about the police interview. The last thing I ever wanted to do was upset you or make you–'

'Vomit into your rubbish bin and faint into your arms?' she boldly completes Jimmy's sentence.

'And don't forget the bump to your noggin,' Jimmy adds before looking down abashed. But when he looks up, there is a lilac glint of cheekiness in her violet eyes, and a tongue planted firmly in her cheek. She's teasing him, he realises with relief.

'Well, yeah,' he smiles and raises one eyebrow in his smoothly sexy way. 'It isn't the traditional way to begin a, I mean, to, ah... So, I'm sorry about all that, Gen. I wish we could have met under nicer circumstances.'

'I also wanted to say how much I admire your work. You call out what's wrong with our world and you fight the good fight, Gen, to make the world a better place for others, and that can take it out of you. It's not easy, I know. I just hope that maybe, now might be a good time for you to fight the good fight for *you*. Maybe make the world a better place for *you*, Gen. Anyway, so, ah, what were you going to say, Gen?' Great recovery Jimmy, *idiot,* he thinks.

'Nothing important.'

She thinks he's an idiot. Yep, idiot box, in he goes.

'Right-o. You're all safe and secure here then. You won't be needing me anytime soon, so I guess that's it then. Someone will be in touch when we know more about the Saucisse brief, but it could all go away with a plea deal.'

'All go away? That would be nice.'

Shit, she really does want Jimmy gone away, he realises. He's most definitely struck out, over and out.

'Yep, okay then, goodbye, Gen.' Jimmy finds himself bowing. *Shit, really, Jimmy?* he berates himself. She's not royalty, and anyway he's a republican. Stand up, pull yourself together. 'It's been lovely meeting you, Gen. Good luck with all your various projects, including the big interview. And, ah, take good care of *you*, hey.'

Gen extends her hand and Jimmy takes it in his. A frisson thrills through him. Goodbye Gen, the most beautiful woman in the world who has ever ripped out his beating heart. This is going to hurt for a while, and no watching *The LoDown*, ever.

Still holding Jimmy's hand, Gen says, 'Detective, Jimmy, would you like a cup of coffee? I still have quite a lot of work to prepare tonight, but I could do with a break.'

Well that turned out to be quite an interesting man experiment, muses Gen as she pops the coffee cups into the dishwasher and returns to her interview preparations. But really, she doesn't want to think about that horrible man again just yet.

She wants to think about the man who has just sat in her kitchen having a coffee with her. A man who is so perfectly wrong for her, he might be perfectly right for her. Gen has just followed, of all people, Mother's advice, which, even more oddly, is exactly the same as Martha's advice: break the pattern. In Martha speak: *You are in a repetitive dysfunctional pattern of romantic relationships. You involve yourself with the same type of man. The same type of unhealthy, harmful relationship and hurtful ending eventuates. Yet somehow you expect, like magic, that the very next time you choose exactly the same type of man, everything will turn out differently. I wonder why that is? I wonder what you can do about breaking that harmful pattern? You deserve to be in a truly loving relationship, Gen.*

Gen is still not sure what a truly loving relationship looks like, but she has just had a cup of coffee and a conversation with a man who is not an older man, but a man about her own age. He's not a charmer sweeping her off her feet, although quite charming in his own kind, goofy way. He hasn't got tickets on himself, but he's humble and funny. She does like his sense of humour. Gen didn't feel pressured or hurried along by him. *Quite the reverse,* she thinks, realising how safe, calm and quite refreshed she feels. Plus, he definitely is not all about him. Jimmy genuinely seemed interested in her. He certainly gets her job and seemed sincere with his concern for her. *Time to make the world a better place for* you, *Gen.* Yes, he is the perfect opposite of the usual men in her life. Jimmy Park is perfectly wrong and so just may be imperfectly right.

From her worktable she stares out at the city lights and the winding river, something unreadable needling at the edges of her mind. Something that is also about how Jimmy is different. Something important? The needling finally turns into neatly stitched words: *Police Officer.*

Gen gasps and her hand covers her mouth in shock. Jimmy is a police detective. Police notice clues about crimes, like say, a smuggling operation or an underground abortion network. What was she thinking?

With a cosmic synchronicity dancing on the same needle point, Gen's phone interrupts with a caller who is all business.

'It wasn't easy, Genevieve, after the debacle at the WTF. He's such a difficult man and quite the sook, but he will be there. He will be at the studio for the interview, as arranged. I'll check in with you on the day, but for now, good luck, Genevieve. No pressure, dear, but we are all relying on you.'

'I understand. I won't let you down,' Gen replies, a sense of excitement, dread and destiny weaving through her. 'Thank you for trusting me with this, Nance.'

# V

# REVENGE

Around the world people's eyes are glued to screens from phone size to giant walls. Huddled in groups or all alone, viewers drink coffee or sip on wine, twiddle chopsticks or nibble chips, eat rations and scull beer. In igloos and mansions, home cinemas and outdoor plazas, in tents and townhalls, people tune in to *The LoDown Exclusive* with Genevieve Parker and the first pregnant man, Prime Minister Julian Pope, *Live And As It Happens*.

The Queen of Great Brexit sits with the champs in her palace in front of her old tele, her slipper-encased feet crossed at the ankles, using her phone to place her horse bets for the day and pouring a cuppa from her bone china teapot.

Motherly Carol cuddles into Reg as they sit on their old couch watching the box and sipping on wine and beer.

Gen's mother sits in front of her large around-sound wall TV, slowly turning the pages of an aged family photo album and waiting for her daughter's exposé.

Detective Senior Sergeant Jimmy Park surveils his latest scene.

The studio executives describe the interview as *a friendly, exclusive chat about Julian's experience of being the first pregnant man,* but Jules and Nance have other ideas. Jules cannot recall studio lights being quite this hot and bright. His armpits are damp and growing damper by the second, even though he's sure he put on his deodorant after his shower. He never found the top seat as sticky as this one. Will this faarking body ever feel like his own again?

It took Jules an age to prepare and ready himself for this *friendly chat*. His brain hurts and, at times, waves roll across his belly freakishly as his alien guests move. He had a tantrum about the XXXXL white shirt he's wearing.

'I can't go out wearing this, I've never worn anything with a faarking X in it in my life. It's not like it's an XXXX beer or an X-rated sex show. These faarking Xs are taunting me, Nance. It's humiliating. I can't go, *I won't go.*'

But Nance explained that Jules was actually wearing King-size clothes.

'Fit for a King,' she said, '*You* are the King, Jules,' she said.

As a surprise, she had a new pregnancy-friendly King size suit run up by Jules' favourite tailor in Jules' favourite steel blue hue to match his famous steel blue eyes and his regal, steely nature. Jules has to admit that the modifications and enhancements cater for the pregnant man beautifully. The fabric is so light, rather like the sensation of his silky boxers, so freeing and unconstrained, like wearing nothing at all. Except his birthday suit. *Ha ha*, he chuckles to himself now as he waits for his world breaking interview to begin.

'You're setting a new trend and igniting a new market,' Nance told him. 'You are the poster boy,' she said. 'Once we figure out how you became pregnant. But not to worry about that for now.'

Nance is sure it will all become clear, eventually. Anyway, this interview is all about retaining the affection of the people, Jules reminds himself. He needs to swing the polls his way and ensure he stays on top in the top seat. The top shelf, top dog in the top house. Top of the top brass. He's just here to top up his top of the pops popularity. He's on top of his top secret topic. He's a top bloke and this is going to top everything. He's going to lop the top off Genevieve Drop Dead Gorgeous Parker.

Jules gives his tie a flap and lets it sit on his round belly, then does up one button of his King size steely blue pregnancy suit, just above his preggy bump. He is feeling regal and quite royal, *yes*, he is a mighty King.

Jules smirks at snooty-nosed Genevieve Parker who is sitting opposite him in a modern chair, a twin to his own. *Rude bitch*, he thinks. Apart from a brief serious nod from her when he sat down, she has not looked up from her papers. Well, two can play at that little game. Jules stretches languidly, arms and legs sprawling in an overdramatic, man-dominating-space nonchalance. Just look at her, he sneers. She wants to play everything by the book and play safe, but she's playing with fire. This is not some playground stoush, Jules is here to play hard ball. He'll play her for a fool. He can play it by ear. Play to the gallery. Play tricks on her. Play havoc with her. It will be game, set and mat–

'Are you aware, Mr Pope,' Genevieve asks him, 'that since you took your seat, you've spent the entire time staring at my breasts?'

Oh faark, he's been eyeballing Genevieve Parker's breasts all this time. Nance will have his balls for breakfast. Little minx has purposely worn a more revealing top to put him off his game. He's not buying it, *he's not* – faark. Jules realises he is staring at Genevieve's boobs again. To anchor himself he very consciously eyeballs Genevieve's boobs and riffs on the word. There must be no booby traps for Jules. Not one booboo, or he'll be seen as a right booby and come out of this with nothing but a booby prize. Who knew it would be so hard to concentrate when Drop Dead Gorgeous Genevieve Jezebel Par–

'... Julian Pope. Welcome,' Genevieve is saying.

Faark! Jules blinks and jumps into an upright pose. The interview has begun. He better get his eyes off her jugs and his mind on the job. Jules' eyebrows twitch with murderous, kingly intent.

'Our audience is dying to know about your pregnancy, Jules. But before we get to that, I'm sure they're also dying to know about the stylish outfit you're wearing. Can you tell us a little about the design and designer please, Jules?'

'Well, er,' Jules has never been asked such an absurd question before. If this is all she's got, he'll be running rings around her in no time. He'll play along. Now, what did Nance say about it all? 'Genevieve, my suit is a bespoke modernist ensemble by Tailor Williamson on the High Street,' he says remembering Nance's exact description. 'The fabric is an unusual and couture blend of silk and cotton. The thread detail provides a sophisticated and chic finish.'

'I'm sure our audience would love you to give us a 360, Jules. Would you mind?'

Jules looks at Genevieve's elegant, pointing fingers, 'Standing,' directing him what to do, 'Turning a full circle,' her fingers twirl.

'What? Er, if you think...' Jules rises from his seat and turns in a tight slow circle with one hand on his hip, before sitting down. His voice has abandoned him in his embarrassment and the muddle of his brain.

'I understand, Jules,' says Genevieve with much interest, 'that the suit has been specifically modified to cater to your pregnancy?'

'Well, er, yes, Genevieve.' Jules is feeling rather uncomfortable with all this focus on his attire and such public discussion around very personal, unusual aspects of his body. 'I think that is self-evident.'

'The colour is divine, Jules,' observes Genevieve smiling.

'You like it? Yes, that particular hue is what I call my steely blue to match my–'

'Steely blue eyes,' says Genevieve, so that they both say the same three words together and laugh. 'And what does Nance think of your new look?'

What the faark has Nance got to do with his big moment on the box where he's going to win the hearts and minds of the country and the world?

'We-ell, she says I look handsome and manly, of course,' smirks Jules.

'Of course. He does, doesn't he, viewers?' agrees Genevieve grinning at the camera.

'Now, Jules, before we get to your pregnancy,' says Genevieve punctuating her words with her signature frown. 'The WTF. What happened there? Are you all right? You certainly look in ruddy health.'

'Ha ha.' What the faark does ruddy health mean? Ruddy sounds like an insult, Jules reckons.

'What about President Betsy—?'

'What about her?' Jules cuts in, his anger getting the better of him as he relives the whole sorry episode again. 'All old Betsy's fault. If she'd just kept her faarking hands off me—'

'Oh, Jules, I didn't mean to upset you, especially in your delicate condition,' Gen smiles serenely.

'I'm not in a faarking delicate state, I'm just faarking angry for faarking good reason,' Jules explodes, before recovering his dignity, his reason and his script. 'No, no, everything is hunky-dory and right as rain. It's all top of the pops and super-dooper. A mere misunderstanding, Genevieve. Poor old Betsy tripped and to stop her fall, her arms reached out to the closest solid object, which happened to be me, ah, my stomach. Then she toppled backwards, smacked the left side of her face on the hard concrete, and all faarking hell broke loose, ha ha.'

Genevieve looks back at him with grave concern.

'You then were detained on terrorism charges for more than a day, Jules.'

'I wasn't detained, ha ha, why no, not at all. I stayed to make sure my dear friend Betsy was all right during her brief hospital stay.'

'So we are not at war, Jules?'

'Ha ha, no no, ha ha, no war with our closest neighbour, ha ha. But, Genevieve,' says Jules as gravely as he can with his steely blue eyes staring down the camera, 'We do live in worrying times, and I'm here to tell the people that they can sleep easy with me at the helm. I'm a man who knows how to be PM and Julian Pope is what the country–'

'Jules, do tell us about your pregnancy. In fact, we understand that you have hit the half-way mark, Jules. Twenty weeks, congratulations! Plus you and I have been keeping a big surprise under wraps, haven't we, Jules? A big, delightful secret in fact.'

'Ah, yes Genevieve, er, as the Prime Minister, I am determined to continue leading this country during these worrying times–'

'Oh no, Jules, not that,' interrupts Gen dismissively and smiling broadly. 'Twins! You are pregnant with twins! Congratulations!'

*Rude*, Jules protests internally, *interrupting me again when I was just getting to the good stuff.* Jules smiles in his most polished statesman-like manner.

'Well, yes, er, I thought it was just the post-Easter, post cholecystectomy puddin'. That's why I didn't find out until–'

'Jules, some people say that this whole thing, your twin pregnancy, is a hoax.'

'How dare people think I would be untruthful about–'

'Others say it is a phantom pregnancy.'

'You mean like a gall stone gone bad? Well, if only–'

'But we have here your official ultrasound.'

'I believe you *do* have the ultrasound that says otherwise, Genevieve, and right there is the more important story. I'm sure the electorate is dying to know about that, Genevieve. How the faark did you get my private medical records, eh?' Jules demands smugly.

'Your government failed to fund the health privacy security upgrade, preferring to fund the Priests in Public Schools initiative,' replies Genevieve pleasantly. 'Also, Jules, your *COC(K)-UPP* Terrorism amendment requires the Justice Department be copied in on all pregnancy sonagraphs. Who can know where the breach occurred, Jules?' Gen sighs and shakes her head.

'But, the sharing of private medical information without consent is, is–'

'Yes, it would be helpful if you could explain all this, Prime Minister. Better still, if you rectified this appalling situation.'

'Well, er, well...' Jules' mind is scrambled.

'We do so appreciate you suggesting this interview to candidly speak about your pregnancy, Jules,' Genevieve smiles warmly. 'Your ultrasound is on screen now for our viewers to see.'

Jules' eyes finally turn away from Genevieve The-Booby-Trap Parker and towards the large screen broadcasting his ultrasound for the whole world to see. 'I, I don't think that's necessary. That's quite private, Genevieve. I am a humble man and a private man, well, as much as one can be private when one has been PM 25 times. As your Prime Minister, I think the time has come–'

'Actually that figure is 43 times, Jules, over the last six months,' corrects Genevieve. 'You have presided over the greatest government leadership instability of all time. But, Jules,' Genevieve says with her violet eyes sparkling, 'the real question on everyone's lips is: How did you become pregnant?'

'Well, Genevieve, the Lord moves in mysterious ways.'

'So you have no idea?'

'No idea,' Jules agrees feeling rather foolish.

'A runaway body, then?' laughs Genevieve.

'Ha ha, yes, I suppose you could say that, er, yes.'

'Runaway fertility?' laughs Genevieve.

'Ha ha, yes, ha ha.'

'Fertility is quite the tricky affair, isn't it?' laughs Genevieve.

'Yes, yes, Genevieve,' Jules laughs in agreement. 'It is indeed, yes, indeed.'

'Thank goodness for modern family planning methods such as contraception, abortion and science-assisted reproduction,' laughs Genevieve.

'Ha ha, thank goodness, indeed,' laughs Jules. 'Yes, thank

goodness. Modern methods, ha ha.' Jules and Genevieve are having such a lovely time, he could still have a chance with her, to do a bit of the old, how's your father, stir a bit of the up-skirt yoghurt, file the old email in the spam folder, do a bit of the old–

'Jules? What do you to say to that?' Genevieve is looking at him with considerable displeasure.

Jules has no idea what she's been saying. Faark.

'Er, ah, well, the important thing to remember, Genevieve, is that currently as the 107th Prime Minister, I have presided over the most impressive religious revitalisation, er, but of course as only the 42$^{nd}$ *different* person to be Prime Minister, and, er, of course, I am the Prime Minister with the most experience of being Prime Minister, having held the seat on 25, oh no, you caught me on that one before didn't you, ha ha, on 43 separate occasions, Genevieve...'

Jules stops. He and Genevieve don't seem to be sharing their little joke any more. Who stole his Genevieve Booby-Bonhomie Parker who wants him in her bedroom rodeo? Who replaced her with this woman staring at Jules like he's some extinct monster?

'Er, would you please repeat the question, Genevieve?' he says rescuing the situation masterfully.

Genevieve ignores Jules and frowns into the camera, 'Hmm. We'll take a short break and be back in a moment.'

'She's wiping the floor with him, RidgyDidge,' Carol says, placing her wine glass on a side table beside the couch. But I'm not sure that Mr Pope really gets it at all. Which reminds me, love, I visited Naomi today. I took her in some of those nut chocolates she loves, and of course the toothpaste, and some tampons to trade favours, and guess who else I saw in there, love? Dr Francis.'

'She works in there part-time does she, Cazza?' asked Reg.

'No, Reg,' Carol shakes her head and her mouth turns down. 'Dr

Francis is *in* there, love, locked up, apparently all for trying to help women like Naomi get an abortion.'

'Well at least they've got lovely company in there, haven't they, Cazza?' Reg says sadly.

'They do, love, but it *is* prison. All those strip searches and gluggy meals. But the worst thing is being separated from their families, Reg. Mums separated from their kiddies, love, and the kiddies without their mums, all for just trying to do the right thing. I mean there is no way little Naomi could possibly have had another kid. Having that last kid almost killed her, Reg.'

'Terrible business,' agrees Reg, 'She had that transfusion and her heart stopped, didn't it and the doc–'

'Doctor told her never again,' Carol finishes Reg's sentence. 'Who would ever have thought that we'd be locking up women who are just trying to take care of themselves and their families. I mean contraception isn't cheap, and none of it's 100% failsafe, and we humans sure aren't perfect, we're always slipping up aren't we? And what about those women Gen reported on, love, in a violent relationship? You reckon they'd have much choice in the matter? And then to lock up doctors who are just trying to do the right thing by their patients.' Carol sighs deeply.

'You're right, Cazza,' says Reg.

'If you can't control your fertility you can't control your life, can you? I mean just look at me, I've had both sides of the flippin' fertility coin haven't I? It's complicated, Reg, isn't it? Whether you're happy to be preggers, or don't want to be and you are, or can't get pregnant when you want to be. Women shouldn't be told what to do by some heartless law made by some heartless, ignorant men.'

'Exactly, Cazza,' agrees Reg. 'I would have thought that as a pregnant man, Pope might finally cotton on to some of this, but I'm not so sure. I'm still not sure that this isn't some weird practical joke. Are you sure – oh, quiet now,' advises Reg, 'Gen's back.'

'Go, Gen!' cheers Carol.

As the ad break draws to a close, Jules watches Nance retreat into the shadows away from the limelight and his dazzling self. Jules loves Nance's description of his interview performance so far as *dazzling*. Yes, a bit of the old razzle dazzle. Nance thinks it's all going very well. Apparently, Jules' natural photogenic handsomeness is quite winning over the audience. Nance has a focus group doing the little caterpillar thingamajig *and the cute little bugger is doing all sorts of delightful jumps*, Jules thinks proudly.

Two make-up artists flit in, expertly dull sweat from Jules' forehead and upper lip, and retreat. Yes, this is all going rather well.

'All going rather well, Genevieve, eh?' says Jules flashing his most charming smile.

Genevieve smiles perfunctorily in Jules' direction and Jules believes he's still in with a chance with his little scrumptious media strumpet. She's just playing hard to get, Jules decides, as he imagines slowly removing Genevieve's clothing one item at a time.

'What was your reaction, Jules, when you discovered you were pregnant?'

'Oh, we're back, are we?' Jules wipes his salivating mouth with the back of his hand. Certain women always make him salivate. 'Right, well, I, er, it was quite a shock. As I said, it was not exactly planned, you see. It's all a bit of a mystery, but, er, yes,' Jules finally finds his place in the script he practised with Nance, 'that's right, every pregnancy is a precious child from the moment of conception, Genevieve and so–'

'You were over the moon with happiness, Jules?'

'Why, yes, of course. Ah, er, over the moon. That's it, over the moon, ha ha.'

'Isn't it true that you contacted the Love Life Help Line demanding an abortion?'

Jules' head quivers as his brain tries to decode the question. Isn't it true, is *not* it true... Why the faark can't she just ask questions in a normal way? Was that a double negative? Or a tricky single negative? He thinks it's a trick question. When in doubt, *attack*.

'What? Outrageous lies and slander, girlie.'

A voice booms through the studio, '*But all I want is an abortion, you faa*-bleep *cu*-bleep.'

Jules startles, thinking God is finally spaking unto him as He spake unto Moses, before recognising the voice as his own.

'Where did you get that? That was a confidential phone conversation. I'll have you know that–'

'So you do not deny that is your voice, Mr Pope?' Genevieve states rather than asks.

Faark, another faarking tricky double negative: do *not* deny? Jules realises he's fallen into a trap. He should have not not denied. He should have not denied, or denied, or...

He recalls his first, second and third rules of jousting with journalists: Deny, *deny*. Deny, then attack, *attack*, Jules orders himself.

'What a disgrace to betray confidentiality in this way. Betray my private phone conversation. Betray the best Prime Minister in the nation's history. Betray the private conversations of all the girls, er, pregnant girls, er persons contacting a help line specifically set up to, well, er, help in strictest confidence and–'

'Your government set up the help line,' Genevieve says.

Jules' tongue laps like a cat as he tries to rid himself of a tinny taste like he's had a cuppa with one of those fake sugars in it.

'I am reading from the Love Life Help Line manual here, Prime Minister,' Genevieve continues, 'All callers must be advised that their call may be recorded for training, quality control or Terrorism purposes, by order of the prime minister. That's by order of you, Jules.'

'I didn't hear that bit,' Jules whines.

'Did you not also speak to the Pope seeking an exemption from the church to have an abortion?'

Jules is not going to fall for that same old trick this time. Double or single negatives or not, denial is the first and only line of defence. Deny, *deny*.

'Ha ha, well Genevieve, I think you do *not* quite have the *im*proper facts *in*correct.' He'll raise her tricky negative with a triple. Let's see her get her pretty little head around that one.

'These are exactly the facts, Prime Minister.'

Jules' puffed up sense of himself deflates as he sees himself appear on the big screen behind Genevieve. Jules' nose is oversized and his chin is more than a double one. The ugly version of himself – whatever the faark he was on when this footage was stolen, is up on the wall, king size all right, begging like a blathering idiot, 'Look a man is fa-*bleep*-ing pregnant! He looks like he's eaten gela-*to*, piz-*za*, pas-*ta* and the tower of Pi-*sa*. Holy Father, *non, non,* please, I need your divine intervention, and failing that, I need a reprieve, an *excusa*, Most Holy Father. I need a *get-out-of-hell-free* card.'

Jules hears laughter from some of the crew. They're laughing at him and his Italian accent and his pathetic predicament. Everyone's laughing at *him*, the Prime faarking Minister. How dare they? He should walk, just get up and faarking walk out, he thinks.

But Jules feels sweat rolling down his chest, puddling on top of his baby bump and dribbling into his undies; sweat rolling down his back and gathering in his undies; sweat dripping from his underarms, soaking his regal King size shirt and flowing into his undies. Faark, if he got up and walked now, he'd look like he'd wet himself and that would be it for his political career.

Nance's voice replays in his mind, *Remember dear, no matter what happens you must be above it all. Stick to the plan and be your charming and regal self.* Jules lifts his chin and looks with Kingly disdain down his nose at the faarking finagling Genevieve Parker.

'And did you not contact Senator Maxine Badlands to enquire about getting an abortion via an underground abortion network?' Genevieve asks.

'You can't trust the word of that radical, hairy-chested woman about anything. If she's what your intel relies on, Genevieve, you've got nothing, *absolutely nothing*.'

God spake unto Moses again, 'I need to know how to, you know, access an a-a-abortion. *Abortion!* Come on Max-een, *Maxee*. I know you girls have a black market out there, an underground abortion network. I need it Maxine, I *need* it. Help me, Maxine.'

Attack, *attack*.

'Outrageous. Despicable. I am very disappointed in you, young lady,' says Jules as royally as he can.

'Not nearly as disappointed as the people of the nation are in you, Mr Prime Minister. Your prohibition of basic family planning options has destroyed families and killed women. Your hypocrisy is breathtaking.'

Jules is not quite sure what has just happened. He has been slapped down again by this faarking woman. But Genevieve's voice and expression suddenly soften. Her seductive eyes see deep into his soul. He is hers forever.

'Jules,' she says kindly, leaning forward to briefly touch his knee, an intimate gesture of care, 'how have you coped with all this? You were desperate to terminate the pregnancy, but found yourself stymied at every turn. That must be so difficult and depressing, especially for a powerful man like you, Jules. To be so helpless when you are the most powerful man in the country. To have your life out of control in this way must be frightening, Jules.'

Jules' chin drops.

'Well, yes, Genevieve, yes, *yes*, it is.'

'With people turning you away at every turn. You valiantly trying to access an abortion but no one, not one person, prepared to help you. Feeling helpless and misunderstood, feeling so alone.'

Jules is caressed by Genevieve Parker's words. Her eyes are so sincere and sublime. Genevieve completely understands him, his intolerable situation and what he has had to endure. She understands him with a depth no other human being has ever reached before.

'Poor Jules, you have no one to turn to, no one to help you out of this disaster. You have been, and are, trapped by your runaway fertility.'

Jules chin begins to wobble. He stares at his blimp of a stomach and holds his focus there as tears run down his cheeks.

'It has been quite lonely, Genevieve, yes. And rather depressing, and confusing. I've felt so desperate at times, I've been frantic with panic and so angry that no one takes me seriously.'

Jules takes a tissue from the tissue box that has magically appeared in Genevieve's outstretched hand. He dabs at his face.

'I mean I have my own destiny to fulfil. My life is being hijacked by some egregious error. This can't be what God planned for me. I can't do this and I don't want this. Nobody understands what this has been like for me – the horror of it all, except,' Jules looks up hopefully, knowing that Genevieve Parker is one of God's angels, she is Jules' angel, 'except perhaps, you?'

Genevieve Parker's angelic violet eyes and loving voice cut through his hopes like Lucifer's hell fire, 'The nation's women understand the horror of it all perfectly.'

As the ad break begins, he looks at her with pathetic longing. Gen stands and says to the make-up crew, 'Please clean him up.'

She walks as far away from Julian Pope as she can, aware of her skin crawling, with his filth clinging to her. She desperately wants a hot shower with lashings of foaming soap and shampoo, but first, Gen desperately wants to knee Julian Pope in the crotch, kick him in the guts and throttle the life out of him. Gen knows she is capable of doing exactly that: kill a man with her bare hands. Paradoxically, that truth makes it easier for Gen to knuckle down and murder Julian Pope now by using only her words.

She inhales slowly and deeply twice and resumes her seat. Colwyn flutters the make-up brush over Gen's face and whispers, 'Gorgeous, powerful Genevieve Parker, go get him.' It is a familiar touch of Colwyn-speak loosening Gen enough to realise anew the importance of this interview. This is it, her one shot.

Gen rolls her shoulders and checks her papers. She takes a sip of water and out of the corner of her eye, watches the hand count-in. Gen takes another calming breath, smiles and says, 'Welcome back.'

'You have struggled with your sister's homosexuality, haven't you, Jules?' Genevieve asks kindly.

'What? Er, no, Genevieve, I haven't struggled at all,' smiles Julian Pope, his eyebrow dance indicating her question has him off-balance again. 'My sister has chosen a disgusting life style. Homosexuality is against the word of God and I'm certain, Genevieve, that while she might evade punishment in this life, she will not escape the smiting hand of God and the hell fire of the devil in the afterlife. It's important, Genevieve, to be aware that as Prime Minister–'

'Do you not think, Mr Pope,' Genevieve cuts across the PM with a perfectly nuanced and naive curiosity, 'that you sitting here telling the world your sister is disgusting, is itself disgusting?'

'Well, Genevieve, *Genevieve,* ha ha, we all know that it's just like your fats. You've got your saturated fat, that's your healthy normal macho sex. Good dollop of saturated toughens you up – your arteries especially, apparently. The unsaturated fats are your homo-sex-sual varieties – polyunsaturated, monounsaturated, all that wanky stuff with no taste and thinking they're better than everyone else when they are an evil, superfluous to God's plan. Then there's your trans-fat that's been adulterated so much–'

'Prime Minister, are you really likening your sister to a tub of fat?'

'Well, Genevieve, er, Miss Parker, it's just a metaphor or an analogy, one of those. Surely you learnt all about those at journalism schoo–'

'Do you love your sister, Mr Pope?'

'What?'

'Do you love your sister, Mr Pope?

'Well, I don't think love–'

'You are so lucky you have a little sister, Mr Pope,' Gen says, feeling a little dreamy.

'Well, I don't think, that is to say–'

'My little sister killed herself ten years ago.'

Silence shrieks through the studio. Gen hears nothing in her ear piece. The shocked crew's jaws drop, heads twist from side to side as they mouth at each other, 'What the fuck?'

'I think you knew her, Prime Minister. Rosalie, *Rosie Parker?*'

In her ear piece, Gen hears the director's gentle voice, 'What are you doing, Gen? Bring it back now.'

'Well I don't think I–'

'Yes, of course you remember her,' Gen cuts in, her mind refocused, and her voice with a ragged edge. 'You were a 46-year old married father of five girls, Prime Minister. Rosie was a beautiful and intelligent 23-year old intern. She was interning for you personally, Prime Minister.'

Gen's ear-piece speaks, 'I hope you know what the fuck you're doing, Gen.'

Gen pulls the bud from her ear casually, glances over to see the producer's mouth in the shape of the word, 'Fuck.'

'Well, ah, I can't be expected to remember everyone who ever worked for–'

'You had just been promoted to the Cabinet as Minister for Women's Affairs and Minister for Social Security. Remember the party function celebrating the welfare cuts to the Single Mothers Pension, Prime Minister?'

'Well, ah, I'm not sure where this is going Genevieve,' laughs Pope in a jokey manner, looking around the studio obviously expecting others to laugh along with him, but finding only the horrified stares of Gen's crew.

'You raped my sister, Mr Pope. You raped my beautiful Rosie, and because of that, because of *you*, Rosie killed herself.'

*OutRageOnLine:*
*GENEVIEVE'S #metoo MOMENT NAILS POKEY POPE.*
*GET FREE $100 FOR FIRST THREE BETS ON BETCHA! WHEN YOU SIGN UP FOR PORN&POPCORN.*

*OutRageOnLine:*
*FIFTEEN WOMEN SPEAK OUT: PREDATOR POPE.*

*OutRageOnLine:*
*66 WOMEN SPEAK OUT: RAPIST POPE*

The screen abruptly goes to an ad as Carol and Reg sit in stunned silence. Eventually, Carol speaks. 'That poor little girl, Reg, as if she hasn't gone through enough. I had no idea. To have her little sister kill herself all because of that pig of a man, Julian Pope.' Tears spill from her eyes.

Reg puts his arm around her, and Carol sobs before she lifts her head from Reg's shoulder and says, 'Reg, I have to do something, Reg. I have to go to the studio.' Carol blinks back tears and stands up. 'She needs someone to be there for her, love. I...'

'It's okay, Cazza,' Reg says reaching for her hands and stroking them with his thumbs. 'Look, love, Gen's a hurt and broken little girl, but she's also strong and capable. There'll be people there for her, love. Just hold up a bit – Oh, here she is back on, love. Look, *look*, she's fine, *she's fine*, love.'

'Welcome back. I'm Genevieve Parker.'

Carol hears the slight tremor in Gen's voice and sees the quiver at her chin.

'You can do it love,' she tells Gen. 'You've done the hard part now, and you did great, Gen. You did it perfect, didn't she, RidgyDidge?'

'She sure did, Cazza. Come on sit down with me and we'll cheer her on,' encourages Reg as they channel their bolstering vibes back to Gen.

'In dramatic scenes just moments ago, police escorted Mr Julian Pope from *The LoDown* studio. *The LoDown* camera crew captured the arrest of Prime Minister Julian Pope.'

Carol, Reg and the world watch as the screen fills with footage of two uniformed police officers entering *The LoDown* set and approaching the pregnant prime minister as he sits opposite Genevieve Parker. The PM looks confused and indignant. He refuses to stand and yells, 'Faark off! Get your faarking hands off me!' Each officer takes one of the PM's arms and with considerable effort lifts him out of his chair.

The footage changes to on-the-run footage following the PM and police through the studio's warren of corridors, the heavy breathing of the hand-held camera operator vying with the PM's unintelligible ranting. A steely blue arm flies up and a clenched fist heads straight for Carol's watching face. The screen becomes a jumbled collage of lights, walls, legs, arms, grunts and thumps, before finally righting itself to show a plain clothes officer handcuffing the PM. Detective Senior Sergeant Jimmy Park gives a quick thumbs up and handsome grin.

The camera operator remains stationary and panting, recording the PM being marched away between police officers, and the PM's plaintive cries, 'Na-ance, *Na-ance!* Help me Na-ance, *Na-ance*!'

Carol and Reg are speechless. Genevieve Parker is not, and says, 'Women here and overseas have contacted police to report serious sexual assault allegations against Prime Minister Julian Pope. Moments ago, Mr Pope was taken into custody by police.'

The footage of the arrest is replayed, before Genevieve reappears.

'Rest assured that *The LoDown* will bring you the latest on this second Exclusive World First, as it happens.'

Genevieve puts her hand to her ear and says, 'Well-placed sources advise that Mr Pope's bail application is likely to be speedily heard and denied. Mr Pope will be remanded at Royal Queen's Prison.'

'One does usually like to hear One's name mentioned,' the Queen of Great Brexit says, sighing, 'but not in the same breath as sexual assault and that pregnant poopy pants.'

The Queen sits on her sofa watching the box and chatting to her doggie champs. 'One's queen should *not* be dragged into such a scandal. That little colony really should be standing on its own two feet by now. What is One to *do* when a country refuses to cut the umbilical cord to the mother country. Honestly, I do think that perhaps Great Brexit might have to do it for them. That country is like one of those never-leave-home grown up children – never growing into actual grownups. I mean it's hard enough in One's own situation with the royal children, but a whole country! One really does get quite tired of it all. Then, this Poop fellow disgraces himself and, by association, One also has One's good name and reputation besmirched, doesn't One, champs?'

In agreement, the champs yap and yelp, and bark and yap some more.

'Because of One's recalcitrant child nation's embarrassing WTF and pregnancy debacle,' the Queen complains to her canine minions, 'One could not possibly have watched this broadcast in the presence of anyone else, and thank goodness for that because One did not see this extra scandal coming, tut, *tut*.

'I do like this little filly though, Genevieve Parker, eh? She didn't even break a sweat while that dastardly prime minister blathered and bullied. Miss Parker KO'd that sexual predator, kapow!' The Queen pants and puffs as she demonstrates her point to the champs by shadow boxing enthusiastically, her handbag twirling and flying about the pivot of her elbow. 'Perhaps One shall invite this Geneveive Parker over for tea at One's palace.'

The Queen slumps with fatigue and humiliation into the sofa and refocuses on what Miss Parker is saying, '…world renowned doctor explains how a biological man could become pregnant.' Genevieve Parker smiles at the queen before the screen displays the edifice of a hospital helpfully emblazoned across the top with *The Royal Queen's Hospital.*

'Oh goodie, much nicer,' approves the Queen.

Genevieve and a white-coated doctor enter the building, and proceed to look at pregnant bellies from the outside and inside, while the world renowned doctor informs the Queen, 'For a man to become pregnant requires the miracle of modern science and complex medical procedures. This is still an inexact science, but we have come a long way in science-assisted reproduction, embryology, fertility, gender reassignment medicine and, of course, the work of our friends in animal research.'

'Oh that's you, champs,' the Queen exclaims as One spies One's favourite champ snuggling up to One's leg and orders, 'Up, *up*, there you go, you old thing.' The Queen picks up the canine from One's lap and lets him lick all about the royal person's face.

'All right, *all right, s*ettle down now.' One returns the dog to the floor. 'This is important stuff. One must keep up with the latest, especially if One is going to cause a constitutional crisis by sacking a government. One swore, *never again*, after the last debacle when One should really have sacked the GG instead, but, oh well, that was then and this is now, so…'

Her Majesty looks forlornly at the segment (shot days ago) and watches Genevieve nod seriously and say, 'I'm sure that despite the complexity, Doctor, our viewers are eager to get some idea of how a man can become pregnant, in as simple terms as possible.'

Medical diagrams, and colourful shots of embryos and

microscopic cells moving like partying balloons, share screen time with the doctor's scientific insights.

'Put simply,' explains the doctor, 'We transplant a donated uterus into the male patient. Babies have been successfully born to women undergoing this procedure for some years now. The male patient receives very specific hormonal treatment, the transfer of a healthy embryo and enhanced implantation. Immune-suppressing drugs prevent rejection of the uterus, while hormones and other supplements ensure everything proceeds well. A twin pregnancy indicates the successful implantation of two embryos.'

'Goodness, champs,' exclaims the Queen, 'anything is possible these days.'

'So this is probably how Julian Pope became pregnant?' Genevieve asks.

'Oh, not probably, most definitely. I undertook the procedure on Julian Pope myself,' replies Dr Roberta Roberts.

As the pre-recorded segment with Dr Roberts continues, all Gen can think is, did she really say, *the latest on this second exclusive world first as it happens?*

Gen shivers and her teeth chatter. She feels chilled to the bone. Oh God, they were right, she realises. After such a personal, public revelation, the whole crew urged her not to go back on camera. She should go home. Fairley Fine could take over with introductions to the pre-recorded segments. No one would expect Gen to resume her place on camera after telling the world about Rosie. Yes, she should have stopped after Rosie. But, no, Gen had to play *the-show-must-go-on* card, and now she feels like an earthquake about to crack wide open.

She left her studio team completely in the dark as to what was going to play out. Until now, even Gen had no idea herself if it would actually happen. Would she be brave enough to confront the PM about Rosie? Would Julian Pope be arrested? Would everything pan out according to plan?

From somewhere, Colwyn produces a rug to wrap around Gen's legs, a jacket to drape around her shoulders and a mug of tea. She takes a sip and another. The warmth seeps through her, and with it the knowledge that she has just killed Julian Pope. It's finally done. She did it. Julian Pope is dead.

Of course this was not how Gen had imagined she would murder him. She entertained so many revenge fantasies: running him down with her car, pushing him from a cliff, bashing his head in…

Her rage at Julian Pope for what he did to her little sister, was eating her alive, until Brian. Brian offered to train Gen in martial arts, and at the time, nothing could have appealed to Gen more. She just hadn't figured out that was what she needed. As she learnt how to kill a man, and that she was capable of killing a man, paradoxically her obsessive rage began to settle and a sad but philosophical acceptance surfaced.

But then, Nance Pope came along.

Nance was persuasive. She described her slow burn realisation that she was 'living with the enemy'. Nance was just another smart woman seduced by a charming snake.

Nance's conspiratorial feminist determination was contagious. Gen was excited to be part of something bigger, a camaraderie amongst women with a common goal. The goal aligned with Gen's own and fed her hatred. Getting even with Julian Pope would transcend even Rosie. The revenge would be for all womankind. Rosie's death would mean something spectacular.

Or, whatever Gen originally signed up for, she despairs now. All Gen's dedication, her heightened emotions before and during the perfect execution of a plan years in the making, everything, all of it, collapse into a porridge of existentialist *ennui*. The elation and pride at the revenge wreaked on Julian Pope is already a grey puddle of anticlimactic apathy. *Who cares?* Gen thinks. All that work. All that preparation. Everything, all of it. *Who cares?*

Nothing can ever bring Rosie back. Nothing can make things right. Nothing can change a reality where Gen could not save Rosie. She could not save Rosie from him. Gen could not save Rosie from herself.

Who cares if one man is called to account? If one bastard of a powerful man is locked up? Who cares about this famous doctor? Who cares if a man is pregnant? Who cares? *Who cares?*

Just as Gen feels she cannot fall any lower, a sudden peeling away of her heart opens up the reality concealed from her by all the feminist scheming and gut-wrenching hatred of Julian Pope. What about the babies? What about those two innocent babies? What have we done? What the fuck have we actually done?

Gen is in the doldrums. Deep, *deep* in the doldrums.

*OutRageOnLine:*
*POPE FACES 666 SEXUAL ASSAULT CHARGES.*
*BAIL DENIED*

'Are you sure this isn't one of them April fools jokes, love?' asks Reg for the umpteenth time.

'Oh RidgyDidge. This is all completely on the up and up. Gen says so, love.' Carol is enthralled by Dr Roberts whose short dark hair and serious glasses are overshadowed by dingly-dangly earrings that Carol finds a bit distracting. She thinks they are seahorses.

When the segment finishes, Reg concedes, 'That Dr Roberta Roberts seems to know her stuff, I guess. But Roberta Roberts? Who names their kids that? Some parents, eh?' They both giggle and shake their heads.

'I bet that fancy pants doctor was once a pants-down victim in the playground with a name like that!' says Reg taking a swig from his beer stubby.

Genevieve frowns solemnly into the camera at Carol.

'We are fortunate to be able to speak with Dr Nance Pope, a PhD in micro-biology, President of Freedom from Reproductive Torture and Control, mother of five, and wife of Julian Pope.'

'There's something not right with Gen, love.' says Carol matching Gen's frown. 'Gen's eyes, her beautiful eyes that sparkle every shade you can imagine of violets and purples and lavenders and – they're dull, love. They look almost grey. Something's really wrong.'

'Well of course something's wrong Cazza. You can't front up after everything that's just aired and be right as rain can you?' Reg shakes his head. 'Everything's wrong, isn't it? And it would be even more wrong if Gen was all fine and dandy, eh? But don't worry love. If there's one thing we know about Gen, she's a young woman who knows how to bounce back, eh?'

Carol feels a little reassured, but is suddenly horrified to realise who Gen is now interviewing.

'Bloody hell, Reg. And she can't be right either can she Reg, that one,' Carol nods at the tele. 'Married to that man. She's very brave, Reg, isn't she? Or very stupid.'

'Dr Pope,' Gen begins.

'Please, call me Nance, Ms Parker.'

'And please, call me Genevieve.'

Both smile, although Gen's is but a poor replica of her usually sublime smile.

'Genevieve,' says Nance kindly, 'I do wish to express my sincere condolences about the tragic death of your sister, Rosie. My husband will feel the full force of the law in this matter, and for any other crimes he may have committed.'

'Thank you, Nance. I appreciate your kind words. All this must be shocking for you too?'

'Well, Genevieve, I have been working behind the scenes for some time to bring my husband to account. As far too many women have experienced themselves, it can be difficult to hold men accountable. This is perhaps particularly so when a woman like me finds herself married to a man like Julian Pope who once seemed so loving and charming but who, shall we say, ultimately showed his true colours,' Nance sighs.

'For most of his life, Jules has been fascinated with religion. But over more recent years, he became dangerously enamoured with the extreme religious right, which as you know, is headed by the pope. This church hierarchy has, I believe, been estranged from the original teachings of Jesus – compassion, inclusion, sharing resources in order to improve the lot of others.

'Instead, the church hierarchy has propagated, abetted and protected paedophiles. It has rejected and doomed to suffering, those who are dying torturous deaths and those who do not fit neatly into an Adam and Eve gender dichotomy. It has excluded women from official church roles other than as slaves. It has damned women to eternal hell if they do not adhere to impossible and cruel reproductive restrictions that doom them and their families to a unique form of torture, poverty and even death. All this it does in God's name, while it accumulates riches beyond our wildest imaginings.

'In short, Genevieve, the church is run by a bunch of cruel, greedy old men living in a corrupt fantasy world of infallibility, celibacy and utter godlessness, telling the rest of us how we should live. It is time to cry out, *The king is wearing no clothes!*'

'What does she mean by that love?' Carol asks Reg. 'What king? We have a queen. And why would he have no clothes on?'

'I think she means that fairy tale, Cazza. You know the one, by that Hans Christian Andersen fella, where swindlers hoodwink the king by pretending to make him clothes that only smart people can see, but there's no clothes at all. No one wants to be called a fool, so everyone just goes along with it, even though it's complete rot.'

'Yeah, I remember the one,' says Carol. 'At the big parade, a little boy finally yells out, *The king is wearing no clothes!* and finally everyone realises the con, and the truth.'

'And Jules?' Gen is asking Nance.

'Well, Jules must pay the price for his own shocking hypocrisy and crimes against women and humanity. If we are to become the best country we can be, we must rid it of violence and misogyny. All women must be able to choose when or if we become pregnant, and when or if we have children. All people must be supported with the very best in family planning methods. Dr Roberts' work is crucial here.'

'Do tell us more, Nance,' prompts Gen.

'Roberta is eminently and brilliantly qualified. As a transgender herself–'

'Oh?' says Genevieve with apparent surprise.

'Dr Roberts is an openly transgender woman, Genevieve. Roberta was born male. Robert Roberts became Roberta Roberts. As you can imagine she is fascinated with all the possible gender combinations and permutations. This has not only been a momentous professional coup for Roberta, but also deeply personal. A medical marvel at the cutting edge of scientific brilliance.'

'I have got here holding onto that man's shirt tails – and the sacrifice that went into that is beyond words, Genevieve, but ultimately, *ultimately*, I grabbed those coat tails tight and strangled the bastard. You, Genevieve dear, carried off your part brilliantly.'

Nance and Gen stand in the studio as post-show housekeeping rolls on around them. *Brilliant it might have been*, thinks Gen, but she is suddenly doubting whether the ends justified the means.

'But what about the babies?' Gen asks.

'We have all that sorted, of course, Genevieve. Once they are born they will be cared for unstintingly in a loving, feminist household.'

'But it's not as simple as that, is it?' Gen says, realising that it was only weeks ago that Gen was devastated by thoughts she herself had been an unloved and discarded baby and now here are twins. Gen glimpses a world where Nance Pope may be as ruthless and self-serving as her husband. Why couldn't Gen see this before?

The answer comes swiftly: Rosie. Gen's overwhelming rage and obsession with avenging Rosie's death possessed and blinded Gen. She fell for the flattery and seduction of powerful women, like Nance.

'Genevieve, dear,' Nance is saying, 'for millennia, women and girls have been forced into unwanted sex and unwanted marriages. We've been denied contraception, forced to have children we didn't want to have, and forced to have abortions we didn't want to have. We've been bought and sold, beaten and murdered. All Jules copped was one little pregnancy. He didn't reap the feminist insights we'd hoped for, but that was always a long shot. Genevieve, you must understand that women have been fucked over by men for thousands of years. We've got a lot of catching up to do. This is one man, just one man.'

*And two children?* Gen thinks. 'But who will look after the little ones, Nance?'

'Jules' lesbian sister, of course. She is the biological mother after all. Jules is his sister's surrogate, dear. Don't worry about the babies, they will be loved and cared for by their mother.'

'Who donated the uterus, Nance?' Gen asks, her brain now fully mobilised and wading through the muck of ethical questions. Can it be right to do, and take, such liberties with other human beings?

Nance replies matter-of-factly, as if she answers such questions every day, 'The uterus, dear, came from a woman who was killed by the strangling hands of her husband.'

Gen gasps. Although she knows about the women murdered by their intimate partners, Nance's answer shocks Gen like a punch to her gut.

Nance continues, 'In case you haven't noticed, dear, women are fighting for their lives. It's a war. The rules of right and wrong are always broken in war, Genevieve.'

Nance reaches out her hand, and Gen automatically mirrors the action to bridge the gap between them. Two women of the sisterhood, hand in hand, eyes and hearts wide open.

'Thank you, dear, for your bravery. Because of you and Rosie, the sisterhood stands on the brink of a glorious new age. You may think that we have only taken down one man, Genevieve. But this will change everything, *everything*. Goodbye, Genevieve. I will see you again soon, I'm sure of it.'

# VI

# RECLAMATION

*Pregnant within body and pregnant with an idea are both worlds of fantasy, possession, obsession, chaos, revenge, and finally, the reclamation of both self and other.*

The Queen quickly intercedes in the ghastly affair of the piddling colony that should have quit the empire decades ago. The Queen's agent, the colony's governor general, sacked the government and called an election. Within a month, the whole thing had been decided. An electoral broom swept through the whole place. Out with the old, in with the new. Never had so many women stood for election, and never had so many women entered the parleyment, including Dr Nance Pope. Women parleymentarians held a clear majority for the first time in the nation's history.

The Queen gave an interview saying, 'How proud One is to be a woman paving the way for other wimin doing it for themselves. With a little nudge from One's queen, surely the likes of Genevieve Parker, Nancy Pope and those miracle baby doctors can cut the colony's umbilical cord at last!'

On the new parleyment's first sitting day, the Concatenate Of Conception and Unborn Person Priority, otherwise known as the COC(k)UPP, was repealed. Pardons were given and victim compensation approved to all those whose lives had been cocked up. Given that the nation was now the world capital for reproductive and gender health, funding for same was increased 100 fold. The reproductive health tourism dollars alone were already bringing in an unexpected budgetary windfall.

On the second sitting day, the Pope and his church were banished from the nation. Church assets held around the country, worth in the order of $80 billion, were compulsorily acquired and confiscated without compensation. Church hospitals and schools joined the public sector. The sale of other assets provided proper compensation to victims of clergy abuse and racketeering.

The Vatican refrained from declaring war, deciding to cut its losses. The loss was a mere '*una goccia nel mare*,' Santissimo Padre proclaimed: a mere drop in the ocean, both monetarily and spiritually speaking.

The Pope has not yet considered *ogni alluvione inizia con una sola goccia:* every flood begins with just one drop.

Carol and Reg continue to watch their favourite news program, *The LoDown* with Genevieve Parker. Carol left the home help agency and keeps house for Gen on a full-time basis, earning double her previous weekly wage. The special relationship with the beautiful woman who could have been Carol's own daughter continues to evolve happily. Carol's capacity for generous mothering provides a warmth to Gen and so many others.

For all the wrong reasons, as usual, Julian Pope stars in another exposé with Genevieve Parker. He slouches uncomfortably in a straight-backed chair in a secure, windowless brick room at Royal Queen's Prison, a TV camera and crew set up around him ready for his live cross.

'Five minutes 'til the live cross, Mr Pope.'

'Live cross,' mutters Jules. 'I don't want a live cross. I'm too cross for a cross. Yes, I'm too cross to do the cross. I'm too cross to be cross-examined. Too cross to cross swords with that double-crosser. Too cross to cross the floor. I'm at the crossroads and it's a cross too heavy to bear. Oh that's a good one,' Jules Jesus Pope decides, momentarily brightening. 'Too many lines have been crossed. I'm a cross-breed now. A cross-dresser. I got caught in the crossfire of feminist, bra-burning whackos. I'm so cross I'm cross-eyed. Cross-legged. I want to cross it all out. I'm all crossbones.' He finishes his word game quite deflated.

Jules stares at the TV monitor and crosses his arms over his now voluminous belly. He's got quite used to this perch for his arms to rest on. Jules watches as Nance chats with Genevieve Parker within the intimacy of a trendy lounge room. The camera frame excises the paraphernalia of technology-power and people-power necessary to produce the illusion, and Jules finds himself caught, caught in a deception and snared in the infidelity of his own being.

'Oh, Nance, how could you do this to me, Nance?' Jules sadly asks TV Nance as if she is actually in the room with him. It is the way of this world, the lack of seams and boundaries, and nothing as it seems. No one really knows anymore what is real and what is fantasy. What is actual or virtual. As-It-Happens Live, or already past. Truth or lies. What is here or what is not. Julian Pope certainly has no idea.

'How could you do this to me, Nance? I go in to get rid of my gallbladder and end up with two faarking foetuses. How could you side with that drop dead gorgeous, treacherous bitch, Genevieve Parker? I'm your husband, Nance. I'm the ex-prime minister for faark's sake.' Jules sniffles and feels sorry for himself.

'Live cross, Mr Pope. In five, four, three, two, one.'

'Our next guest needs no introduction, although his new affiliations do,' Genevieve Parker tells her viewers and her live studio audience of intimate soiree guests. 'Ex-Prime Minister, Julian Pope, resident of Royal Queen's Prison, Ambassador for Sexual and Gender Diversity and Reproductive Rights, President of Rape Prevention Initiative, Special Advocate for Shame on Church Abusers & Racketeers, and of course, Patron of RESPECT and star of that organisation's latest remake of a classic chart stopper.'

Vision cuts to the beautiful Royal Queen's Prison garden. A thriving vegetable garden and colourful roses bobbing like pom-poms provide a cheer-leading backdrop to a sensational performance. With overall-clad prisoners as back-up dancers, Jules dances in a sparkling orange wig, matching figure-hugging jumpsuit, and full drag. Jules watches the footage of his pregnant tummy rolls and seductive gestures, as he gyrates and lip syncs, 'Wooah, R, E, S, P, E, C, Tee, wooah, that's all it takes to be...'

Then, Genevieve smiles broadly.

'Wow, Julian Pope as we have never seen him before. What do you think of that?'

The live audience claps and hoots with approval before Jules sees himself coming live and magnified ten-fold on the wall behind Genevieve Parker. Buttons protesting for gender rights, SCAR, RESPECT and all his other projects of desperate reclamation cover his prison-issue orange XXXXX size overalls. His face looks ugly and horrified. Is that him? Jules quickly grits his teeth in a furious smile.

'Welcome, Jules,' says Genevieve.

'Thank you, Genevieve, delighted to be here,' Jules replies through his teeth.

'First up, Mr Pope, why would you sign up for such a dramatic experiment, to become the first pregnant man?'

'Well, er, well,' *Just do it, it's just politics*, Jules tells himself. If he ever wants to get out of here, just do it. Cross the faarking floor! 'Well, Genevieve, as you know, as a man it can be difficult, to say the least, ha ha, to understand the mysteries of the female mind and, er, body. Nance, the love of my life, helped me to understand that I was quite off track, had crossed a line in fact, in my eagerness to make a better world.'

Nance interrupts at this point, and there is a slight delay between her voice being heard and Nance's face coming onto screen as she sits on set with Genevieve. 'The point is, if I may Genevieve?'

'Of course, Nance, do, please,' encourages Genevieve.

'Jules, you actually raised the whole topic one morning at brekky, didn't you?'

Jules nods soberly, 'Yes, er, quite.'

'Jules knew how much his sister wanted a baby, but there were issues there, you see, so with brotherly love, Jules put his hand up to be the surrogate. To maintain some privacy around it all of course, Jules' gall bladder became a cover story, and under that small subterfuge Jules was able to embark on becoming the medical marvel he is today.'

'Exactly,' Jules concurs. 'While I am highly intelligent, I had what I now see were very simple ideas about the roles of men and women and a blindness to the multi-gendered narrative of humanity.' Phew, after all that practice he nails it. Jules sticks that faarking *multi-gendered narrative of humanity* like a gold medal gymnast sticks a dismount. 'I also, as you'd understand,' Jules continues buoyed by this success, 'am a deeply spiritual and religious man and was always guided by the church, from when I was very young.'

Gen nods, and asks sympathetically, 'And it was the church that guided you towards sexual harassment and rape of women, Mr Pope?'

'None of that has been tested in a court of law,' Jules replies tersely. She's not going to get him this time, no, she is not. 'I am innocent until proved otherwise, Ms Parker.'

'Yes, I wonder why that is so, Mr Pope. That in our judicial system, men have the presumption of innocence, but women and children have the presumption of guilt. Men are to be believed, but women are not. Mr Pope, in fact your bail applications were all denied, indicating the seriousness of the charges and the overwhelming nature of the evidence.'

'Well, I don't think, Genevieve, er,' Jules says with an attempt at a smile. But when he looks at himself displayed on the big screen behind Genevieve Parker, he has to admit it's more creepy predator than charm offensive. Jules wonders why Nance is not interrupting again to get him off the hook.

'I don't think, Ms Parker, that here and now is the forum for an analysis of jurisprudence. Ha ha. Well yes, er, yes, but the point is Genevieve, *the point is*,' flusters Jules ruing the now incontestable fact that Genevieve Parker is both bimbo and faarking brainiac, which is an appalling, God-fearing combination. 'Your interpretation is *not* altogether *in*accurate, Genevieve.' Jules is rather proud of his double negative. 'Yes, your interpretation of the church's role is *not* altogether *in*accurate.'

'How so?'

'Like many who have devoted their lives to the church, I am disgusted by the church hierarchy. The Bell, er, Archbishop Bell, has been found out for embezzling 66 hundred million dollars from the Vatican. Although he always was one for the money. The Bell even saw my miracle of modern medicine pregnancy as an opportunity to make money.

'Then there's the church's perpetration and cover-up of child sexual abuse. SCAR worked tirelessly to uncover the truth and support victims, and I, er, I now work tirelessly with SCAR. And of course, also, I see now that, er, the whole reproductive health sins thing put women in an impossible position.

'So one day I had a crisis of faith and saw the light. I am suing the church, Miss Parker. I am suing the church for brainwashing me into believing that I had a God-given right to possess women as I wished. It was the church that made me do it. It wasn't my fault, Genevieve. It was the faarking church.'

Jules is not quite sure what he has just said, but drop dead gorgeous Genevieve's face is so serene and so beautiful that a smile plays on his mouth. Jules is in with a chance here, he thinks, yes, still could be in like Flynn for a romantic tryst with drop dead gorgeous Genevieve. After this whole faarking nightmare is over.

'Jules,' she whispers to him and him alone, 'welcome to your eternal purgatory on earth. No matter what good deeds you may perform, what excuse you may provide, you will never, ever see the light of day outside Royal Queen's Prison.'

Julian Pope looks aghast. He squirms.

'Ouch,' he says, rubbing his 35-week pregnant stomach. 'Ooouch!!!' he screams. 'What the faark is this agony? Call an ambulance. Call Roberta faarking Roberts! Call Zig and Zag. Get me the faark out of here! Aah! What the hell is this? Oow! Oh good, it's gone away. Everything's fine. No problemoooo – aaah! It's back. It's happening, isn't it. AAAH. Get me out of here. They said they'd do something before it hurt. This is not hurt. This is agony. This is faarking torture! EEEOOOOOOOOOW!'

As the plug is finally pulled on the cries of the labouring ex-PM Julian Pope, Gen smiles and frowns down the camera lens. 'Ouch,' she says.

Genevieve Do-Not-Mess-With-Me-No-Facefreeze Parker rather likes her more expressive face and the hint of wrinkles that make that particular expression possible. An expression that says, *wisdom, compassion and adorable imperfection.*

She glances over to the studio wings, and there he is. His eyes follow her. A finger points to his chest. Hands come together in the shape of a heart. A finger points at Gen. The mouthed words, 'I love you,' silently float across the studio.

With cheekiness and love, Gen's hands and mouth respond in kind, 'I. Love. You.'

The voice in her ear says, 'Gen, we're not out yet. That just went to air.'

Live on screen, Gen whispers, 'Who the fuck cares,' smiles and winks. 'Good night'.

*OutRageOnLine:*
*GEN FINDS TRUE LOVE AT LAST!*
*Parents and kiddies jubilant.*

Hours later, Gen sits at her writing table and gazes out from her penthouse window. Pen in hand, she stares at a blank piece of paper. Nearby, Rosie's diary lies open at a page of desperate scrawls where one line catches the light. *He said I must get rid of it.*

Gen puts the pen down, folds the blank paper and places it in an envelope. Gen can talk to Rosie in her mind and out loud, for always. She removes her robe and slips into bed and sleep.

When A-Pop plays at 6 am, her hand reaches for the snooze button and Jimmy.

# THE END

# Book Club Discussion Questions

- Who was your favourite character and why?
- How do you think the title of the book related to the story?
- Which scenes and plot twists did you enjoy most?
- Did the book give you insights to situations outside your experience?
- What was left unresolved and what might be in store for your favourite character?
- Do you think you can know too much about the world?
- Do you think psychotherapy was helpful or dangerous to Gen?
- What did you think of the gender-bending premise of the book?
- How might the world be different if women dominated positions of power?

Thank you for reading my book. If you enjoyed it, please buy another copy for a friend, recommend *Genevieve Knows Too Much* to your friends and family, or take a moment to leave me a review at your favourite retailer.

# Acknowledgements

Thank you to the Shawline Publishing team especially: CEO Brad Shaw for seeing the potential and fun in *Genevieve Knows Too Much*, production manager Alana Lambert for her delightful efficiency and reassurance, editor Samantha Elley for astute and playful guidance and Elissa Sanchez who created the mesmerising cover.

My author mentor and dear friend Myf Jones continues to be a generous guiding hand and a ray of sunshine. Genevieve owes much to Myf's kind wisdom and learned encouragement. Heartfelt thanks to my cheer squad of friends – you all know who you are! Deepest thanks to the oldest through to the tiniest members of my family: my love and rock Pete, Beccie and Anthony, Mike and Laura, Steve and Jia, Benjamin, Georgia and Jules. *Genevieve Knows Too Much* would never have seen the light of day without their insightful and unwavering encouragement, sense of fun and love.

I am grateful to have written this story on the lands of the Wurundjerie Woi-wurrung people of the Kulin Nation. Traditional custodians are the oldest and first storytellers of the world and are an inspiration. I pay my respects to traditional elders past, present and emerging.

Shawline Publishing Group Pty Ltd
www.shawlinepublishing.com.au